RIDERS OF FORTUNE

RIDERS OF FORTUNE

A WESTERN TRIO

WALT COBURN

SAGEBRUSH
Large Print Westerns

Copyright © 2007 Golden West Literary Agency

First published in Great Britain by ISIS Publishing Ltd.
First published in the United States by Five Star

Published in Large Print 2010 by ISIS Publishing Ltd.,
7 Centremead, Osney Mead, Oxford OX2 0ES
United Kingdom
by arrangement with
Golden West Literary Agency

British Library Cataloguing in Publication Data
Coburn, Walt, 1889–1971.
  Riders of fortune.
    1. Western stories.
    2. Large type books.
    I. Title II. Coburn, Walt, 1889–1971. Ride 'im
  cowboy. III. Coburn, Walt, 1889–1971.
  Sun Dance Kid.
  813.5'2–dc22

ISBN 978–0–7531–8507–0 (hb)

Printed and bound in Great Britain by
T. J. International Ltd., Padstow, Cornwall

CONTENTS

RIDE 'IM, COWBOY

By 1924, Walt Coburn was a regular contributor of
stories to Street & Smith's *Western Story Magazine*,
which had a weekly circulation of 2.5 million copies.
Jack Kelly, who was the chief editor of Fiction House's
pulp magazines, went to Santa Barbara, California,
where Coburn was living at the time, and negotiated a
contract with Coburn whereby the author was to write
a 25,000-word novelette each month for *Action Stories*,
a monthly magazine that cost 20¢ when *Western Story
Magazine* was priced at 15¢. Coburn was to be paid
$100 a week by Fiction House as a guarantee against
his income from writing stories and would be given top
billing. "Ride 'Im, Cowboy" appeared in *Action Stories*
(1/25). It was later filmed as *Between Dangers* (Pathé,
1927) directed by Richard Thorpe and starring Buddy
Roosevelt and Alma Rayford.

CHAPTER
ONE

Tom Rawlins groaned, then opened his eyes. To be exact, it was only one eye that opened for the other one was swollen shut. Slowly, painfully he hoisted himself to a sitting posture. His head felt like it had grown to twice its normal size and shooting pains ran like knives from the base of his skull to his bruised, blood-caked forehead.

"Wow. Sufferin' rattlesnakes. They must 'a' hit me with a double-bitted axe," he muttered as he gained his feet, swaying dizzily.

Save for a round-topped poker table, the room was empty. A dingy, dusty hole. Tom seated himself on the edge of the table and went through his pockets, one by one. Except for a few matches and a couple of crumpled cigarette papers, his pockets were empty.

"Clean." He grinned ruefully. "Clean as a gutter rabbit. They done rolled me like I was a drunk sheepherder and made a shore good job of it. Gee, this here head of mine is shore a-bustin'. Don't look like solid bone could ache thataway. No ma'am. Wonder what become of the big feller that was pilotin' me around the city? Don't recollect seein' much of that gent after the ruckus started in the barroom. It was him that begun it. They must 'a' beefed him early in the game. Mebbyso the bartender kin kinda shed some light on it."

Tom eased himself off the table and made his way to a door at the end of the room. He shoved it open and stepped into a small barroom.

Save for the white-aproned, red-faced man behind the bar, the place was empty. This individual looked up with mild curiosity from his business of polishing a row of whiskey glasses. Apparently he was not unaccustomed to seeing disheveled, black-eyed men emerge from the back room in the early hours of the morning.

"Sleep good, bo?" he inquired, shoving forth a glass and a half filled bottle of whiskey.

"Fair to middlin'," returned Tom with a grin that was a bit one-sided due to the swollen condition of his face. "Reckon it was what the wimmenfolks calls a beauty sleep, only she kinda backfired on me."

The bartender smiled faintly and held a freshly polished glass to the light, examining it critically. A bit too critically, thought Tom.

"Where was *you* when the cyclone hit us, pardner?"

"Off shift. Slip an eye-opener under your vest and the world'll look merrier, brother." He nodded toward the whiskey bottle.

Tom shook his head. "I took on aplenty of the firewater last night. And it'll take more'n a shot of hooch to open this here left lamp of mine."

The bartender shrugged and replaced the bottle under the bar.

Tom surveyed himself in the mirror on the backbar for a moment. Apparently the white-aproned dispenser of drinks had forgotten his presence.

"I don't reckon you know what become of that big gent that was with me last night. Kinda dude feller. His name was Harris. Claimed to be one of these law sharps?" Tom eyed the other hopefully.

A shake of the head was the only satisfaction Tom gained to his query.

"You see, mister, it was like this. I had some papers on me. And letters. Kinda important, they was. In fact, there's about half a million bucks tied up in them papers. Whoever got the roll of greenbacks I was packin' is plumb welcome to 'em. But I shore do hate to git cut loose from them papers. Half a million ain't . . ."

"Listen, brother." The burly bartender leaned across the bar, a sneer on his thick lips. "I'm fed up on this millionaire chatter, see? I'm a busy guy. Too busy to listen to any hophead's tale of half a million bucks. Them swingin' doors behind you is in good workin' order. Beat it before I call a cop." His pudgy hand slipped beneath the bar to grasp the wooden handle of a bung starter.

"So that's the idea, eh?" Tom's good-natured drawl was as deliberately slow as ever but there was a different tone to his voice somehow.

"That's the idea exactly. Take the air. You need it." The bulky shoulders of the man hunched forward meaningly.

5

Tom had been leaning idly against the bar in an attitude that was the picture of dejection. Suddenly, with the lithe swiftness of a cat, he cleared the bar, landing astride the thick shoulders of the startled bartender who crumpled under the impact. A moment and Tom was astride him.

Smack! Smack! Tom's open hands landed simultaneously on either side of the bloated, liquor-mottled face.

"Talk and talk fast, you barrel-paunched shorthorn! What 'come of that law sharp?" Tom's steel-like grip on the man's arms tightened.

"*Ouch!* He beat it, you fool, after he'd frisked you! Lemme up!"

"It was him that rolled me?" Tom increased the pressure.

"Sure! *Ouch!* Cut it out! You was framed, you hick! Help!"

The voice of the bartender had risen. Tom's ears caught the sound of running footsteps outside. With a parting slap, Tom leaped to his feet, cleared the bar, and was out the rear door and down an alley when the blue-uniformed policeman halted pantingly in the front entrance.

A passing truck afforded a safe means of escape for the fleeing cowpuncher. He swung aboard the rear of the big machine and, unseen by the busy driver, crouched among the crates and boxes. From his place of concealment, Tom saw the policeman dash out of the saloon entrance into the alley, peer about in a puzzled manner, then return to the saloon.

"Broke, beat up, and a dang' long ways from home," groaned Tom. "And that smooth-talkin', dude-dressin', di'mond-totin' law sharp played me for a pilgrim." Tom chuckled mirthlessly. Then he crawled over the boxes and crates and slid into the seat alongside the startled truck driver.

"Gosh. Strike me blind. Where'd you come from, pal?"

"From Montana." Tom grinned. "I'm startin' to Arizona now. How far in that direction do you go, mister?"

"To de freight depot." The driver grinned. "Who t'rew de load of bricks at you, buddy?"

Tom grinned back and, ignoring the question, inquired further.

"Ary train leavin' that freight shed that's headed my way?"

"Plenty of 'em. Hittin' de rods?"

"Huh? What rods, mister?"

"Meanin' are you beatin' de freights back?"

"Reckon so. Can't seem to locate my ticket. They done a good job of friskin' me last night. I'm due in Arizona next week, too."

"Arizona, eh? Gonna be a few minutes late, ain't you?"

"Some, I reckon," admitted Tom. "How does a man fork one of these here freight trains?"

The truck driver looked him over critically. He liked the cheerful way that this lanky man from the range treated misfortune.

"Broke flat?"

7

"Flatter'n a tortilla." Tom slapped his empty pockets. "And these here high-heeled boots ain't built fer walkin' in 'em."

The truck driver, manipulating the wheel with one hand, fished out a roll of bills and peeled off a $10 note.

"If you was the whinin' kind, bo, you couldn't nick my roll for a thin dime. But I like a game guy, see, and I'll take a chance on you. I know a couple guys at the yards. They'll put you in right with the brakies. This ten'll buy scoffin' on the road." He shoved the $10 in Tom's pocket.

"Scoffin'?"

"Grub," explained the driver, weaving the van neatly in between a streetcar and a line of trucks.

"Dog-gone. Darn me for a polecat, mister. You're a white man. My name's Tom Rawlins. I'm hittin' the trail for Arizona to take over a cow spread left me by an uncle I never seen. The lay is worth half a million. This here ten's a-comin' back to you someday, pardner. Comin' back with *poco* plenty int'rest, savvy. Jest write your name and range on a hunk of paper. And when I gits located, I shore am goin' to have you visit me. You're white, pardner, and Tom Rawlins ain't the kind that fergits a favor."

The truck had been skillfully halted beside a high platform beside a freight shed. The driver shut off the engine and half turned in his seat to look into his companion's face.

"Listen, Rawlins," he said earnestly, "don't go spoutin' off about dis million-dollar ranch too much, see. I ain't callin' no guy a liar, buddy, but when a bird wit' his clothes half torn off, no dough in his pocket, and a map on him that looks like a tractor had just passed over starts tellin' folks dat he's worth a million or two, he's gonna wind up in de funny house or sumthin'. Take it from a bird that's listened to many a hard-luck tale, bo, and keep yer trap shut about wotcha got in Arizona. Here's one of me cards. Nifty, eh? A guy in a circus done me two dozen while I waited. No arms on him and he held de pen wit' his toes. Make the name out? Barney Nolan and me address underneat'. And here comes a brakie dat'll putcha hep to a smooth-ridin', side-door Pullman."

CHAPTER
TWO

A far cry from Chicago to Arizona, far indeed to the ragged, unshaven cowpuncher who was learning by bitter experience the life of one who rides the freights. To Tom, it seemed that he was making but little faster time than the frontiersmen made with ox teams. Each division point meant a new train crew and each new train crew meant a fight or the parting with a dollar or two from the ten that had sadly dwindled. These railroad men, and the wandering tramps who rode the rods, were an alien breed to the man from the open ranges. He hated the former, and shunned the latter clan. But 53¢ remained in his pocket. Twelve days' beard covered his cinder-grimed face and could not hide the bruised cheek and swollen eye that still were in evidence to remind him of his visit to Chicago.

Slipping from a freight car at Gallup, New Mexico, Tom dodged between lines of freight and stock cars, deftly avoided the yard detective, and slipped into a cheap lunch counter. Ten minutes and he emerged, the inner man fortified by ham and eggs. He puffed contentedly at the tightly rolled cigarette and jingled the three pennies in his pocket. A man who bore the earmarks of a law officer strolled down the street toward him and Tom moved on.

A passenger train whistled in preparation for departure. Tom quickened his step. He had not yet attempted beating his way on a passenger train, but he had heard more than one knight of the cinder road speak carelessly of riding the blind baggage. He was alongside the train now. The blast of the locomotive whistle and the ringing of the bell quickened the heartbeat of the weary cowpuncher. A hasty glance told him that he was not being watched. The line of cars jerked and the locomotive slowly dragged them ahead. A short run alongside the slow-moving train, a quick leap, and Tom flattened himself in the tiny compartment at the forward end of the express car that is known as the blind baggage.

The long train crept forward at a snail's pace. Then came an interruption that caused Tom to swear softly beneath his breath. Someone had pulled the air cord, signaling for a stop.

It had grown dusk hard on the heels of the setting sun. An irate conductor, swinging a lantern, came forward at a trot, pausing at the open door of the mail car.

"Who pulled that air cord?" he demanded with a fervent sprinkling of profanity.

A portly mail clerk, clad in striped overalls and wearing an Army automatic strapped clumsily about his rotund stomach, stepped to the door of the car and leaned against the pouch catcher.

"Search me, doc." He grinned. "Must 'a' been that fresh brakie of yours."

The conductor shoved his head inside the mail car.

"Thought so. Only one helper in here. You sent the other one to the Harvey House for lunches and you're tryin' to hold up this train while he chews the rag with some bobbed-haired hasher over there. Pull that cord again and I'll report you. Get me? Holdin' up a through train because you're too lazy to fetch a lunch with you from Albuquerque. I'll turn you in for this!"

He gave the signal for the start again, whirled on his heel, and strode angrily down the platform. Tom, fearing he was about to be thrown off the train, had slipped from the blind and ducked between two empty freight cars on a siding. Now, as the conductor moved toward the rear of the train, he left his hiding place with a leap that catapulted him squarely into a youthful mail clerk laden with three box lunches. The boxes slipped to the ground, their contents spilling out.

Tom halted. The train was creeping forward. Stooping, he gathered triangles of pie, sandwiches, and pickles, thrust them into the boxes, and shoved the boxes back into the arms of the astonished youth who had not quite recovered his wind.

"Excuse me for bein' so danged clumsy, pardner," apologized Tom hastily. "Never seen you till we bumped. Lucky them hunks of grub was wrapped in paper thataway."

He and the mail clerk were running side-by-side abreast of the slowly moving mail car.

"Step aboard with them lunches, son!" called the grinning mail clerk from the car door. "Better hop that blind and make it snappy, bo!" he advised Tom.

Tom obeyed. He breathed freer when he was again standing in the narrow compartment and the train gained momentum.

The keen eye of the brakeman had spotted him too late. Condemning all hoboes to a warmer place, the brakie swung aboard the now swiftly moving train.

Clickety-click. Clickety-click. The thrum of the swiftly moving train was music to the soot-grimed ears of Tom Rawlins. At this rate he should be in Cactus City, Arizona in twelve hours or so.

The *clicking* of the rails hummed a lullaby. Tom gazed sleepily at the narrow strip of stars visible between the express car and the tender. The dust swirled up into his face but he did not seem to mind. To stave off sleep, he reviewed the events that had caused the journey. His humdrum life at the Circle C Ranch in Montana. Hard winters and hot, dry summers. Breaking horses, feeding cattle, working at odd jobs between roundups, and squandering his money across the bar or poker table. No better, no worse than the average cowpuncher. Taking what little fun he could get out of life, living from day to day with no thought of the future. No regrets, no great hopes of a future. In short, a cowhand.

Came the day when he received a letter from the county attorney at Malta. A letter that told of a wealthy uncle in Arizona. An estate worth half a million and

Tom Rawlins, cowpuncher, the sole heir. Weeks of delay, customary red tape while Tom proved his identity. No easy task for the wandering cowpuncher whose mother had died while he was an infant and whose father had been killed in a saloon row when Tom was a boy of fourteen. Vaguely he remembered his father speaking of a brother Joe down in the Southwestern country. Joe and Harvey Rawlins, Tom's father, had never got along. Joe had been the thrifty one, Harvey the black sheep. Occasionally they had written each other and it was these old letters, together with the certificate of Tom's birth at Helena, Montana, that were to identify him in Arizona. A letter from the county attorney accompanied these documents and now they were stolen from him.

Tom caught himself wishing that he had not taken that train of cattle back to Chicago for the Circle C. He had taken the job because there was nobody else handy to take charge of the train. The Circle C had been his home for many years and loyalty figured strongly in the make-up of the carefree cowhand.

Thus musing, Tom fought off the drowsiness that swept over him. He dared not go to sleep for fear of falling beneath the wheels of the speeding train. He lost all sense of time. Minutes seemed hours and hours eternity. He opened his sack of tobacco and rubbed flakes of the stinging particles in his heavy eyes. In spite of himself, he drowsed.

The *hissing* blast of the air cord brought him to wakefulness. The grinding *squeak* of brakes and the train ground itself to a reluctant halt.

Tom's ears, humming and throbbing from the hours of roaring wheels, began to pick up sounds now. He tensed suddenly and straightened his cramped limbs. On either side of the train there came the *pop-popping* of rifle fire. Then shouts. No doubt about it, the train was being held up.

Tom was about to peer around the end of the car when a shadowy figure crawled up the side of the tender.

"Uncouple that mail car and the express car!" ordered a gruff voice.

From the engine cab came the sound of a shot. Louder, deeper than the staccato bark of the rifles. The boom of a .45.

Uncertain as to what he should do, Tom flattened himself against the wall of the express car. A second figure clambered over the tender.

"All right?" called this man.

"Settin' purty!" called a voice from the cab. "The engineer come at me with a wrench and I had to kill him. Got the fireman at the throttle. Cars uncoupled?"

"Yeah. Let's go!"

The puffing of the laboring locomotive. Spinning of wheels as the shaking hand of the fireman opened the throttle. Then Tom felt the car lurch forward.

Shots from the top of the car told Tom that the hold-up men were riding there. A mile down the track and the engine and two cars halted. Tom suddenly thought of the portly, good-natured mail clerk and the boy that was his assistant. There would be a man in the express car, too. Locked in there with the packages that he would guard with his life until he went down. Judging from the voices, the hold-up men numbered ten or twelve. The mail clerks and the express messenger were hopelessly outnumbered.

Men were running about now. Tom's eyes were glued to the figure of a man that was sliding down from the tender. His mind was made up. He would help equal the odds against those men in the mail car. The man slid off the tender, almost into the waiting embrace of Tom. The dull *thud* of a hard fist and the man went limp. Another instant and Tom was slipping along the shadow of the car, a .45 in each hand.

"Open that mail car or we blow 'er up!" called a big man who seemed to be the leader.

"Blow and be hanged!" came the muffled reply from inside the car, accompanied by a shot.

"Git the powder!"

"Here y'are, Cap!" Two men approached, carrying a box.

Four men had taken a stand a dozen feet from the car and were methodically drilling its sides with rifle fire. Muffled shots from the mail and express cars told that the men within were making a brave stand.

Unseen by the outlaws, Tom clambered to the top of the mail car. Lying flat, he peered over the edge of the car. Several men were grouped about the box of dynamite. To them Tom called in a loud enough voice to be heard above the rattle of rifle fire.

"Back off from that powder, *hombres*, or I'll turn this cannon loose. One shot in that box'll blow you all over the desert! Stand back from it, dang' you!" He pulled the trigger of the .45 in his hand and the well-aimed bullet kicked dust in the faces of the men. They recoiled, reaching for their guns.

"Try to pot me and I'm aimin' closer! I'll live long enough to take a lot of you with me if I'm killed, so don't go droppin' lead this away." Tom's threat was convincing. There came a lull in the firing. A glance down the track told Tom that a crowd of men were coming on down the track from the abandoned section of the train. It would be some time, however, before they could reach the mail car. The outlaws drew back away from the car for a hurried consultation. They, too, had seen the crowd approaching.

"You win that pot!" called the leader who held a lantern. Tom caught a glimpse of the man's face. Smooth-shaven, lean, with a vivid white scar across the sun-reddened cheek. A scar that ran from the lobe of the left ear to the corner of the thin-lipped mouth. Then the lantern lowered and the evil-looking face faded into the shadow. But Tom knew that he would know the man if ever he saw him again.

The rifle fire ceased and, like ghosts, the shadowy forms of the hold-up men faded into the black night.

Tom grinned to himself. His ruse had been easily successful. Much simpler than he had hoped for. His grin of satisfaction was short-lived, however. A lurching jerk and the car under him was in motion. The man in the cab had started the engine!

"Blow up the powder and yourself with it, mister!" called a derisive voice. "You won't hurt nobody but yourselves!"

17

Fully well Tom realized the truth of the leader's statement. The outlaws, save those in the locomotive cab, were all out of range if the powder was exploded. To shoot into that box of powder meant only the possible destruction of himself and the men whose lives he was fighting for. With a grunt of disappointment, Tom edged along the car until he gained the forward end. The little section of the train was traveling at a decent rate of speed now.

Keeping pace with the train, although fifty feet from the tracks, the outlaws rode their horses at a run. The spot of the hold-up had been well planned. While part of the men had ridden on the train, others had been waiting with horses at the designated place where the train was to be stopped.

Tom gathered himself to a crouching position, gathering his legs well under him and bracing himself against the swaying of the car. Mentally he gauged the distance between the tender and where he stood. The darkness obliterated all outline of cars. There was one chance in 100 that he could land safely. Fear gripped at his throat and all but choked him. A chance in 100 . . . in 1,000 perhaps. With a short, reckless laugh, he leaped.

A sickening moment that seemed hours as his body suspended in the air. Then a swift, jolting impact that threw him forward on his face on top of the tender. He felt himself sliding, then, as the tender lurched sideways with a sickening motion, he rolled over. Grasping, clawing frantically, his left hand fastened on something solid. His body swinging alongside the tender, he slowly drew himself upward. When he had again gained footing on top, he heaved a sigh of relief. Then cautiously he moved forward.

Foot by foot he made his way along the swaying tender. He could see the glow of the fire in the firebox. Another lurch forward and he lay flat, peering down at the men in the cab. There were three besides the chalk-faced fireman at the throttle. Tom reached for the .45 that he had shoved in the waistband of his trousers. It was gone! The other gun had been discarded as superfluous when he had made the leap. Unarmed, one man against three who would show no quarter if he lost.

He hesitated an instant. Then his jaws clamped tightly and he crouched. A cat-like leap and he landed squarely on the shoulders of the nearest man. They went down in a heap. He had the man's gun now and the feel of its hard butt sent a thrill of hope through him. He swung it in a short arc. It *thudded* against the head of his struggling antagonist and the man lay quietly. At that instant the other two men were upon him. A blinding flash as a gun exploded. A gun barrel crashed against his head and Tom went limp.

CHAPTER
THREE

Clickety-click. Clickety-click. And vaguely, indistinctly at first, but gradually becoming clearer, the murmur of voices. For some seconds Tom was content to let his eyes remain closed. The words of the men talking were taking shape now. He caught himself piecing together the scraps of conversation. One voice, a booming bass voice, rose above the rest in a domineering fashion.

"Can't tell much about it, folks, till we gets the brush mowed offen his face, but I ain't doubtin' but what he's wanted bad. Shore a ornery-lookin' cuss. A heap tougher lookin' than them two dead 'uns. He put up a plumb nasty fight but I beefed him. Could 'a' shot him easy but wanted him alive, savvy? I'd tell a man there was goin's on there in that locomotive cab. You betcha. Fireman knocked cold and four ag'in' one. You boys got there in time to see the other two git away."

"It was quick work, Sheriff," came a voice that Tom recognized as that of the train conductor. "Look sharp, though, he's coming alive."

Tom, blinking in a dazed fashion, had opened his eyes. He was riding in a Pullman car. About the seat where he lay crowded a throng of curious passengers, pushing and crowding to obtain a better view of him.

Tom made as if to move and a rough hand shoved him back. He realized with a shock of surprise that his hands were bound by handcuffs that bit into his wrists with unwarranted cruelty. For the moment he forgot the terrific pain in his head. Twisting over on his side, he looked into the pale blue eyes of a big man who stood over him.

"What's the idee in treatin' a man like this, mister?" Tom asked hotly.

The blue-eyed man laughed harshly. "Did you hear him, folks?" he boomed. "Whinin' a'ready. Bet he squeals on his pals afore I git him locked up."

"I don't savvy the play," Tom went on. "I done my best to help them boys in the mail car and this is what I get fer it. Ask the mail clerk fellers. They'll tell you how I held that gang off from blowin' up the car. They'll . . ."

A ribald laugh cut short Tom's speech. With a sneer on his lips the big man looked down at him.

"You're either loco or drunk, feller," he said contemptuously. "How about it, clerk?"

For the first time, Tom noticed the big, good-natured mail clerk, swathed in bandages, propped up in the seat on the opposite side of the section. The clerk shook his head slowly.

"He boarded the train at Albuquerque. He rode the blind. I let him climb aboard to spite that grouchy con. As for him keeping the car from being blown up?" He smiled grimly and looked down at an arm that was wrapped in splints. "He did a bum job of preventing.

All that saved us boys in the car was that they didn't use enough powder."

"You mean to say you never heard me when I yelled at 'em to back off from the car that first stop they made?"

"Hear? With that bombarding going on? Listen, guy, don't kid us." The clerk's tone was heavy with bitter sarcasm.

"Better quit runnin' off at the head," put in the big man with the pale eyes. "You hired out fer a tough hand. Now play your string out."

"And who in tarnation are you, big feller?" growled Tom, now angry.

"Special officer from Cactus City and you're my prisoner." The man drew back the lapel of his coat, revealing an officer's badge.

"Cactus City?" repeated Tom, his hopes rising. "Then I reckon me and you kin talk turkey. Know Joe Rawlins from there?"

"Joe Rawlins?" The officer started perceptibly, then recovered his self-composure to survey Tom through narrowed eyes that seemed to be trying to convey a message that Tom could not fathom.

"Yeah. Joe Rawlins. Know him?"

"I knowed him afore he was . . . afore he died. He's dead now."

Tom nodded. "Yeah. And I'm Tom Rawlins, his nephew. I'm on my way to claim the estate."

The officer's expression suddenly changed. Tom, watching him narrowly, wondered. It seemed as if the man was greatly relieved. Suddenly the big man threw back his head and laughed.

"That's a good 'un. You heard him, folks? Nephew of ole Joe Rawlins of Cactus City. He'll be tryin' to tell us he's President of the United States next. Say, Miss Tuttle, did you hear what this gent said?"

The crowd parted and all eyes were turned to a girl seated across the aisle. Tom, following the glances of the throng, saw a somewhat tanned young lady whose mass of reddish-brown hair shone like spun copper in the sunlight of the early morning that streamed through the car window. Forgetful of his aches and pains, of his sad plight, Tom looked squarely into the large brown eyes of the girl. She met his gaze calmly. Contempt and loathing were dominant in the girl's level survey of the ragged, blood-caked man who lay manacled. Tom winced beneath that stare and for the first time became conscious of his disreputable appearance.

"The man lies, of course, Mister Edwards. Tom Rawlins is in Cactus City and has been there for five days. It was you that introduced him to Dad and me."

Tom suppressed a groan. Sick at heart, he looked at his manacled hands. Fully well did he realize the odds he was up against. These people all thought him one of the band of train robbers. Without a paper of any sort to prove his identity, it was useless to argue further. Apparently someone had appeared in Cactus City and by some means proved himself to be the nephew of Joe Rawlins. Plainly this Edwards was claiming credit for having knocked Tom on the head and capturing him. Edwards was making a hero of himself. Tom knew the type well. He smiled bitterly to himself and made an attempt to sit up. The officer allowed him to do so and seated himself alongside his prisoner.

Tom gazed moodily out the window. The curious crowd slowly broke up and went back to their seats. The mail clerk lay back on his pillows and closed his eyes.

"Best thing you kin do is come clean with me, tell who your pardners are, and I'll see what kin be done fer you when you come up fer trial. You got a life sentence starin' you in the face, feller. I can't promise nothin', but I'll do what I kin to see you git a fair trial."

Tom turned his head to fix the officer with a cold stare.

"Listen, mister," he said in a flat, menacing tone that caused the burly officer instinctively to reach for his gun, "I read your brand and earmarks plumb good, savvy? There's a heap about this here lay that I don't savvy, bein' as how I was sleepin' some. But I know that it wasn't you that put me away nor was it you that done ary fancy fightin'. It was all over when you got on the job, I'm a-thinkin'. And now you're tellin' it shore scary to these folks. The cards're all stacked ag'in' me, but a run of bad luck don't ever last always. When my luck does turn, Mister Two-Bit Officer, you better be a long time gone because I'm gonna be on the prod."

"Yeah?" Edwards's tone was sneering. He glanced quickly about. No one in the car seemed to be looking that way. Drawing back his hand, he struck Tom squarely across the mouth.

24

"That's a little sample of what you'll get if you make any more nasty cracks, get me?" he hissed in the prisoner's ear.

The girl across the aisle had apparently been gazing out the window. But there was a tiny mirror that ran upward along the window casing and in this mirror she had seen the cowardly blow struck. Now she whirled in her seat, a crimson spot of anger in her cheeks.

"Is that necessary, Mister Edwards?" she called in a low tone that despite its quietness was cutting.

Edwards flushed. "He . . . he was tryin' to make a break, Miss Tuttle," he explained hastily.

"So? It must have been a mild attempt. I've been watching in the mirror and he seemed quiet enough."

"Thanks, ma'am," said Tom through his bleeding lips.

She turned her head without meeting the prisoner's eyes. There was a look of pity in her eyes now instead of contempt. She had turned her head to keep the prisoner from seeing that look.

Edwards edged a bit closer to his prisoner, cursing him beneath his breath.

"Cactus City!" called the conductor.

Tom was pushed down the aisle of the car to the platform. The officer's grip bit into his forearm with an unnecessarily cruel pressure but Tom gave no sign. Grim-lipped, his eyes blazing defiantly, he allowed himself to be pushed down the steps of the car to the plank platform in front of the station.

News of the hold-up had reached Cactus City and the entire town was assembled to greet the arrival of the prisoner. The few women in the surging, milling crowd were in the background. Tom went a shade white as he saw the glowering, scowling expression on that sea of faces. A low, rumbling murmur swept over the waiting crowd as they saw the prisoner.

"String him up!" called an angry voice from the rear of the crowd. Other tongues took up the cry. The muttering crowd surged forward a little. Half a dozen ropes were held high by uplifted arms. Here and there the sun struck the glittering steel of a gun barrel.

Edwards, a faint sneer on his lips, made no move to protect his prisoner. His attitude was one of resigned helplessness.

A sinewy hand darted forward from the crowd and yanked at the bosom of Tom's shirt. Tom swung backwards, pulling the owner of that hand clear of the crowd. A flash of shining metal as the prisoner's manacled hands swung upward and descended, crashing into the astonished face of the man who held him.

"Any more of you dirty cowards want a taste of these?" he snarled at the hesitating crowd. "Come on, blast you! I ain't got a gun but I kin still use my fists! Step up and try your luck!"

"Grab him, some of you!" called a voice from the hesitating crowd.

"Here! Here! None of that!" Edwards stepped alongside the prisoner but those at the front of the crowd saw the officer wink broadly.

Suddenly Tom's fettered hands darted downward to the officer's hip. Then they raised again, a fraction of a second later, holding Edwards's gun. Stepping behind the officer, Tom jabbed the gun barrel in the center of the broad back.

"The first man that makes a bad move, I'm drillin' this officer!" called Tom. "Up with your paws, Edwards. I'm rearin' to kill you!"

The crowd gasped. Edwards obeyed the order with alacrity. His face went pasty white. "For God's sake, boys, step back!" he pleaded. "He means it! He'll kill me!"

"You're danged right I'll kill you," grunted Tom.

Behind him, on the platform of the car stood the girl who Edwards had addressed as Miss Tuttle. Her face was tense and drawn. She seemed about to speak, then halted, her eyes fixed on a rider who was pushing his mount through the crowd. A moment and the rider was alongside the train. He swung from the saddle and walked deliberately toward Tom and Edwards.

He was a small man, barely five feet five, dressed in shabby range clothes, dust-covered and none too new. A man of perhaps fifty, tanned the color of an old saddle, chewing at the corner of a ragged, snow-white mustache. Pinned to his vest was a sheriff's badge.

Tom looked squarely into the cold, gray-colored eyes of this little man who made no attempt to draw a weapon, although his right hand crooked claw-wise above the ivory butt of a low hung .45 on his thigh.

For a long second Tom held the gaze of the little sheriff. Then with a twisted grin, he stepped from behind Edwards and tendered his gun, butt first.

"I'm right glad to see you, Sheriff," he drawled. "You're my kind, I reckon. I'm your prisoner."

A faint smile crossed the lips of the girl on the platform. The color came back into her cheeks and she drew a deep breath. The little sheriff faced the crowd. Not a word passed his lips. Not a muscle of his face moved. But his cold gray eyes swept that crowd with a look that made those in front flush shamefacedly and push backwards in an effort to get somewhere else. Then those in the rear slunk off and in no time the platform was empty save for the sheriff, Edwards, Tom, and Miss Tuttle. The train was slowly departing.

The sheriff, seeing the girl for the first time, smiled and the effect was like a stone being tossed into a still pond. The gray eyes twinkled. Tom, watching the weather-beaten face, smiled in sympathy without knowing that he did so.

"Sue. Drat my spotted hide. Thought I'd shipped you off to the coast fer the summer."

"I wouldn't stay shipped, Dad. Got as far as Albuquerque and turned back. Now don't scold." She kissed him, squeezed his arm, and the smile left her lips. "You got here just in time to stop a lynching, Daddy," she said in a barely audible tone that did not reach the ears of Tom or Edwards some ten feet away.

"*Humm.*" Sheriff Tuttle strode toward Edwards and his prisoner. His cold gaze fastened on the officer and that gentleman squirmed uneasily.

"This your cannon, Edwards?" Sheriff Tuttle tendered the red-faced officer his gun.

Edwards muttered some inarticulate reply and shoved the weapon back in its holster. Tom grinned into the little sheriff's face, and, while the weather-beaten countenance of the officer was as expressionless as a mask, a spark akin to humor lit up his keen eyes, then, as suddenly as it had come, died out.

"I'm takin' charge of the prisoner, Edwards." The sheriff's attitude left the big man no alternative. With an attempt at passing the affair off as a joke, he left Tom in the sheriff's care and swaggered off.

Tuttle's eyes narrowed slightly as he watched the retreating form of the big man.

"Folks in these parts must 'a' bin grazin' some on locoweed when they let such a gent as that git to be a law officer," said Tom.

"Edwards ain't a native," put in Tuttle quickly. "He's what you might call an imported product. Hails from Wyoming or somewhere in that section. Kinda stock detective and bodyguard fer young Rawlins and the big law sharp. Rawlins hired him on the way down. Like as not he done got wind of the fact that fallin' heir to the Cross P Ranch had its drawbacks. Come on, pardner, I'll git you locked up afore you start another ruckus."

Tom followed obediently. He was thinking, thinking rapidly, as he pieced things together and jumped with some accuracy to several conclusions.

"This law sharp of young Rawlins's, Sheriff? What's his name?"

The sheriff gave him a quick look. "Calvin Prentice."

"Then it ain't the same gent I had figgered out," replied Tom disappointedly. "You were speakin' of drawbacks hooked to this Cross P Ranch that belonged to Joe Rawlins. Meanin' what, Sheriff?"

Tuttle surveyed the disreputable-looking cowpuncher with a gaze that seemed to read Tom's innermost thoughts.

"You seem all fired curious concernin' this Cross P layout, stranger," he said slowly, never taking his eyes from Tom's face.

Tom nodded. "Yeah. Seein' as how Joe Rawlins was my uncle, I'm kinda curious, mister. Oh, I ain't expectin' you to believe it," he finished with a wry grin as he saw the look on Tuttle's face.

"Why not?" snapped the sheriff. They had reached the jail now and the little officer was unlocking the door. "Why not?" he repeated. "You're a heap more like ole Joe's folks than that shifty-eyed dude that's claimin' the Cross P. I knowed Joe Rawlins and his brother Harve since they was kids down on the Brazos. Harve was ornery enough to have a kid that'd turn out to be a bad 'un. But he weren't yaller nor sneakin', Harve weren't, and this young Tom is both. And the yaller in him is goin' to grow some afore long, I'm a-thinkin'. He'll be needin' this here Edwards afore he's much older."

He pulled open the door, let in his prisoner, and the two men were alone.

"Hold out your paws, son. I think my key'll unlock them handcuffs."

"I don't foller your meanin', Sheriff." Tom frowned as he rubbed his galled wrists, now free from the handcuffs.

"Joe Rawlins was murdered. Shot in the back. Whoever killed him is more than likely to git the nephew in the same way."

Tom's eyes widened with surprise. "Feud?" he asked.

The sheriff shrugged. "*¿Quién sabe?* I'd give a heap if I knowed."

"The papers said Joe Rawlins was dragged to death by a bronc'."

"Yeah, he was dragged by a bronc', all right. But he was dragged *after* he'd bin shot. I was aimin' to keep that plumb quiet so don't spill it to nobody. Me and you're the only ones that know."

"You mean you're tellin' me somethin' that nobody in these parts knows about?" asked Tom, surprised and more than a little flattered that this apparently close-mouthed officer should talk to a prisoner with such freedom.

The sheriff nodded, smiling oddly.

"Why?"

"Why? Because, even with them whiskers and your face kinda swole like a lump-jawed steer, you're the spittin' image of Harvey Rawlins when Harve was your age. Now shed them clothes and crawl into the bathtub yonder. There's shavin' tools on the shelf. I'll rustle some clean clothes fer you."

Before the astonished Tom could speak, the sheriff was outside. Tom heard the *click* of the lock as Tuttle secured the door.

CHAPTER
FOUR

A shave, bath, and clean clothes did wonders for Tom. He looked and felt like a new man as he sat on the rickety little bunk, blowing cigarette smoke in luxuriant clouds toward the steel bars of his cell.

Sheriff Tuttle, reared back in an armchair in the corner, vied with the prisoner in filling the jail with tobacco smoke. Through the blue haze, he eyed Tom through lowered lids.

Tom had been telling the story of his adventure in Chicago and Tuttle listened attentively.

"Sounds like a likely enough yarn, son. And mebbyso this feller Calvin Prentice is your Harris gent. Like as not he'd change his brand when he moved West. But you ain't in no position to go claimin' your rights now. You got a danged serious charge starin' you in the face, and, unless one of these here miracles comes along, you're due to draw a life sentence. The engineer on that train was killed and it's plumb likely the fireman'll cash in his chips. A technical charge of murder will be filed ag'in' you. Bein' Tom Rawlins ain't goin' to help you none. You come by that ornery streak plumb nacheral. Harve Rawlins was a fightin' fool. Got killed in a drunken row, didn't he?"

Tom nodded. Plainly Tuttle was convinced that he was one of the train robbers. He noticed that the little sheriff was on guard every minute, and, unless he read the sign wrong, Tuttle was mighty fast with a gun.

"You aim to let this gent that claims he's me git away with his game?" asked Tom in an annoyed tone.

"If he kin. He's tackled a man's job. There's them gents that downed ole Joe, waitin' fer the chance to down him, remember that. He ain't had time to git to the ranch yet. Bin busy provin' his identity. It's a case of dog eat dog and I'm standin' off, givin' 'em room to lock horns."

"He might sell the place," suggested Tom.

"Sell the Cross P? Reckon not. Nobody wants to take a chance on it. It lays to the south, on the edge of the Crazy Mountains. Rough country, chock full of rustlers and renegades. Let a stranger take over that spread and they'd steal him blind. They was stealin' from ole Joe but he was too danged bull-headed to quit. He knowed they'd git him someday, and they did. And they'll git the next man that takes the place. They need that range and they'll fight to keep it. Not in the open, mebby, but from the brush."

"Looks to me like a big posse could wipe 'em out."

"It does, eh? Well, you'd change your mind if you was to take a ride in them hills. An army could hide there and you couldn't find a man of 'em if you hunted a year, it's that rough. Brush so thick a snake'd rub the hide offen hisself crawlin' through, box cañons with walls a hundred feet high, cricks with quicksand bottoms that'd bog a hoss fly. Wipe 'em out? I reckon not, young 'un. A man might crawl into a bear hole and pull a grizzly out by his ears, but he can't go into the Crazies and come out with nothin' except a carcass full of lead."

Tom smoked thoughtfully for some minutes. He was wondering if the men who had held up the train had fled to those hills. Perhaps. If he could only escape, he would head for the Crazy Mountains. If he could manage to capture the man with the scar on his face, there was a possibility of clearing himself of the charge against him. Once clear of that charge, he could somehow prove his claim to the Cross P Ranch. The problem was to escape from the jail. The log building was solid, the bars new and well embedded in the huge logs. Tuttle was on his guard constantly. And he had not a single friend on the outside to lend him aid. Tom frowned thoughtfully into space. It was growing dusk now and the tiny square of sunlight on the jail floor faded.

A knock on the outer door shattered the silence that had fallen over the two men.

Tuttle rose, tossed the cold butt of his cigarette into the brass cuspidor, and started for the door.

Tom swung his legs up off the floor preparatory to lying down. The rickety little bunk *creaked* ominously, then the legs at the foot of the bunk suddenly gave way.

"Dog-gone! I plumb fergot to wire up them laigs, son," apologized Tuttle. "You'll find some hay wire in the corner yonder. You'll have time to wire 'em up, I reckon."

Tom nodded, grinning, and crossed over to where several long lengths of wire lay along the wall. Then the sound of a loud, grating voice wiped the grin from his lips.

"Edwards," he muttered, and paused to listen.

". . . so I told him I'd bring it over, as long as I was headin' this way," came the tail end of the sentence.

"Now what in tarnation is anybody telegraphin' me for?" growled Tuttle in a petulant tone. A moment of silence, then: "Hang the luck!"

"Somethin' gone wrong, Sheriff?" asked Edwards.

"Huh? Wrong? Nope, reckon not. Only this telegram calls me away fer the night, that's all. Means I gotta leave this prisoner alone. My deputy's out on a case. Tarnation!"

"I'm at your disposal, Tuttle."

Tom, listening intently, was sure he caught a note of triumph in Edwards's voice.

"*Humm.* Yeah. Uhn-huh, so you are, Edwards." He paused as if thinking deeply. "I'm obliged, but I reckon I won't be needin' you."

"Aim to leave the prisoner unguarded? A man charged with murder left without a guard? He's a hard egg, Tuttle, and without a guard that hen coop of a jail 'ud be pickin's fer him to break outta."

"Yeah? Dunno about that, Edwards. This here cabin's held some right ornery gents. Uhn-huh. But I ain't leavin' him unguarded, pardner."

"No?"

"No." And the little sheriff deliberately turned his back on the big man. When he came to the steel bars that separated Tom from the front part of the jail that served as an office, he halted.

"Hey, young feller!" he called, peering into the shadowy interior of the cell.

"Yeah?" returned Tom, looking up from the bunk that he was mending.

"I'm called outta town. Won't be back afore noon tomorrow. I'm sendin' Sue over with your supper and she'll act as guard, *sabe?*"

Tom's eyebrows lifted in surprise. "A girl stand guard?"

"It won't be the first time. She kin shoot straighter and quicker than heaps of men that claim to be fast with their irons. And she'll not hesitate none if the play comes up right, savvy?"

Tom nodded. Edwards, standing a few feet back of the little sheriff, snorted his skepticism. "Now here's another thing I want settled afore I leave." Tuttle paused to light a big ceiling lamp, adjust the wick, then went on, speaking in a quiet drawl. "There may be another try made to lynch you."

"Yeah?"

"More than likely. That engineer left a wife and kid behind when he crossed the Big Divide. The hull town's het up. Consid'able het up, young feller. Your life ain't worth two-bits Mex if they lay hands on you. *Sabe?*"

Tom nodded gravely and waited for Tuttle to continue.

"If it comes to the worst, Sue will stake you to a gun. You ain't to use it lessen you jest nacherally have to. You gits that gun on one condition."

"Name it, Sheriff."

"Give me your word as a man that you won't try to make a getaway and that you'll return that gun when the gal asks you fer it."

Tom hesitated for a moment. "It's a go, Tuttle."

"I protest!" exploded Edwards. "Givin' a killer a gun. It's as good as givin' him the key to his cell and tellin' him to git out. I won't stand for it. I took this man prisoner and, by Harry, I'm seein' he ain't allowed to escape. I won't stand for it."

"Jest what d'you aim to do about it, Edwards?" The sheriff's tone was as soft as ever but his eyes were cold as steel.

"I'm stayin' right here in this jail to see that he don't git out or try any funny tricks. I'm an officer and I'm actin' within my rights. This man is my prisoner and I'm boggin' down right here to stand guard over him."

"And if the necktie party comes to carry him off?"

"I'll do my duty as a officer of the law."

"Don't lose your gun again, Edwards." Tom grinned.

"Don't worry," came the hot reply. "I won't."

"Better keep it in your hand or tie it around your neck with a piece of whang leather," suggested the prisoner.

"That'll be about enough of that," put in Tuttle, the ghost of a smile hovering about his lips. "Stay here, if you're a mind to, Edwards. Sue'll be over directly with the prisoner's supper. I'm lockin' up now."

"You mean you're lockin' me in?"

Tuttle nodded.

"Suppose a fire broke out? I'd be roasted like a rat in a trap."

Tuttle grinned. "Reckon you would, Edwards," he agreed.

"That man in the cell is ornery enough to set fire to the place. He's facin' a life term at Deer Lodge. I wouldn't put it past him."

"Neither would I, Edwards." The sheriff smiled.

He turned and walked to the outer door, fumbling in his pockets for his keys.

"Hold on, Tuttle, I'm comin'!" called Edwards with a curse that caused Tom to chuckle.

"Figgered you would, Edwards," said Tuttle dryly as he let the big man out the door.

Followed the rasping *click* of the lock and Tom was left alone.

CHAPTER
FIVE

By standing upright, Tom's head was level with the small window at the end of the long cell. Tuttle had opened the outer window so as to allow the breeze to enter. The short twilight had come to an abrupt end and night had enshrouded the little cow town in its black blanket. Here and there, lights shone in the adobe houses. Voices, dim and weird in the dark, came to the prisoner as he gripped the thick steel bars and peered into the night. The laugh of a woman floated toward him, gay, carefree, youthful. Tom caught himself wondering if it was Sue Tuttle that laughed. Blending nicely with the laughter of the girl came the musical *tinkle* of distant bells. Some Mexican goat herder corralling his charges at the edge of town. The barking of a dog, the strum of a guitar. The lilting refrain of a Mexican love song. Tom smiled bitterly and was about to leave the window when his ears caught the soft *thud* of a horse's hoofs in the dusty street.

Curiously, for want of something better to do, he watched the slow approach of a rider whose mount traveled at a running walk. Horse and rider came abreast of the jail now. The flare of a match pulled across the saddle cantle and the cupped flame rose to light a cigarette. For a long moment the face of the rider was illuminated. Tom gasped and his hands gripped the steel bars tightly. The rider was none other than the leader of the train robbers. The man with the scarred face.

Choking back the mad desire to call after the man, Tom watched him ride boldly down the main street of the town. Only when he had turned the corner of a building and was lost to sight did Tom relax.

Had Tom Rawlins been able to follow the movements of the scar-faced bandit, he would have seen him halt his horse at the long hitch rack in front of the Oasis, Cactus City's only hotel. Boldly, with the cool nonchalance of one who is sure of his ground, the scar-faced man slid from the saddle with the practiced ease of an expert horseman. For a moment he stood in the shadow of his horse, unfastening the snaps of his batwing chaps. Tossing the chaps across his saddle, he shoved the .45 that he had taken from the pocket of the leather leggings into a low-tied holster. Then he walked unhesitatingly into the lobby of the hotel.

A picturesque, striking figure, this tall, lean man whose amber eyes swept the place with a sure, swift glance. A bit over-dressed, in comparison with the average rider of the Southwest range. The high-crowned hat was a bit too high, the California pants, tight fitting and faced with buckskin, were a trifle too fancy, the stitched boots with three-inch heels were more ornamental than comfortable. But it was the man's face that held one's gaze. Lean, smooth-shaven save for a slender mustache twisted to needle points, dark as an Indian's except for the ugly scar that ran like a chalk mark across his jaw. Beneath straight black brows, the amber-colored eyes shone with the cold cruelty of a cat's.

The hotel proprietor greeted him with a smile of welcome that seemed a bit forced.

"Howdy, Santine," he called with uneasy heartiness. "Long time no see. How's tricks?"

The scar-faced man smiled and the effect was chilling. The man's smile seemed to add to the cruelty of the sinister face. "I'm looking for Tom Rawlins," he said in a voice that was well modulated. "Is he in?"

"Room Five. Head of the stairs and two doors down the hall on the left. Prentice and Edwards're with him."

"And who," inquired Santine in the level tone, "might Prentice and Edwards be?"

"Law sharp and detective that young Rawlins brung with him."

Santine smiled again and nodded slightly. Then he reached for the pen that stood in a tumbler filled with shot. He bent over the register and in a bold, vertical hand wrote: Santine, Cross P Ranch.

"Room Thirteen vacant?"

The proprietor chuckled. "You bet. Funny how some folks hate Room Thirteen. Now with you it's just the opposite. You . . ."

Santine reached out a slender, well-kept hand for the key. The cold look in his eyes cut short the hotel man's speech as effectively as if he had been throttled.

Key in hand, Santine mounted the uncarpeted stairway, the high heels of his boots *clicking* to the music of the silver-crusted spurs that he had not removed. Every eye in the lobby followed him. Not until his picturesque figure had disappeared in the long hallway above was the hushed silence in the lobby broken.

"He's a queer 'un, that Santine," the hotel man confided in a guarded tone to the group of loungers.

Half a dozen heads nodded in silent approval of the statement.

"And a bad 'un if he's crossed," added a cowpuncher. "But he's the best all 'round cowman in the country even if he does wear dude clothes."

"Wonder how him and young Rawlins will hit it off?" inquired someone.

There was no reply to this question. Silence, an uncomfortable silence, fell like a pall over the group. The man who had asked the question spat nervously toward a convenient cuspidor and shot an uneasy glance toward the head of the stairs.

But Santine was well out of earshot. With unguarded step, he walked past the closed door of Room 5, down the hall until he reached a door marked 13. A moment's pause as he unlocked the door and entered. His hand resting on the pearl butt of his low hung .45, he peered into the dark room. He stood in the shadow, letting the light from the hallway illuminate the room. Then, before lighting the Rochester lamp on the washstand, he crossed over to the window and pulled down the blinds. This done, he closed and bolted the door and lit the lamp.

He pulled a chair up to the washstand and took a square of white paper from his pocket. Then with the sharpened lead of a .45 cartridge, he carefully wrote on the paper.

A thin smile twitched at the corners of his thin-lipped mouth as he read what he had written. Then he carefully folded the paper and tucked it in his pocket.

His next act was to remove his boots. This done, he extinguished the lamp and stood for several moments in the darkness. Now he made his way with uncanny accuracy to the door and with guarded care unbolted it. Without a sound, the door opened on its oiled hinges.

Santine stood in the threshold now, peering up and down the deserted hallway. Then with long, swift strides, making not a sound in his stocking feet, he slipped down the hallway, pausing at Room 5. He stooped to a crouching position. Then, taking the note he had written, he pushed it under the closed door, leaving one corner protruding. Crouching a moment, he listened to the steady flow of low-toned conversation that came from within the room. Then, as swiftly and silently as he had come, he made his way back to his own room.

Without lighting his lamp, he stood in the shadow of his room, his eyes fixed on that corner of white paper that showed beneath the doorway of Room 5.

Five minutes passed. Ten minutes. Then the watcher saw the bit of paper disappear within the room. Someone in there had discovered it. Closing his door, Santine lit the lamp, pulled on his boots, and smiled at his reflection in the cracked mirror above the washstand. He hummed softly as he flicked bits of dust from his well-tailored flannel shirt. It was a bit of Italian opera that Santine hummed, the words half forming as the thin lips moved imperceptibly.

Once more the lamp was extinguished and again Santine moved down the hall toward Room 5. There was no stealth in his movements now. His boot heels *clicked* on the pine-board floor, his big, rowelled spurs chimed a merry accompaniment to the opera aria that he still hummed.

At his abrupt knock, the low murmur of voices in Room 5 ceased. A moment of silence. Then the stealthy turn of a key in the lock. Another brief interval of silence. Then: "Come in!" called a tense voice.

Santine, a smile on his lips, opened the door and paused on the threshold.

Three guns covered him where he stood.

"A strange welcome, gentlemen. A strange welcome, indeed." Santine's hand rose to twist the tiny mustache.

"Who the devil are you?" growled Edwards from a corner of the dimly lit room.

"I am Santine, foreman of the Cross P Ranch. I was told I would find Tom Rawlins in this room. I fear I'm intruding."

"Intruding? Santine? No, no, not at all."

It was a man even bigger than Edwards who spoke. A carefully groomed man. Tom would have recognized him as Harris. He gave Edwards and the younger man who crouched behind the folding bed a look that caused them to lower their weapons. Shoving his own automatic back in the side pocket of his coat, he advanced, his right hand outstretched in welcome.

"We've heard of you, Santine. Mighty glad to know you. I'm Calvin Prentice, Tom Rawlins's attorney." He paused embarrassedly as Santine made no offer to grasp his extended hand.

"Pardon my not shaking hands, Prentice. I never shake hands with anyone. Odd habit of mine. No offence meant, I assure you."

Prentice, a bit taken aback, smiled. Hastily he introduced Edwards and his client. Santine acknowledged the introductions with a formal bow.

This Tom Rawlins was a youth of medium height, wiry of build, a bit sallow, with beady black eyes that constantly shifted. His sharp features were stamped with a cunning craftiness.

Santine surveyed him with a slight narrowing of the eyes, then his yellow eyes fastened themselves on Edwards with an intentness that caused the officer to flush uneasily.

"Has the Casino at Cheyenne closed, Mister . . . ah . . . Edwards?" he asked pleasantly.

Edwards gave an almost imperceptible start and laughed shortly. "Casino? Cheyenne? You got me wrong, mister."

"Then I apologize." Santine smiled. "Odd that I should make such an absurd error. Fact is, I rather pride myself on my ability to remember names and faces. You must have a double, Edwards. Same voice, same face, same mannerisms."

"Queer, ain't it?" Edwards's voice had the hint of a threat in it that did not miss Santine's quick ears.

"Remarkably so, Edwards." Santine had suddenly tensed. His eyes were mere slits of yellow flame now. His upper lip lifted in a smile that was animal-like. His thumbs hooked in his cartridge belt, he stood with legs spread far apart.

The other two men shrank back out of line. The atmosphere of the room was charged with a tenseness that so often is the forerunner of violence.

Prentice and the younger man exchanged a swift glance. Their hands crept toward their guns.

"Careful." Santine's voice cracked like a rifle shot in the tense silence. His eyes had never left Edwards's face but he had stepped back until his spur rowel touched the closed door. Poised easily on the balls of his feet, he waited, his hand on his gun. "Three to one, gentlemen," taunted Santine. "Open up the jackpot if you're feeling lucky. I'm staying."

His tone was contemptuous, insulting. Yet none of the three moved to resent the insult. Of the three, the sharp-featured youth who claimed to be Tom Rawlins seemed the most formidable. Half crouched, his beady eyes like two spots of black fire, he seemed to be waiting for an opening. Santine seemed to sense this.

"I'm accommodating you whenever you're ready to open the show, Rawlins." He sneered. "Edwards seems to have changed his mind."

"Look here, boys, we're all acting, like a lot of fools," cut in Calvin Prentice with what was meant to be a hearty laugh. "Why the devil should we be quarreling?

Friend Santine mistook Edwards for someone he knows. Is that any reason why we should go shooting each other? We three are strangers in a strange land and it hardly behooves any of us to begin our sojourn in Arizona by shooting folks."

"Or being shot," finished Santine dryly. "I quite agree with you, Prentice." He relaxed, leaning idly against the door, and deftly rolled a cigarette. The other three seated themselves, relief plainly written on their faces. "If my memory serves me right, gentlemen, my reception here was an odd one," he went on easily. "You seemed to be expecting a visitor. An unwelcome visitor apparently."

The three men exchanged uneasy glances. Each seemed to be waiting for some sign from the other. Then Prentice nodded to Edwards as if in approval of the message he read in the other's eyes. The man who laid claim to the name of Tom Rawlins smiled mirthlessly and hitched his chair forward.

"We found this under the door a few minutes before you came," said Prentice grimly as he tendered a sheet of folded paper to Santine. "See what you make of it."

It was the note that Santine himself had shoved under the door. Yet, so far as his demeanor went, he was seeing it for the first time.

" 'Go careful,' " he read aloud, measuring his words carefully. " 'Cross P Ranch is bad medicine. Your lives ain't worth tobacco money if you go out there. Santine's a snake. Watch him.' "

With that twisted smile that made his dark face more sinister, Santine handed Prentice the note.

47

Edwards, watching the visitor closely, seemed disappointed.

Santine blew a smoke ring, watched it drift ceilingward, then laughed softly. "Well, gentlemen?" he inquired softly, visibly amused.

"Who do you suppose wrote the thing?" growled Prentice.

Santine shrugged. "*¿Quién sabe?* There is no signature. I am not without enemies. It would seem that one of them is poisoning your minds, no? He refers to me as a snake. You intend to heed his warning about going out to the ranch?"

Prentice, catching the note of banter in the speaker's voice, flushed slightly. "We were discussing the advisability of such a move when you rapped. We are men of peaceful habits, Santine. But if necessary, we will fight for our rights. Edwards is an officer of the law. I am an attorney. We intend to look out after Mister Rawlins's interests to the best of our ability. Whoever wrote this anonymous letter, no doubt intends bluffing us into leaving the country. In due time, we *will* leave. Mister Rawlins has no intention of keeping this ranch. He has other interests in the East that are vastly more important. Therefore, as soon as he has established a clear title to the Cross P Ranch, he will put it up for sale. Meanwhile, however, we will allow no man to hamper our movements in any way. If we choose to visit the ranch, we shall do so. Any interference will be overridden, I assure you."

"Quite so." Santine smiled. "I admire your stand in the matter. My services, naturally, are at the disposal of my employer." He indicated the sharp-featured youth with a nod of his head.

Again the youth smiled mirthlessly and Santine somehow felt annoyed. He could not help but feel that, in spite of his habitual silence, the owner of those beady eyes was a crafty thinker and a far more dangerous opponent than either of the larger men. He wished this silent individual would speak. He had his wish.

"Your services include the gun you're wearing, Santine?" he asked in a thin, colorless voice.

"Sorry, Rawlins, but they do not. My gun is not for hire. It comes out of its holster in defense of one man only. That man is Santine. In other ways, I'm ready to serve you."

"You mean you would not fight for a friend?" asked Prentice.

"Friend? Santine has no friend. That is why I never shake hands. I create no false impressions. I stand alone. I ask no favors. I grant none. I run the Cross P Ranch to the best of my ability."

Twisting his pointed mustache, he glanced from one to the other of the three men, an enigmatic glint in his amber eyes.

From the wooden sidewalk below came the tramp of booted feet and the murmur of many voices. If Santine heard, he gave no sign. The others, however, seemed to attach some significance to the unusual sound below. Edwards smiled as he met the glance of Prentice, then he addressed Santine.

"Looks like I'd better be goin'. Sounds like that lynchin' party was gatherin' and I told Tuttle I'd be on hand when they got too unruly."

"Lynching party?" Santine's voice was but mildly curious, but his jaw muscles twitched with some hidden emotion.

"Yeah. That train robber I brung in. The town folks is rearin' to git at him."

"Train robber? What train robber?" The yellow eyes narrowed slightly.

"You must 'a' jest got in." Edwards grinned. "There was a train hold-up and I managed to bring one of 'em in alive. I was on my way back from Albuquerque and happened to be on hand when the play come off. They'd've got away with a purty haul, too, if I hadn't took a hand in the game. They'd orter reward me good fer that piece of work."

"You captured one of the men?" asked Santine carelessly.

"I'd tell a man. And now I'd better be goin'."

Edwards got to his feet, winked meaningly at Prentice, and swaggered to the door.

Santine let him out and closed the door after him. "I'm leaving early in the morning for the Cross P," he announced. "We're mighty busy this time of the year. I just ran in to say howdy. I'll be looking forward to seeing you soon. Meanwhile, if you need me, send a messenger out to the ranch. Gentlemen, I bid you good night."

With a bow that hinted of mockery, he let himself out the door.

CHAPTER
SIX

Again in his own room, Santine closed and locked the door. Then, without lighting the lamp, he stepped to the window and for some time stood gazing at the rapidly gathering crowd that swarmed in front of the hotel. Snatches of profane comments drifted from the crowd. Comments that without exception were filled with condemnation of the man who was locked in the nearby jail.

Santine made out the bulky frame of Edwards who seemed bent on encouraging them instead of making any attempt at dispersing the lynching party.

The watcher had raised the window blind to gaze out. Now he lowered it until some twelve inches of space remained between the base of the shade and the window sill. He crossed over to the lamp and lit it, frowning the while in a puzzled manner.

Scarcely had he taken a seat and built a cigarette when there came a tapping at his door. Once, twice the peculiar tap was repeated. Santine unbolted the door and resumed his seat.

"Come in!" he called in a low tone.

A short-statured man in brush jumper, overalls, and rusty boots entered and closed the door. He seemed ill at ease as Santine's eyes stared at him unblinkingly.

"Who's that man they've got in jail, Bill?" snapped Santine in an annoyed tone. "We short any men?"

"Nary one, not nary. Dogged if I know who it 'ud be."

"They have a man in the coop. And they think it's one of the gang. You were in that mob across the street?"

"Shore thing. I stood in the shadder, watching your winder. I was shore gettin' a earful of information when I got your winder-shade signal."

"What's the dope on it?"

"They're rearin' to string this boy up, whoever he is. And a big gent named Edwards is ribbin' 'em up to it. This Edwards feller is a officer of some kind. Fine officer, him. Seems like this Edwards and ole Tuttle done locked horns over the pris'ner and Tuttle bein' outta town, the Edwards polecat aims to make this here necktie party a plumb success. Sue Tuttle's guardin' the boy now. If you're askin' me, boss, I'm claimin' it's a danged shame to go fightin' wimmen and stringin' up a boy that ain't done nothin'."

"But I don't recall asking you your opinion," replied Santine dryly. "Recall the tramp that made the play from the top of the mail car?" His voice had dropped to a hissing whisper and the yellow eyes were mere slits.

Bill nodded.

"I'm making a big bet that it's the tramp that's in jail."

Again Bill nodded, shifting uneasily from one foot to the other.

"Well? What else is on your mind?"

"Nothin'. That is, nothin' to speak of. Only I was jest recallin' a talk some gent in the crowd was mouthin' off. He claimed he was on the train when the Edwards feller brung this boy into the chair car. He said the pris'ner claimed to be Tom Rawlins. Danged nonsense, of course."

Santine nodded absently and seemed intent on some subject far removed from Tom Rawlins. In reality he was mentally comparing the sharp-featured youth in Room 5 to Joe Rawlins. This city-bred youth was far from the counterpart of Joe's nephew as Santine mentally pictured him. Also, even in the West, a man is judged by the company he keeps and this man Edwards was bad. Bad to the core. His memory for names and faces had not failed him. Beyond a doubt, this Edwards was the man he had seen in the Cheyenne gambling house. Moreover, Edwards knew that. Where had Edwards and the sharp-featured youth met? Was the youth an innocent victim of Edwards and this man Prentice or was he hand in glove with them, an imposter?

"The Edwards feller's done gone down to the jail," Bill cut in on Santine's musing. "He 'lows he's goin' to separate Sue Tuttle from her pris'ner."

"How?" Santine was smiling now.

"Either by some trick or else by main strength an' awkwardness."

"He might trick her, Bill, but if he tries any rough stuff, my money's on Sue. That girl's game. And Edwards, unless I'm going blind, is a four-flusher and yellow clear through."

"From his brisket to his hocks," agreed Bill. "You met him?"

Santine nodded. "Twice. Once in the Casino at Cheyenne. Across a poker table. He was running a stud game. Cold-decked a greaser and some idiot kept the Mex from killing him. I met him for the second time, this evening. He's sort of bodyguard for the young man who, if no one by some mischance puts out his light, will be signing our pay checks next week."

"He's ridin' herd on young Rawlins?"

Santine nodded. "Perhaps," he said softly, as if musing aloud, "that is why he is so anxious for the lynching party to be a success."

"I don't get you, boss."

"No, Bill." Santine smiled. "I didn't expect you to."

Bill fidgeted. He felt that he was being made fun of, somehow. His loose lips spread in a half-hearted grin as he fumbled with cigarette makings. Down in his heart, he hated Santine. Hated him for being so superior. Hated him for the way he wore his clothes, the way he smiled, the way he had of making a man feel like a whipped cur that comes whining back to its master for another kick. But he hid his hate beneath that loose grin and waited for his employer to speak.

But Santine remained silent, apparently absorbed in thought. To Bill, that silence became torture. He hated these lapses in conversation. It made him feel even more ill at ease than Santine's barbed remarks.

"You're . . . you're aimin' to kinda help this gent they're aimin' to lynch?" he finally blurted.

"Help him? Hardly. It's none of our business if they want to hang a man in this town. Why should I help him?"

"I thought that mebbyso, him bein' kinda innocent-like, and the gal bein' kinda up ag'in' big odds thataway, that we might kinda take cards in the game?" Bill's tone was hopeful.

"You shouldn't do so much single-handed thinking, Bill. You aren't built to stand the strain. Nobody's going to hurt old Tuttle's daughter, rest easy about that. As for the man . . . ?" Santine snapped his fingers.

"But if we was to save his pelt fer him, he'd be plumb grateful and with them two boys bein' killed and leavin' us shorthanded down in the hills . . ."

"Suppose you let me do the suggesting, Bill?" Santine's voice was soft as silk but the sneer on his lips belied the quietness of his tone.

Bill gulped, grew red, then white, and red once more. He had heard Santine use that same soft tone before. He had seen two men mistake the softness for a weak strain in the boss' makeup. They had paid the penalty of their mistake with their lives.

"Shore, boss. I was meanin' no harm," he muttered.

"Good. You might take a stroll toward the jail, then. When the show is over, report back and give me the details. I'll be interested to learn how friend Edwards came out with Miss Tuttle. And you might as well put my horse in the barn on your way there."

CHAPTER
SEVEN

It took some time for Tom Rawlins to survive the embarrassment of a lady jailer. Long ago, the luckless captive had decided that Sue Tuttle was by far the most attractive girl that he had ever seen. This, despite the fact that she had not by so much as a single glance let him think but what she loathed and despised him.

As she handed him his supper through the steel bars, she was as cool and self-possessed as if he were some animal.

"I'm . . . I'm shore obliged, ma'am," he managed to say as he set the dishes of savory viands on his bunk. "This grub looks plumb good . . . I ain't had nothin' fer so long the smell of food makes me kinda faint."

He fumbled with his napkin, flushing brick red as she smiled faintly. Standing there beside his bunk, he gazed at her as if fascinated. He knew that he was staring at her and grew all the more embarrassed. Yet he could not tear his gaze from her face.

For the first time, Sue Tuttle lost her superb self-possession and blushed.

"Shucks, ma'am, excuse me fer bein' a starin' idiot," gulped Tom, dropping his gaze to his boots, all but upsetting his food in an embarrassed move to seat himself. "I didn't aim for to be smart-alecky, ma'am."

The girl nodded, and laughed softly. Tom grinned down at the thick steak.

"Please eat before everything gets cold," she told him, then made her way to the outer room to remain there while the famished prisoner hungrily devoured the meal that she had prepared. Her father had warned her that the prisoner would be able to stow away considerable food and the meal she brought was more than ample for a hungry man. Yet there was not a particle of food left when she returned to the cell bars.

"Best meal I ever tackled," was Tom's grinning comment as he passed the empty dishes through the bars. "I'm shore grateful, ma'am."

"I'm glad you managed to make out," she returned with a disconcerting coolness.

Tom noticed that she wore a well-filled cartridge belt about her waist and the gun in the holster was a .38 special, light but effective.

"Dad told me there might be trouble," she announced, seeing the direction of his glance.

"Yes'm."

"If it comes to the worst, I'm giving you a Forty-Five. You'll use it only to defend yourself. If you must shoot, aim for a gun arm. I reckon you can handle a gun with enough control to wing a man without killing him?"

"Yes'm. Reckon I kin."

"And when things have quieted down, you'll return the gun?"

"I give your dad my word that I would. I wouldn't lie to him or to you, ma'am."

"No." Sue smiled. "I don't believe you would. You know, since you've shaved and gotten cleaned up, you don't look near as villainous as you did on the train. Queer what whiskers and . . ."

A loud rapping at the outer door interrupted her. She shot Tom a meaning look as she started for the door.

"Careful," cautioned Tom in a guarded tone. "It may be the mob."

She nodded and kept on until she reached the bolted door.

"Who's there?" she called sharply.

"That you, Miss Tuttle?" called a muffled voice in what appeared to be a tone of great agitation.

"Yes."

"Thank the stars I found you! This is Charlie Simms. Brakie on the through freight. The missus is sick, Miss Tuttle. Awful sick. And that fool doctor's dead drunk again. She's bin callin' for you for more'n an hour, miss. Says you set with her durin' one of these heart spells last month. She's in a bad way and . . ."

The man's plea swept away her suspicions. She unbolted the heavy door and peered into the night, half blinded by the inky blackness in front of her.

"Where are you? I can't see well in the . . ."

A sudden, unexpected movement in that cavern of darkness. Four men leaped simultaneously upon the girl before she could move. Another instant and she was carried away into the night.

"Sorry I had to lie like that, miss," came the apologetic voice of the railroad man, "but the engineer that was murdered was my buddy."

Tom, back in his cell, had not caught the plea of the man. He had heard Sue unbolt the door, then the muffled, indistinct sounds of a scuffle, followed by silence. Now he heard the *click* of a man's boot heels on the floor and the scraping of the bolt as the door was fastened. The sounds of the boot heels approached.

Suddenly Tom choked back an oath and slipped to the far corner of his cell. For it was Edwards, vastly pleased with himself as he dangled the jail keys in his hand, who stopped at the cell, peering through the bars.

"The boys'll be here in half an hour, pardner," he sneered at the prisoner. "If your mammy ever learned you ary prayers, you better be thinkin' em up. Sorry we can't accommodate you with a sky pilot to hunt a easy crossin', but we're kinda pressed for time and can't be bothered huntin' up no psalm singers."

"Listen, Mister Plenty-Belly," said Tom, striding toward his cell door, "if you or ary man in that gang has hurt that lady, you'll pay, if I have to come back from across the Big Divide to do the collectin'. I ain't no ways scared to die, Edwards, and I ain't askin' no favors of you or the men that're doin' your dirty work. But I'm goin' to make it plumb interestin' for them that has the guts to tackle me without shootin'."

As Tom stepped to the bars, Edwards instinctively recoiled. He was chewing vigorously on a wad of fine-cut. Now he spat, squarely at Tom's face. Tom dodged just in time.

Edwards laughed harshly as Tom retreated to his bunk. Then turning his attention to the empty dishes that Sue had placed on the floor, he shattered the china with a well-placed kick.

Despite the fact that it was a matter of minutes until the mob stormed the jail, Tom did not lose hope. Desperately he glanced about the bare cell in search of a weapon. He decided on the chair that Tuttle had left there. An effective weapon that would make things interesting for a few moments, he decided. Unconsciously he had picked up a six-foot strand of the smooth hay wire and run the end through the spliced loop at the other end. The thing reminded him of a hangman's noose as it closed, and he shuddered. He was about to cast it aside when an idea stabbed his brain with a suddenness that made him look up quickly at Edwards to see if the officer had read his thoughts.

Edwards was pacing leisurely up and down in front of the cell, taunting his prisoner with vile remarks. Tom, with head lowered, but furtively watching his captor, made no response. After several minutes of this profane abuse, Edwards seemed to tire of the cowardly baiting. Tom's unresponsiveness was galling.

On the opposite wall of the narrow corridor were posted placards with photographs of various criminals who were wanted. Curiously Edwards fell to studying these. His back was toward the cell.

It was the opportunity for which Tom had been waiting. With cat-like tread, he slipped across the floor of his cell, making no sound. In his right hand was the looped wire. He was at the bars now. A barely audible *swishing* sound as the looped wire swung upward, then flipped down over the officer's head and around his thick neck. With a terrific jerk that threw Edwards off his balance, Tom pulled the noose tight.

An agonized, choking cry as Edwards sought to free his neck from the tight noose. Another heave on the wire and the struggling form was alongside the bars. Keeping the wire taut with his left hand, Tom's right hand reached through the bars and plucked the officer's gun from its holster.

Edwards was growing weaker now. His struggles were but feeble, child-like attempts. His purpling face, the protruding eyeballs, the thickening tongue made Tom shudder. The choking man's wind was coming in awful whistling gasps. Then Tom let go the wire and picked up the keys that had fortunately fallen within reach. A moment and he was in the corridor. It was the labor of a few minutes to jerk free the wire, then drag the unconscious officer into the cell, and toss him on the bunk. Then, working with swift sureness, he bound and gagged Edwards, locked him in the cell, and extinguished the light.

Still moving with the utmost caution, he let himself out the door into the velvet darkness of the night. For a moment he crouched in the darkness beside the log wall of the jail, his gun ready for instant use.

Not a sound betrayed the presence of anyone near. From the direction of the hotel came the muffled sound of voices and the tramp of booted feet on the board sidewalk. He could see lanterns flitting about in the distance.

Tom's first thought was how to get a horse. From experience, he knew that the feed barns were usually at the end of town. Which end? After a moment's debate, he decided to go in the opposite direction from the hotel. He set off at a brisk walk. Keeping to the dark streets, he pursued a zigzag course, glancing over his shoulder every few feet to see if he were being followed.

Just when he gained the impression that someone was dogging his footsteps, he did not know. He saw no one, heard no sound, yet he was certain that someone was behind him. The hair along the back of his neck seemed to rise and he quickened his pace a trifle. A big, frame building loomed up in front of him. The feed barn. He could hear the nicker of a restless horse inside.

Breathing freer, Tom slid around the corner of the barn and flattened himself against the boards. Gun in hand, he waited for the man who had been following him.

A minute passed. Two minutes. They seemed hours to the impatient Tom. Perhaps, after all, he thought, he was wrong. Then, out of the wide opening of the barn, a man came, swinging a smoke-grimed lantern.

For the moment Tom forgot the man who had been following him. He devoted his entire attention to the man with the lantern.

The man walked with a bent-over, rheumatic gait. The gait of a man past sixty. The barn man, no doubt. Tom sank to a crouch as the yellow rays of the lantern fell fully upon him. But the man with the lantern was looking straight ahead. Pausing for a moment to light a corncob pipe, he pinched out the match between thumb and forefinger, then went his way, puffing contentedly.

Still grasping his gun, Tom rose with a sigh of relief. He was about to move to a more advantageous position when a harsh whisper caused him to whirl in his tracks, his gun leveled at the spot in the darkness from whence the sound had come.

"If you're holdin' that gun on me, mister, hold your fire," came the whisper, over to the left now.

Tom swung his gun barrel toward the new spot, making no reply.

"I'm your friend, pardner," came the whisper. "If I'd wanted to plug you, I'd 'a' done it when you was in the lantern light. I'm comin' toward the barn now with my hands empty."

"Light a match," growled Tom.

A scraping sound as a match head was pulled across an overall-clad leg. Then with the flame cupped in his upraised hands, he walked toward Tom. It was Bill, Santine's man.

Tom let him get within a few feet, then halted him.

"What's the idee?" he asked.

"I follered you from the jail," replied Bill in a cautious tone. "So danged dark I couldn't tell if it was you or that Edwards polecat. I'm right glad it's you."

"Why?"

"I got my reasons, pardner. No time to go arguin' about that. You're after a hoss, ain't you? Well, I'll stake you to one. A danged good 'un. Good outfit, too. Kinda fancy but plumb good." He chuckled.

"What's the joke?" growled Tom, still suspicious. He had gotten to the point where he trusted no man.

"I was just thinkin'," Bill explained, "how Santine will fight his head when he finds his hoss gone in the mornin'."

"Who is Santine?"

"You'll learn soon enough if you stay on this range long. Come on, feller. Shake a leg. We ain't got all night."

With Tom's gun still covering him, he stepped into the barn and boldly lit a lantern that hung on a wooden peg.

A big roan horse stood in the end stall. Tom needed no second glance to tell him that the roan was an animal far superior to the average cow horse.

"Lead him out," ordered Bill. "He's plumb gentle. And the fastest hoss in the Cross P remuda."

"Cross P?"

"Yeah." Bill had produced a saddle, blanket, and bridle. An outfit worth far more than most cowpunchers care to put into their rigs.

"And here's Santine's carbine. You'll find shells aplenty in the saddle pockets."

Not a little puzzled at this stranger's efforts on his behalf, Tom watched him furtively as he saddled the roan. The man's face and voice were vaguely familiar. But he could not recall where he had met him. In spite of his apparent friendliness, Tom suspected some sort of trick. Not until he was mounted and had ridden into the open did he feel secure.

Bill had blown out the light and followed him outside.

"You'd orter be across the Mexican line by noon tomorrow," he advised. "She lays south and east of the Cross P Ranch."

"Which direction do the Crazy Mountains lay?" asked Tom.

"South?" gasped Bill. "You ain't headin' fer the Crazies?"

"Reckon I am, stranger. And I'm obliged to you for the help. Excuse me for bein' too danged superstitious about you but I've bin gettin' some raw deals lately."

"Pardner," said Bill solemnly, "Santine'll locate you, shore as shootin', if you go to the Crazies. You're forkin' his pet hoss. He'll kill you shore."

"Mebby." Tom grinned. "I'm riskin' that. I don't care much for this silver-trimmed outfit. You might tell him I'll send it to him when I get hold of a good hull without jim-cracks on it. Reckon I'll keep the roan, though. Kinda like the feel of him between my laigs."

"I ain't carryin' no messages like that to Santine." Bill grinned. "No, ma'am. And this here hoss-stealin' deal is between you and me, savvy? Santine's bin rawhidin' me hard and I'm evenin' up a mite, that's all. Between you and me."

"That goes as she lays, pardner. Say, if you were there when Edwards busted in the jail, mebbyso you know what become of the gal?"

"They took her to a deserted cabin at the edge of town. I heered Edwards tell the gents to take her there. He 'lowed there'd be two gents there to guard her."

"Know where this cabin is?"

"If you're takin' the south trail, you pass right by it. It stands about fifty feet from the trail. Creaky windmill in front. But dog-gone it, feller, don't do nothin' foolish. The gal's safe enough there. They won't dast hurt her."

"Mebby not. I aim to make sure. I'm obliged, mister. I'm returnin' the favor someday. So long." He held out a hand, dimly visible in the light of the half moon that had risen.

Bill took his hand. Then Tom whirled the impatient roan and was gone.

CHAPTER
EIGHT

Sue Tuttle, her wrists and ankles tightly bound, sat in a chair facing the two masked men who stood guard over her. Her cheeks pale with anger, her dark eyes blazing defiance, she eyed the two men without speaking.

They were well masked, these two, with black hoods that covered their heads and fell about their shoulders. Each of them wore a long yellow slicker, buttoned to the throat. For Calvin Prentice and the young man who claimed to be Tom Rawlins had no desire to be recognized.

"You'll pay for this insult," panted Sue, her usually musical voice now a husky whisper.

"Don't be holdin' it against us, miss. We're just two well-meaning cowboys, trying to see swift justice done." It was Prentice who spoke, disguising his voice.

"Cowboys?" retorted Sue. "With low-cut shoes and tailored trousers creased like that?"

Prentice suppressed an oath. The slicker lacked several inches of being of sufficient length to disguise his feet. And beneath the slicker of his companion showed polished tan Army boots.

"Your masks are so warm," went on Sue in a sarcastic vein. "Really, you should take them off, Mister

67

Prentice . . . and Mister Rawlins." She smiled grimly as her two captors squirmed uneasily. "Aren't you afraid to be out after dark without your faithful protector, Edwards?" she went on, getting what enjoyment she could out of a miserable situation.

The smaller man did not answer but muttered some remark to Prentice.

Prentice shrugged. "What good will it do us to beat it now?" he growled in an annoyed whisper. "The idiot got us into it. Let him get us out of it tomorrow."

"Mister Edwards, I presume, is taking charge of the murder party." Sue's voice trembled with emotion.

"Is it murder to hang a man who has done what that prisoner did?" retorted Prentice in a nettled manner.

"He has the right to be tried for his crimes, Mister Prentice. Believe me, you'll wish you had kept out of this, when Dad returns."

"Now look here, Miss Tuttle," Prentice began in a soothing tone, "things could be much worse for you, you know. Those men who left you here were ignorant of our identity. Suppose something should happen to you? Suppose you were gagged again as you were when they turned you over to us to watch? And, for the sake of argument, let us say that the gag, hastily applied in the dark, strangled you. There would be no one to try for the crime, unless your efficient father placed every man in Cactus City under arrest and brought them to trial. And that, of course, is too absurd to think of."

"Am I to understand that you are threatening to kill me, Mister Prentice?" Sue's lip curled in defiance.

"You put it very . . . ah . . . bluntly, Miss Tuttle."

"Unless you want me to tell my father who the two men were who held me prisoner in this cabin, I advise you to go ahead with your murder, Mister Prentice."

Inwardly quaking with fear, for she had no doubt but what Prentice would carry out his threat if he had to, yet the girl gave no outward sign that she was afraid.

On the floor lay the rude gag that had been removed when Sue was brought to the cabin. Moving with deliberate slowness, Prentice picked it up and advanced a step toward the girl.

"My God, Cal! You don't mean to . . . ?"

Prentice whirled on his companion, his big fists clenched. "Shut up, you fool! Can't you see we're up against it? If you're going to turn yellow, get outside. I'll tend to this alone!"

"You will like . . ." The younger man's hand darted to his gun but the heavy automatic in the big man's paw covered him.

"No gun play, pal. It's not your line of work, you know. Toss your gat in the corner, then take the air. When you've cooled off, come back."

The two men were too intent in their clashing of wills to hear the door behind them *creak* faintly as it swung cautiously open. Sue, however, saw it and schooled her features to a mask-like immobility as she saw the door open, an inch at a time. The slight draft caused the lamp on a nearby table to gutter, and then flicker, shooting odd shadows across the cobwebbed ceiling. The door was open now and in the open doorway stood Tom Rawlins, a .45 swinging idly in his hand.

In spite of his hood, Prentice felt the cool draft of air on the back of his head. His big frame tensed. Yet he did not turn his head or make any sign that he knew someone stood behind him.

The big man's confederate, seeing Tom, stood motionlessly, the eyes behind his hood fixed on Tom's gun. Then the automatic in the big man's hand spat a streak of flame, its heavy leaden slug shattering the lamp and plunging the room into sudden darkness.

With a curse of chagrin, Tom sprang. A heavy *crash* as he flung himself upon Prentice. The *thudding* of blows, and then the two men rolled over and over on the dusty floor, locked in deadly embrace. They crashed into the chair where Sue sat, helpless, pitching her to the floor. With ready wit, she rolled clear of the fighting men, tearing frantically at her bonds.

"Sap him, Eddie!" croaked Prentice. "Sap him! He's got my gat! He's killin' me! Quick! I'm . . ."

A thudding *crack* as Tom's gun barrel met the big man's skull. Tom jumped to his feet, ready for the second man.

But Chicago Eddie, alias Tom Rawlins, was in no hurry to mix in the fight. Fighting was not his game. He was accustomed to winning his battles by his nimble wits, not with his hands. Besides, he was sickening of Calvin Prentice and his murdering tactics. Outside the door, he crouched in the darkness.

"All right, ma'am?" called Tom anxiously.

"All right," came the reply from a far corner.

"Where's the other 'un?"

"He ran, I think!"

Tom cautiously made his way in the darkness to where she lay. She made no sound as he cut the ropes that bound her.

"Keep right behind me," cautioned Tom in a barely audible whisper. "We'd better drag it while the goin's good."

She obeyed. Together they gained the door. There they paused, listening intently.

Chicago Eddie, crouched a few feet away, slipped a keenbladed knife from beneath his shirt. He had already shed the cumbersome slicker and hood. A twig *cracked* under his foot as Tom and Sue stood, peering into the night.

"Wait here," Tom whispered in the girl's ear. "If I seem to be gettin' the worst of the scrap, run. Use this if you got to." He shoved his gun into her hand. Then, before she could offer protest, he was gone without making a sound.

Eddie moved with a faint rustling sound. The next instant Tom was on top of him. He had leaped blindly toward that rustling.

The knife swung in a short arc, burying itself in Tom's chest muscle under his left shoulder. The blow was a glancing one, or else it would have found his heart. Tom's fingers found the soft throat of his antagonist and his other fist crashed time and again into the face of the man. It was a short struggle. One of the blows caught Chicago Eddie under the point of his jaw and he went limp.

71

"All over, ma'am!" called Tom. Panting, he again guided her through the darkness to where he had left his horse.

"You . . . you killed them?" she asked in awed tone.

Tom laughed shortly. "No, ma'am. That is, lessen they run themselves to death when they wake up. I just put 'em to sleep. Who are they? Don't reckon you know, though, masked like they were."

They were standing beside the horse now. Tom no longer felt embarrassed in the presence of this girl. Without a word of explanation he lifted her into the saddle and swung up behind.

"If this pony ain't broke to ride double, it's time he was learnin', ma'am." He laughed.

But the big roan offered no protest at the double burden. He set off along the trail at a running walk.

"Where are you taking me?" asked Sue.

"Wherever you say, ma'am, so long as it ain't back to jail. I changed places with that Edwards gent. If you must have a pris'ner to show your dad, use Edwards."

"Oh." The monosyllable might mean anything or nothing.

"Got ary friends near town, Miss Tuttle?" he asked.

"Two miles out of town. On this trail. They'll take care of me until Dad gets here."

"Good. Miss Tuttle, I've done give my word to you and your dad that I'd act on the square. D'you reckon I'd be breakin' that word if I was to leave you at that ranch and go on?"

"Under the circumstances, no. You ceased to be my prisoner when I let myself be tricked into opening that jail door. You saved my life a few minutes ago. I think Dad will agree with me when I tell him my story. You risked capture and death when you came into that cabin. I'm thanking you now. Here is your gun."

Tom shoved the gun back into his holster. "You mean, those two gents aimed to kill you?"

"Prentice did, I'm sure. The other one, Tom Rawlins, tried to prevent him. They were quarreling about it when you came in."

"Prentice? Rawlins? The hounds. Let's go back and I'll . . ."

"And you'll run square into the mob that will be hunting you. Dad will fix them when he gets home."

Tom did not speak for some moments. At last he broke the silence that had fallen over them.

"Tell me what this Prentice gent looks like, ma'am."

Sue described him to the last detail. Her father's training in being able to give an accurate description of people had been passed on to his daughter.

"That's Harris, all right," said Tom, when she had finished. "Shore as shootin'. Ma'am, when you meet your Dad, tell him about tonight's deal if you want to. But tell him not to bother this Prentice or the gent that calls himself Tom Rawlins. Tell him to let 'em play their game. He'll savvy what I mean. Tell him to give 'em all the rope they need to run on. I'm the one they're hurtin' most and I'm goin' to beat 'cm at their own game, savvy? The same goes for Edwards. These gents will be crawlin' to you on their knees tomorrow, like as not. Let 'em. Don't throw 'em in jail. I want to see what they'll do next. Promise?"

"I don't in the least understand." She frowned.

"Your dad will. I never had no hand in that hold-up, Miss Tuttle. I was beatin' my way when the play came up. I'm huntin' for a gent that I'll make prove what I say. I got a hunch he hides out in the Crazy Mountains and I'm goin' there to drag him outta his hole. You heard me tell Edwards on the train that I was Tom Rawlins. I told the truth. Ask your dad if you don't believe me . . . dog-gone!"

From the distance came the shouting of men, riding along the trail from town.

"Looks like they were shore after me, ma'am." Tom grinned.

"Yes. You'll have to ride for it. Yonder's the ranch. See the light through the window? Let me off here. It's only a hundred yards to the house."

"You're right sure you'll be plumb safe there?"

"Safe as if I were in church."

Tom slipped to the ground and lifted her from the saddle. The dim light cast by the moon hid the twinge of pain that for a moment shot across his face. The wound in his chest, while not in the least dangerous, was a bit painful. But the girl's next words drove all thought of pain from his mind.

"I'm mighty grateful to you, Tom Rawlins," she said in an earnest tone that thrilled him like an electric shock. "And I believe you. I promise to do as you wish. But the Crazy Mountains . . . those hills are not safe for honest men."

Tom nodded briefly. "Your dad told me about 'em. And that's where my man will be, I'm plumb certain. I never cared much, up till now, what folks thought of me. But you and your dad have treated me mighty fine. I'm aimin' to prove to you-all that you ain't wrong in your judgment. Those gents are gettin' closer, ma'am. I'll say so long."

The girl held out a slim hand. Tom held it for a moment.

"It's worth a heap to a man to have a girl like you believin' in him, ma'am."

"Thank you. Good bye. And good luck . . . Tom."

With the girl's farewell ringing in his ears, Tom rode at a stiff trot along the trail. For the first time in weeks, he felt happy.

Once in the ranch house, Sue Tuttle gazed with tremulous lips at her hands. On them was fresh blood. Tom Rawlins's blood. He had been wounded in his fight to save her life.

"There, there, honey," said the rancher's wife in a motherly tone as she listened to the girl's story of Tom's escape. "If the lad was hurt bad, he'd've let you know. Cowpunchers are mighty tough material and it takes more than one or two scratches to stop 'em from bein' in good workin' order. Lawzee, child, I'd orter know. Ain't I married to one of the critters? Look at him yonder, waitin' for those murderin' hounds! Tougher'n an old rooster, Hank is, when he's got his fightin' shirt on. Only thing that gets him down is lumbago. Then he's wuss'n a baby. Why, Sue Tuttle, you're cryin'! Fust time I ever seen *you* cry over ary man!"

"It's . . . it's the first time I ever met one worth crying over," sobbed Sue as she buried her head on the ample bosom of the rancher's wife.

"I thought the same when Hank was a-courtin' me, honey. There's times when I think so yet, but it don't do to let the varmint know it."

She spoke in a husky whisper but her words carried to the gray-bearded man who stood by the door, fondling a sawed-off shotgun. Catching Sue's eye, he winked, and Sue smiled at him through her tears.

"Don't go to worryin' your purty head, Sue," he said in a deep, sonorous voice. "That young feller'll come back. Young Rawlins, eh? And he 'lows he'll tend to these polecats hisse'f. Sounds like Rawlins talk. Pore old Joe fit 'em till they downed him somehow. Folks says he was drug to death, but I ain't tyin' to no sech idee. Ner does your dad. And now the young 'un is takin' up the scrap and I'm bettin' a spotted hoss he comes out winner. Dang my ornery ole hide, if I was young again, I'd go down there an' . . ."

"That'll be about all of that kinda talk, Hank Roberts," put in his wife in no uncertain tone. "Hear the ole rannihan, Sue! Ain't he a caution? Lawzee but a woman has to put up with a heap when she ties herself up to a bench-legged cowhand. But Hank's right. The lad will win out. Bound to, honey."

"You think so?" asked Sue hopefully.

"Think so? Bless your heart, child, I know so! Didn't you jest hear Hank tell us? I never knowed Hank to judge a hoss ner a human wrong."

Hank swelled visibly.

"But that ain't sayin' the old codger's got good sense," she added as she led Sue into the bedroom.

CHAPTER
NINE

Room 5 at the Oasis held a battered, surly trio who sat about nursing their hurts and eyeing each other with sullen glances.

"A fool's game from the start," groaned Edwards.

"I'm sick of the thing," added Chicago Eddie. "Let's chuck it."

"And let half a million slip out of our mitts?" growled Prentice. "Not if I know it. You'll stick or I'll know the reason why. I picked both you guys out of the gutter, paid your fares here, put some clothes on you, and staked you to scoffin'. Now you dope it out that you'll throw me down because the going's a bit rough, eh? Well, you won't, see? I'm out a nice piece of change on you guys. And here's where you begin to earn your salt."

"By croakin' the sheriff's gal?" sneered Eddie. "Guess again, Cal. I'm not ready to spend the rest of my life in stir."

"And that goes fer me," added Edwards. "That was about the foolishest idee that I ever . . ."

"Cut it," snarled Prentice. "If you'd had the sense of a half-wit, you'd never have passed the skirt on to us to keep. And if you hadn't been so obliging as to turn this

Rawlins loose and stake him to your gat, we'd be setting pretty now. You said the boys croaked Rawlins back in Chi."

"They bungled the job," growled Prentice. "Let's not go into that again. We have to dope out a new plan, that's all. I'm open to suggestions. Eddie, you claim to be a slicker. Open the pot."

"There's a train for Chi in about an hour." Eddie grinned. "Let's hop it."

"If you go East, my young friend, you'll go in a wooden kimono, get me?"

"Or with nice shiny handcuffs on if we linger in this hick burg after this evening's cute little performance," supplemented Eddie with a wry smile.

"Lay off the crêpe hangin', laddie. You should be sweating! Didn't you play the little hero at the cabin? Didn't you put on a neat little sketch when the villain got rough? I'm the bird that's in wrong. Listen, you guys, I've got a scheme."

Edwards groaned. "Let's have it, Cal. We can't be much worse off than we are."

"Let's draw cards from a fresh deck. Trot out the fresh brain throb, Cal. But don't have any fireworks in it. We ain't here to wipe out the West with bullets."

"Here she is then. Edwards, you and I are in rotten bad in this burg. We're shaking the dust of Cactus City from our shoes before daylight."

"Now you're talkin' sense, Cal." Edwards sighed.

"This Tom Rawlins is somewhere loose in this part of the world." Prentice smiled. "You and I will get horses and trail the slippery gentleman. When we locate him, we'll fill him so full of hot lead that it'll take a derrick to lift him from where he's layin'.'"

The smile on Edwards's lips died a quick death.

"Where does that leave me?" asked Eddie.

"Right here, pal. You're the foolish victim of a couple of crooks, see? Tonight's little play opened your eyes. You tell the admiring throng how you gave us the air, see? You ran us outta town. You'll be a hero, Eddie! Play up to the girl, kid the hick sheriff into thinking you're an innocent young man who has fallen into bad company. You know how to spread it on. You claim you're the slickest con man that ever worked the game. Now's the time to do your stuff. You've got a cinch. When the time comes, sell this cow farm. Edwards and I will have the Rawlins party put away. We'll join you at some town where they don't know any of us. We split the pot and go home. Slick idea, what?"

"Slick for Eddie," grumbled Edwards. "But I don't like the idea of you and me goin' after Rawlins all by ourselves. He's a tough hand, that gent."

"Then I'll show you how to handle tough eggs," said Prentice dryly. "He's my meat."

"All right," agreed Edwards with little enthusiasm as he caressed his discolored throat.

"You're overlooking one bet, Cal," put in Chicago Eddie.

"Name it, pal."

"That note that some guy slipped under our door. I don't like the way it reads. That Santine bird looks like he'd kill his own grandmother without batting an eye.

Cool guy, him. You saw how he took it when we let him read the note."

"That's why I handed it to him. Wanted to watch his face. I'll admit he looks bad, but I don't think he's going to try anything on you, Eddie. That note was written, as he says, by some guy that has it in for him."

"He read my brand, blast him," snarled Edwards. "He's a wise hand, that Santine *hombre*."

"Bah! Because he wears trick clothes and plays to the grandstand, you birds think he's a mean proposition. Are we going to let a bird like that scare us away from a nice stake? Are we going to let a fool note run us away from half a million berries? Rather not. We're men, not a pack of superstitious kids. Forget it."

"All right, Cal," consented Eddie. "But I don't like the lay. I got a hunch that things are going to break tough for us. But the only thing to do is play it the way you say or chuck it. And the boss says play ball."

"Now you're talking like the real goods, Eddie. We'll make monkeys outta these hicks."

"But don't forget for one second, Cal," added the cautious Eddie, "that the Santine bird is not a hick."

Down the hall, in Room 13, Bill was having a tense fifteen minutes with his employer.

"So the prisoner gave Edwards the slip, stole a horse, and made a clean getaway, did he?" Santine's voice betrayed his chagrin.

"A plumb slick getaway, boss. Unless I'm badly mistaken, that feller's a plumb wolf."

"So? You met him?"

"A man don't have to meet him. His actions speaks plainer'n ary talk he could make."

"Where were you when he got away?" asked Santine.

"With the gang that was gatherin'. I goes with 'em to the jail. Here's the Edwards gent tied hard and fast on his bunk. Alongside him lays' the hay wire that the pris'ner uses fer to rope him with. The Edwards feller is shore givin' up head, when he's cut loose and the gag took outta his mouth."

Santine smiled thinly. "He's the bawling kind, friend Edwards is. And which way did the prisoner go, Bill?"

"South," said Bill without thinking. "That is, I reckon he headed thataway. Most gents do. It ain't far to the border."

"South," repeated Santine, ignoring the latter part of Bill's remark. "South, eh? You seem certain of the trail he took, Bill. A bit too certain. It would not surprise me if you helped him get out of town. You seemed to be wasting a lot of sympathy on him when you left here a while back."

Bill squirmed under the sharp scrutiny of the yellow-eyed cross-examiner. Every muscle in his body rigid, he waited for Santine to continue.

"The man that escaped tonight is dangerous," Santine went on. "I want him put out of the way. I'm giving you ten days to do the job."

"Supposin' I fail?"

Santine eyed the man for a long moment, his narrowed eyes glittering in the haze of cigarette smoke that drifted from his nostrils.

"Ever hear of the Spartans, Bill? No, I suppose not. Well the Spartan mothers gave their sons instructions to come back with their shield or on it. In other words, get that man or don't come back!"

"I savvy." Bill nodded. "When do I start?"

"Now."

Bill shuffled to the door and with the sneering Santine watching him in silence let himself out into the hall and closed the door. Not until he had saddled his horse and taken the south trail did he draw a free breath.

"*Whew*," he sighed as he rolled and lit a cigarette. "I've done pulled a bone-head play when I staked that boy to Santine's hoss. That yaller-eyed snake seen plumb into the innards of my brain, seems like. Dang him, he knowed I helped that gent. Knowed it like as if I'd told him. And when he finds that roan boss and his fancy rig gone! Mama! Bill, ole hoss thief, you done cut loose all bolts tonight. You shore did. You're a marked man from tonight on. The law a-proddin' you on one side and Santine on the other. Looks like your best bet is old Mexico. Oh, well, it might be wuss."

He inhaled a draft of smoke, let it ooze slowly from his nostrils, and hummed the tune of "The Dying Cowboy" as he rode into the night.

CHAPTER
TEN

With a light heart, Tom rode along the dim trail that led southward toward the Crazy Mountains. High above him were the stars and a white moon. Between his legs paced as fine a horse as ever he had ridden. His troubles forgotten, he whistled softly as he let his mount pick its own way. It was a half-forgotten love song that he whistled, and the tune conjured up visions that made him blush at his own temerity. Until now he had always banished love with a shrug and a laugh. Always until tonight, he had told himself that love and punching cows did not mix. But with the sweet face of Sue Tuttle visioned in the star-dotted sky, all seemed different. It seemed like a different world, somehow, since this girl had entered his life. A cleaner, better world.

Daylight came but Tom hardly seemed aware of the fact. So wrapped up in his dreams was the young cowpuncher that he had almost forgotten the predicament he was in. He saw a rider approaching along the flat mesa that seemed endless. His first impulse was to take to the brush. Then he shook his head, reassured himself that his gun was within easy reach, and boldly kept on along the trail that had assumed the proportions of a well-traveled road.

The rider pulled his horse to a halt, eyeing Tom in scowling silence. The man was unshaven, his jumper and chaps ready for the trash heap, but his outfit was an expensive one and he rode a good-looking horse. Instinctively Tom read the brand. Cross P. This must be one of the Cross P riders. Unless the man had been making a night ride — and the horse appeared too fresh for that — he must have come from either a range-branding camp or the home ranch.

"Howdy." Tom grinned pleasantly enough despite the fact that he did not like the man's looks.

The Cross P cowpuncher looked him over insolently, then returned the greeting with a nod.

"Stranger, ain't you?" he growled.

"Shore am," acknowledged Tom.

"Figgered you must be. Which way you headin'?"

"South." Tom was becoming nettled at the man's surly manner. He noticed that the man's right hand had dropped with seeming careless movement to the butt of a low-hung .45.

"And jest how fur south," returned the man with an open sneer on his loose mouth, "did you aim to go *on that hoss?*"

Light dawned. As if deluged with a pail of cold water, Tom suddenly realized that he was riding a stolen horse. He had not seen the brand on the roan but he recalled Bill's remark about a man named Santine and Bill's boast that the roan was the best horse on the Cross P Ranch. This man, Santine, must be the Cross P foreman, he guessed. He met the other's suspicious gaze with a grin.

"I was in a kinda rush when I pulled outta town," he explained. "I needed a fast hoss under me. Santine claims this roan is the best mount that wears the Cross P iron. But he's had a plumb hard ride. I was aimin' to fork a fresh mount at the Cross P Ranch, then drift on into the Crazies."

Realizing that boldness was his greatest asset, Tom had quickly resolved to bluff the thing through.

"Santine staked you to Roany and his own outfit?"

"I'd be a plumb fool to ride here if he hadn't, wouldn't I?" countered Tom.

"*Hmmm*. Fool? Yeah, I'd tell a man. But I never knowed Santine to lend ary man anything. I'll go on back to the ranch with you, stranger. How come that blood on your shirt?"

"I had a little trouble gettin' outta town." Tom grinned. "A gent scratched me with a pen knife."

"*Hmmm*. A close call, I'd say. Either it was dark or he was a shore clumsy hand with a Bowie."

"Both," admitted Tom. "She bled some, though, and I could take on some grub and coffee without tryin' hard."

Tom was telling no more than the truth. Slight as the wound was, it had bled profusely until he had gotten it bandaged and he felt weak and fatigued.

"Then let's git goin'," growled the Cross P man as he watched Tom closely.

Together they started, each man on his guard. As they rode side-by-side in silence, Tom mapped out his plan of action. He was badly in need of food and a fresh horse for he had ridden hard despite his dreaming. He would have to risk the chance of this man not being convinced that Santine had loaned him the roan horse. If his bluff worked, well and good. If not, he might have to fight his way out of it. They had reached the edge of the mesa and the trail dipped abruptly to the level land below. Among a grove of tall sycamores, Tom caught a glimpse of adobe buildings and several corrals.

"Did the boss say when he'd be back?" asked the man as he took the lead along the narrow trail that descended precipitously.

"He didn't say. Right soon, I reckon."

Ten minutes later they drew rein at the barn. As if by magic, half a dozen armed men sauntered into view. They made no hostile move but divided their glances between Tom and his companion.

"Friend of Santine's, so he says," the man satisfied their curiosity. "He had to make a quick getaway and the boss staked him to Roany. Light, stranger. Yonder's the mess house. Tell the cook I said to feed you."

Tom dismounted, nodded his thanks, and sauntered with well-assumed carelessness toward the building mentioned. He did not like the derisive leer on his erstwhile companion's face, or the receptive grins of the other men. At the doorway of the cook shack, he halted, half turning to survey the group at the barn. They seemed to be laughing at something Tom's guide was saying. With a frown of suspicion, Tom's eyes lit on the roan. He gasped audibly as he recognized the horse. Until now he had not had a fair look at the animal.

There could be no mistake. It was the horse that the scar-faced outlaw had ridden into town. The horse he had seen from the jail window. Santine, then, was the leader of the outlaws who had held up the train. His brain whirling with the astonishment of his startling discovery, Tom stumbled into the mess shack.

A slovenly-looking Chinaman brought in platters heaped with steak, potatoes, and soggy biscuits. Then planting a huge coffee pot at Tom's elbow, he departed without having said a word.

Heaping his plate with food, Tom ate hurriedly, washing the food down with gulps of steaming black coffee.

Santine, the outlaw, he mused. *Santine, the Cross P foreman*. And old Joe Rawlins, his uncle, had been murdered. Those men at the barn were no doubt part of the gang. Others were hidden in the Crazy Mountains. Had Santine killed his uncle? It was more than likely.

He looked up as three of the men he had seen at the barn stepped into the cook shack. The man who had guided him to the ranch followed closely behind them. They seated themselves as Tom swung his legs over the bench on which he was sitting and reached for his papers and tobacco.

"Us boys has bin talkin' you over some," volunteered the sneering individual who Tom was beginning thoroughly to despise. "And we done decided you'd better hang around the ranch till the boss shows up."

"Meanin' you think I was lyin' about the roan hoss?"

87

"Not persactly, stranger. We ain't cravin none to hurt the feelin's of ary man who's Santine's friend. But on the other hand, if the boss was to find out that we'd let you go afore we was plumb certain, he'd skin us alive. If you're Santine's friend, you're as safe here as you'd be in the Crazies. If you stole that hoss, you'll pay for it."

"I savvy," replied Tom quietly. "You figger on keepin' me here till Santine arrives, eh? Well that suits me plumb purty. I'm rearin' to talk over somethin' with him. Yeah, I shore am."

For a minute Tom's grin disarmed them. His next words, however, brought them to attention with a gasp.

"You see, I want to tell him the story of how come I stole the roan hoss last evenin'. Gents, you couldn't drive me off this place with a flock of machine-guns."

"Goshamighty, man," gasped one of the group. "You mean to set there and tell us you stole that roan hoss and you're goin' to tell Santine why you done it? I reckon you don't know the boss good."

"Never knowed him at all, good or bad," admitted Tom coolly as he lit his cigarette. "What little I seen of him was at a distance. But I aim to git acquainted right soon."

"Then you was lyin' back yonder along the trail?" snarled the big-mouthed man, triumphant hate in his narrowed eyes.

"Easy, pardner," replied Tom, his eyes glinting dangerously. "You're usin' fight words when you call Tom Rawlins a liar. I ain't used to it. I never said Santine staked me to the hoss. You jest called me a liar, mister. I'm waitin' for you to take it back." Tom's legs were gathered under him and his hand poised above his gun. "I'm waitin'," he repeated through clenched teeth.

The roar of the two guns blended. Tom felt the zip of the lead slug as it passed his cheek. Across the room, his antagonist sank into a chair, groaning and cursing as he held his gun arm, broken above the elbow.

Tom, now on his feet, his lips bared from his clenched teeth, his eyes blazing, swept the others with his gun. "I'm shootin' to kill the next time!" he shouted. "Keep your hands off your guns! I'm Tom Rawlins, owner of this ranch, and I'll start in by plantin' the whole low-down lot of you if you crowd me. Reach for the ceilin', you low-lived polecats! *Pronto*, damn you!" Three pairs of hands reached upward.

"Face that wall! Hey, Chinaman, gather their guns!"

The frightened Chinaman who had been standing in the doorway hastened to obey, chattering in his own tongue. The guns were placed on the table where Tom had seated himself, one foot on the floor, the other dangling rhythmically.

"Now, boys, we'll have a little powwow, you and me," he told them. "How many more gents're hidden around the place? I'm talkin' to *you* yonder with the sorrel whiskers." His gun barrel indicated one of the trio who looked cowed.

"And if I was you, Red, I wouldn't try to lie, *sabe?* I'm kinda touchy this mornin'. How many men outside around the barn?"

"This is all of us, so help me! The others is in the hills, holdin' a herd of beef. The three boys you seen at the barn has done pulled out fer town to see what's come of Santine. We was aimin' to hold you here till they come back with the boss or with the straight story of how you got that roan hoss."

"You Tom Lawlins?" asked the Chinaman. "You ole bossy man Joe's blotha's kin?"

Tom nodded. "Yeah. I'm Joe's brother's kid."

"Long time stay here, mebbyso?"

"If I don't git killed a-tryin', I aim to linger for some time, Charlie."

"No name, Cholly. Ling Sing mo' bettah. Savvy Ling Sing? All light. Bimeby Ling Sing makee talk. Lotta talk. After Santine dead. Ole bossy Joe good to China boy. Bossy man Santine alle time cly. Cly at China boy. Tleat 'im belly bad. Callem heap bad names. Dam' Chink, callem. Bimeby you killem bossy man, Santine?"

"Mebby," replied Tom.

"Good. Ling Sing makee talk then." His slanting eyes glittered as he looked at the prisoners. Then his glance flitted to the rear door. The hand beneath his blouse slipped into view and in the claw-like yellow hand was a long-barreled six-shooter. It swung upward to cover a man who had stepped into the kitchen. The next instant Tom's gun was also trained on the newcomer.

"'Lo, Billy!" called Ling Sing, grinning widely. The long-barreled gun slipped out of sight as quickly as it had appeared. "New bossy man, Billy. Tom Lawlins. Shoot like helly." He turned a grinning visage toward Tom. "Billy all light. Tleat China boy alle same like white man. Shake hands."

"Howdy, pardner." Tom smiled as he recognized the man who had given him the roan horse and Santine's outfit. But he did not put away his gun.

Frankly puzzled, Bill stood in the doorway, an uncertain grin on his lips.

"I forgot to tell you," explained Tom, "that my name's Tom Rawlins. I'm takin' charge of this spread from now on. I could use a good foreman. Want the job?"

"How about the posse that's a crowdin' you?" asked Bill.

"I figger on meetin' up with Santine afore they git here. He'll be hot-footin' it this way a-huntin' that roan hoss, I reckon."

"Which he shore will," agreed Bill. "He'll be shore on the prod. Like as not he's a-burnin' up the trail between here and town right now. He give me orders to trail you and kill you, mister."

"Account of the hoss?"

"Nary bit. He hadn't found out about the hoss yet." Bill paused, looking askance at the unarmed men who eyed him intently.

"Ling Sing," said Tom, "suppose you take these gents to some place outta sight and guard 'em. Have 'em fix up that groanin' polecat yonder." He indicated the wounded man who, cursing and groaning, had busied himself with a makeshift bandage.

Again the long-barreled gun popped into sight and in an instant the Chinaman had herded his prisoners outside and was driving them toward a potato cellar dug-out.

"Just why does Santine want me outta the way, pardner?" asked Tom.

"Because he wants the Cross P Ranch, I reckon. I've bin thinkin' it over as I rode this way. He was smart enough to figger you wasn't lyin' when you told folks you was Tom Rawlins, savvy? And if Tom Rawlins was outta the way, Santine could git hold of the Cross P hisse'f. That's why he told me to kill you or quit the country."

"And you figgered on doin' which?"

"Quittin' the country, Rawlins. I ain't no bushwhackin' killer and I've stood all Santine's rawhidin' as long as I kin. You was offerin' me a job as boss. I'm takin' it. Not because I think either of us'll live long enough to make any money. But because I hate to see a game man buckin' big odds without ary man to back his play. I'm with you, Tom Rawlins, right or wrong. Santine's a snake and the fastest man I ever see handle a gun. He hates me. Hates me like pizen. And he knows I'm scared of him. I took the Chinaman's part once when Santine was whippin' him with a quirt for not havin' the coffee hot enough. I had the drop on Santine then and I've wished a thousand times that I'd pulled the trigger. But I didn't. He jest kept lookin' at me with them cat's eyes of his'n until I put up my gun. Then he laughed at me. Laughed at me fer not havin' the guts to kill him. He's that way with all his men. Has 'em kinda hypnotized-like. If they ever git the nerve to break the spell, he kills 'em like a man kills a mean dog that's gone mad. Mister, if you kin stand up to Santine without layin' 'em down, you're the gamest man in the West."

"Sounds scary, Bill, but that's what I aim to do."

CHAPTER
ELEVEN

If ever a man rode with black hate in his heart, it was Santine. Mounted on the best horse he could hastily pick up, dawn found him in the saddle, headed for the Cross P Ranch. His spur rowels were red with blood and clogged with matted horsehair, for the Cross P foreman was a horse killer to whom a horse was but a means of transportation, not a dumb beast that had feelings akin to those of a human.

Alone on the trail, his mask of cold indifference slipped from him. His face convulsed with anger, his yellow eyes glowing red, he gave way to a passion that was terrible in its intensity. Cursing, blaspheming, choking as the words stumbled hoarsely from his foam-flecked lips, he rode at a reckless speed along the trail that twisted through the chaparral. Raking catclaw limbs scratched his face and tore at his clothes but he paid no heed. Mile after mile he rode at a killing pace. All because a man had stolen his horse and rig. It was not the physical loss that goaded him to mad anger. It was the pride of this strange man that was wounded. One thing only could salve that wound. The life of the horse thief. Slowly his fit of rage burned itself out, leaving him white-lipped and trembling. The horse slowed to a trot, its sides heaving and dripping with bloody sweat.

A twist in the trail brought him within shouting distance of two riders who were traveling leisurely along the dusty way. At the sound of his horse's hoofs, they swung about in their saddles, startled. For Prentice and Edwards were a trifle nervous.

Santine, again master of his emotions, eyed them with cold suspicion as he rode alongside.

"You are in the saddle early, gentlemen. Thinking of paying the Cross P a visit?" he inquired.

"*M-m-m*, yes," returned Prentice in a somewhat annoyed tone, acting as spokesman. He chose not to reveal the true reason of their ride.

"Anticipating trouble? You're both rather well supplied with artillery."

"With that train robber at large, it rather behooves us to go armed, docs it not?" retorted Prentice with a frown.

"I suppose so. In fact, I'm rather surprised that your companion dares travel at all, after the rough manner in which he was treated last night. How about it, Mister . . . ah . . . Edwards, is it?" Santine sneered openly at the officer.

Edwards made no reply save to spit viciously at the dusty trail.

"And someone seems to have manhandled you a bit, eh, Prentice? Rawlins must be handy with his fists as he is with a gun."

The sneering, bantering tone of the Cross P foreman prodded Prentice into hot anger. He rose to the cleverly cast bait. "We're not through with him yet. He gave us the slip last night but we're taking no more fool chances."

"So it was Tom Rawlins that was in jail?" Santine smiled nastily.

Prentice flushed crimson. "Who said it was Tom Rawlins?"

"You just now admitted it," replied Santine in a flat voice. "Prentice, I'm going to give you a bit of free advice. Take this tinhorn, Edwards, round up that pasty-faced kid that claims he's Tom Rawlins, and go back to where the white lights shine. You aren't wanted here. You haven't the guts to play the game. If the real Tom Rawlins was to show up, you'd take to the brush like two rabbits. Why, you fools, it was I that wrote you the little note that had the three of you jumpy as three old maids with a mouse in the room. You white-livered, petty larceny coyotes. I've a good notion to take those guns away from you and make you eat 'em."

He had not raised his voice above a monotone. He was actually smiling as he watched the pair reach toward their guns.

They were riding three abreast, Edwards next to Santine.

"You seem to hesitate about dragging out the popguns," taunted Santine. "Edwards, I saw a greaser make you take water once. Your name was Robbins, then. You ran a crooked gambling game and weren't man enough to go through when this greaser sheep-shearer jumped you out. Law officer? Why, you idiot, you're wanted in half a dozen states for piker jobs. Tuttle should jail you for a vagrant. Go for that gun and I'll show you . . ."

With a bellow of rage, Edwards drew. A spurt of flame from across Santine's saddle cantle and Edwards gazed dazedly at a bloody, paralyzed hand.

"Show you how to shoot the gun out of your hand," finished Santine coldly. "You're next, Prentice. I'm drilling you above the right elbow, midway between there and the shoulder. A nice, clean break that will knit in about three weeks, with proper medical attention. Go for your gun!"

"But I don't want trouble!" protested the white-faced Prentice. "I don't want . . ."

"Draw!" snarled Santine.

"I won't! I won't be killed by . . ."

Again Santine's gun roared. With a howl of pain, Prentice stared in terror at his right arm. It dangled sickeningly at his side.

"You'll be able to make town before you bleed to death . . . if you ride hard," advised Santine as he calmly reloaded his smoking gun. "I'll be in town in a day or two," he went on, paying no heed to their groans, "and it won't be healthy for either of you to be there when I arrive. Arizona is a large place, but it's too small to hold buzzards of your stamp. Take the third member of your masquerading trio with you when you catch that east-bound train. And be thankful that I let you off with your miserable lives, you cheap crooks! Get!"

The *clicking* of his gun punctuated the command. Prentice and Edwards lost no time in getting under way.

"I've known men to bleed to death in half an hour!" Santine called after them. "So ride those crow-baits like you owned 'em!"

Cursing and moaning, the two wounded men rode back along the trail toward town.

"We'll land in the hoosegow if we go back," snarled Edwards with a curse.

"And we'll die out here if we don't go back," lamented Prentice. "I'd rather do a few years in stir than die in this god-forsaken place. Not even a flower to put on a man's grave. What a fine egg you turned out to be. You claimed to be a gunman when I hired you in Wyoming. Gunman? Take off that tin star and throw it away. It only cost two-bits when I got it in Chi, but it's going to cost us a lot more than that if we don't make a slick getaway. Gunman? You're as yellow as a whipped nigger!"

"I showed more sand than you did," growled Edwards. "I never tried to beg off. I'm damned glad he busted your arm. You're the gent that claims to be brainy. Start workin' at your job. Get us outta this!"

"I'm bleeding bad and getting sick," protested Prentice weakly. "Maybe I'll die before this slow-moving beast can carry me into town."

"Mebbyso you will," agreed Edwards petulantly. "I hope so."

His torn hand was paining terribly but he managed to grin at his companion's discomfort. Thus they rode into town.

Chicago Eddie, standing in front of the hotel, had just finished talking to Sue Tuttle and her father. Once

98

warmed up to his subject, the former confidence man had talked volubly, dwelling at length, in no uncertain terms, upon the perfidy and crookedness of Edwards and Prentice.

Sheriff Tuttle and his daughter had listened patiently, even with remarkable earnestness, to his story. Chicago Eddie felt that he was talking himself with ease into the good graces of his listeners. Words slipped glibly from his tongue. He grew more confident each minute of his success. After all, thought the city crook, these Westerners were boobs.

Suddenly, in the middle of a sentence, he stopped short. His jaw dropped. His pale eyes widened with fear.

Tuttle whirled about to stare at the two riders who came down the dusty street.

At the hitch rack in front of the hotel, Prentice slipped to the ground. Edwards followed suit.

Tuttle and his daughter exchanged a quick look of understanding. The sheriff's face hardened into grim lines as he viewed the two men. Sue's story had riled him to the depths.

"Call a doctor!" groaned Prentice. "I'm dying!" He staggered toward the sheriff.

"Dyin'? I reckon not," said Tuttle grimly. "You'll live long enough to serve about twenty-five years in the pen. And Edwards will keep you company. Yeah, you'll live. Unless the boys take it into their heads to string you up. And I won't fight more'n a week to hinder 'em from doin' it."

Chicago Eddie, a frightened look in his eyes, sidled off to make a run for it.

"Surely you aren't going, Mister Rawlins?" Sue smiled. She was toying with an effective-looking six-shooter.

"No, no, cer-tainly not," stammered Eddie.

Prentice glanced toward Eddie. Their eyes met. In spite of his pain, the thought of self-preservation was uppermost in his fertile brain. With Eddie free, there was a chance that he could somehow get them out of jail. Now, as their glances met, Prentice's left eyelid dropped almost imperceptibly.

"Well, Rawlins, I hope you're satisfied!" he snarled. "You ran us out of town and that yellow-eyed foreman of a Santine winged us. Now that you've got us, what do you aim to do with us?"

Eddie, quick to grasp the meaning of his confederate's speech, straightened his drooping shoulders. The color came back into his cheeks and he managed to smile.

"Put you both where you belong," he replied. "You'll see that these two criminals are locked up, Sheriff?"

Again Sue and her father exchanged a meaningful look.

"Shore thing, Rawlins," drawled the sheriff. "I'm lockin' 'em up as soon as the doc patches 'em up. Let's go into the hotel. You and Sue might take a walk down to his office and send him up."

Eddie grasped the chance eagerly. With Sue at his side, he set out on his mission.

The train from the East was just pulling in and, as usual, the entire town had sauntered over to watch its

100

arrival. Tuttle and his prisoners had the hotel lobby to themselves.

But one passenger alighted from the train. He got off the tourist sleeping car. A heavy-shouldered man was this passenger. His suit of cheap check was wrinkled. Lavender socks showed between the wide cuff of the trousers and the screamingly yellow Oxfords. A brown derby, cocked with insolent rakishness over the left eye, completed the costume of the man who viewed the gaping crowd with a good-natured grin.

"Is dis boig named Cactus City?" he inquired of a bystander.

"This is her," the native admitted proudly.

"Well, I'm lookin' for a guy named Tom Rawlins. He's a pal of mine, see? I was canned off my truck-drivin' job in Chi fer beatin' up de boss and t'ree of his flunkies. Bein' lousy wit dough, I come West to look up dis Rawlins boid. Here's me card. Nifty, eh? A guy in de circus done it wit' his toes. Barney Nolan, dat's me, brother. And I ain't as hard a guy as I look. It's me busted beak that keeps me from bein' purty."

By now a crowd of curious citizens had gathered about the newcomer and Barney was enjoying it as much as anyone. His bulk rather awed them but his wide grin was infectious, and in less than five minutes the truck driver from Chicago was shaking their hands with a heartiness that caused more than one man to wince. Barney's grin had spanned that great gap that lies between East and West. He was one of them. As the crowd drifted toward the hotel, Barney in the center, towering above the laughing, bantering men, they were addressing him with profanity that usually denotes a comradeship of years' standing. And he was giving them as good as they sent.

His curiosity aroused by the unusual attitude of the throng, Sheriff Tuttle met them at the hotel door.

"This is Barney Nolan from Chicago, Sheriff," announced the hotel proprietor who led the jubilant crowd. "He's a pardner of Tom Rawlins and is huntin' him."

Tuttle looked up at the grinning face that towered above him.

"It was me that put him on de train," announced Barney. "He was busted." He thrust out a huge paw and Tuttle thought his hand was being crushed for a moment.

"Friend of Tom Rawlins, are you?" said Tuttle slowly. "Well, yonder he is."

Tuttle nodded toward Chicago Eddie who, accompanied by Sue and the doctor, had halted at the edge of the crowd, unable to pass.

Barney turned, a grin of welcome on his face. A blank look wiped away the grin. Then with a leap that was surprisingly swift for a man of his bulk, Barney had Chicago Eddie by the coat collar, lifting him in the air as if he were a sack of feathers. A knife flashed in Eddie's hand, only to be sent spinning by a slap that temporarily paralyzed his arm.

"A year's a long time, bo." Barney grinned. "A long time. But I ain't forgot dat mug of your'n. Chicago Eddie, de rat dat sold me a phony di'mond fer five hundred smacks. Shall I turn you over to de cop here, or take me five hundred berries outta your hide?"

He shook his captive like a mastiff might shake a rat. Then he turned suddenly to Tuttle who stood by, watching curiously.

"Did I hear you say dat dis boid was me pal, Tom Rawlins?" he asked solemnly.

"So he claims." The sheriff smiled.

"Den he lies. Tom Rawlins is a *man*, Sheriff. A real guy, see? Wears boots with high heels and a black eye. And he's square. Dis rat says he's Tom Rawlins? Say, mister, you better lock him up. Somethin's wrong here."

It took the better part of an hour to explain Tom's escape to Barney Nolan. At the termination of the sheriff's story, Barney rose.

"Got a horse around here that'll pack a guy my size?" he asked grimly.

"Where you aimin' to ride to?" asked Tuttle, smiling slowly.

"To wherever me pal Tom went. He needs a friend, see. And I'm the lad for de job."

"Ever ride a hoss?"

"Merry-go-round. Dat's all. But I'm loinin' today, see."

"Got a gun?"

"A gat?" Barney laughed heartily. Then he held up his clenched fists.

"Dese is me weapons, mister. I couldn't hit a mountain wit' a gun."

"And you figger on goin' into the Crazies?"

"You said it, pal."

"Then that settles it. Reckon we'll go together. It'll take a draft hoss to pack you but you'll git a hoss. I reckon that stallion at the barn'll do the trick. He's gentle as a kitten and broke to ride. Sutkin, guard the three pris'ners."

An odd pair it was that rode out of Cactus City. The diminutive old sheriff looked smaller than ever beside the huge Barney who sat the thick-necked stallion with uneasy pride. The shouts and cheers of the entire town followed them.

"I'm beginnin' to think we shore done Tom Rawlins a lowdown trick, Barney," volunteered Tuttle.

"You said it, mister. Say, how does a guy brace his feet to keep from skiddin' off a horse?"

CHAPTER
TWELVE

Santine pulled his horse to a halt as he met the three Cross P riders.

"Well, what's the row?" he inquired. "Looks like you've been riding hard."

Briefly they explained the arrival of Tom on the roan horse.

"We 'lowed we'd hold him till we made sure he was all right," finished the man who acted as spokesman.

Santine nodded. "You boys can ride back with me and see how I treat horse thieves," he told them, his sinister face dark with suppressed rage.

In silence they followed their leader along the trail. Santine rode alone, as was his wont, saying nothing, engrossed in his own thoughts. They knew better than to interrupt him. Only once did he speak.

"See anything of Bill this morning?" he asked them without looking back.

"Some gent rode into the ranch about the time we pulled out. It looked a heap like Bill."

Santine spurred his jaded horse to a swifter pace, impatient to find Tom before Bill had a chance either to help or to shoot the man who had stolen the roan.

Down in his heart he was almost certain that Bill would not kill Tom. For Santine had a way of reading men.

He was a man who took no unnecessary chances, was Santine. Therefore, he and the three men approached the ranch warily, lest there might be a trap of some sort. Swinging off the trail, they approached by a circuitous route that kept them hidden from sight in the brush. 100 yards from the ranch they dismounted and left their horses in the brush. Then they crept on foot toward the barn.

"Stay there," Santine whispered when they were within 200 feet of the corrals. "If you hear any shooting, come on the run. I've a hunch Bill has gotten cold feet and squealed about the train job. If he's acting bad, when you show up, get him. The horse thief is my meat."

Leaving them in the brush, he stealthily crept toward the big clearing between the barn and the other buildings. Selecting a hiding place, he squatted on his heels, his eyes on the clearing. He drew his .45 and prepared to wait.

Ling Sing was puttering about the potato cellar, piling some empty crates and barrels on top of the slanting trap door that led to the dug-out. Santine frowned in a puzzled manner. Ling Sing was one human whose mind he had never been able to dissect.

A slight noise came from the cook house. A noise such as the scraping of the bench legs upon the board floor. Santine's yellow eyes narrowed as a man stepped to the doorway. It was Bill.

"Reckon it's time I was driftin' up the trail a ways, Tom!" he called over his shoulder to someone within. "The yaller-eyed snake orter be showin' up in a hour or two. I'll watch the trail where she drops off the mesa. When I ketch sight of him, I'll come back a-hellin'. Then the show'll open. He'll have them three Cross P gunmen with him, but I reckon we'll be ready fer 'em, eh, pardner?"

"Reckon so, Bill," replied Tom from within, his voice carrying to where Santine waited.

The listener had heard all he wished to learn. With the swift, silent tread of an animal, he skirted the clearing and slipped through the rear door of the barn. The interior of the building was in deep shadow. With the same swift, sure stride, he gained the stall where Bill's horse stood, bridled and saddled. A moment and he was lying hidden in the manger. No sooner had he hidden himself and the horse had ceased snorting at the strange performance than Bill entered.

"Whoa, boy," he said soothingly to the horse as the animal jumped nervously. "What in tarnation ails you? A man 'ud think you was a bronc', the way you take on. Easy on that tie rope, hoss. What's a-eatin' on you, to make you spooky thataway? Snake in the manger?"

He bent to untie the hackamore rope. A swift movement as Santine's arm swung upward. A dull *thud* as a gun barrel crashed against Bill's skull. Then Santine crawled from the manger to smile twistedly at the huddled form that lay still on the ground.

"A quiet and effective method of disposing of *you*, William," muttered the Cross P foreman as he threw

107

the limp form into the manger. "Now I'll interview Mister Tom Rawlins."

He brushed the hay from his clothes, sheathed his gun, and, whistling a gay air, swaggered boldly across the clearing toward the cook shack.

Ling Sing, hearing the whistle, looked up from his task. For a moment his yellow visage registered blank amazement. But only for an instant. As if he saw nothing unusual in the coming of Santine, he went on with his task of shoving the boxes about in a rather aimless fashion.

Tom, glancing out the window, saw Santine. No detail of the man's appearance was missed in that quick scrutiny. What had become of Bill? No time for idle guessing now. Gun in hand, he stepped to the door.

"I want you, Santine!" he called. "Reach for the sky!"

"You're quite dramatic." Santine smiled, his hands raising slowly in obedience to the command. "The new owner of the Cross P missed his calling. He would have made an excellent road agent."

"I'd have sense enough to keep my mask on if I was in the hold-up game. And that's better judgment than you used, mister."

"I don't quite follow you." Santine continued smiling, advancing a step.

"Stand in your tracks!" warned Tom. "Mebbyso you kin savvy this. I seen you the night you bossed the train hold-up. I was on top of the mail car."

"Ah! The tramp. Pardon me if I didn't recall you, old-timer. Being in the dark, you rather had the advantage of me that night."

"You admit it?" barked Tom.

"Why not? Dead men aren't talkative and you'll be quite dead before you ever get a chance to do any talking, my observing friend."

"Where's Bill?"

"Bill? The misguided William has left us. He's probably telling his hard-luck tale to Saint Peter at this moment. You'll oblige me by getting into action, Rawlins. A man's arms become cramped in this position. Bad for the circulation. I'm about to go for my gun. You quite ready? Any last message I can convey before I snuff out your lights?"

"I'll kill you like I'd kill a snake, Santine, if you start for your gun. I've got you covered."

"Kill me? Perhaps. But I'm taking you with me. Ready?" The fingers of Santine's gun hand, high above his head, flexed as if the man were restoring circulation. His form stiffened to a crouching posture.

"Wait!" Tom's voice cracked like a pistol shot.

"Why wait? Getting nervous? Or is there, after all, some last message? You'll not kill me, you know."

"I can't let ary man do what you're aimin' to. You'd never get your gun outta the scabbard. I ain't a murderer."

"One of us is going to die here," returned Santine coldly. "You are either a sentimental fool or a brave man." Deliberately he lowered his hands until they hung at his sides.

Tom, watching him like a hawk, made no answer. Was this man Santine insane or was he merely too sure of his ability as a gunman. Tom had never yet seen a man who would go after a gun when an antagonist had the drop.

"You should have killed me when I lowered my hands, Rawlins," said Santine, a sneer on his lips. "You've signed your death warrant."

"You're determined to fight it out, Santine?"

"Absolutely." For a moment Santine's yellow eyes left the gaze of the man who held him covered. Then they came back to Tom. "There are two buzzards yonder on the corral. See them? I'll shoot the head off the fartherest one. The other will take wing. You and I will watch him until he lights again. The moment his feet touch the ground, we fire. Does that satisfy your sense of fair play?"

Santine's tone was insolently taunting. He laughed openly as he saw the look of blank amazement on Tom's face. Then he turned half about. There was a flash, an accompanying roar, and one of the buzzards fluttered to the ground, its head torn off. The other took wing. It was a remarkable exhibition of marksmanship, for the shot would have been a fairly difficult one with a rifle. Tom's lips pressed into a firm line as he looked at the sneering Santine who was calmly blowing the white smoke from his gun barrel.

Suddenly there came a crashing in the brush and the three men who had lain hidden in the brush burst into view.

"Trapped like a fool," muttered Tom.

"Watch the buzzard!" called Santine harshly. "Hold your fire, boys. If he's lucky enough to pot me, get him. The buzzard is settling, Rawlins."

The black winged carrion swung in a low circle, its ugly, blood-hued head outthrust.

Santine, his eyes glittering like those of an animal, faced Tom, his gun held carelessly ready.

Tom fought off the sickening faintness that swept over him. He knew that he was facing a killer, a man who for the moment was as insane as the most violent lunatic. The butt of his gun felt moist in his hand. As if in a dream, he saw that sneering face, dark with suffused blood, with the dead white scar across the face.

Black wings outstretched, the buzzard swooped lower.

"That bird'll pick your bones tonight," croaked Santine. "They cheated him when they buried Joe Rawlins. Cheated the poor bird. You might remember me to old Joe when you meet him. He may have forgotten his faithful Santine. It was I who killed him, you know." He laughed, and the sound was like the cry of a hyena. "He's lighting, Rawlins! The bird's lighting!"

It was not fear that paralyzed Tom. Rather, it was some uncanny, hypnotic power behind those yellow eyes that blazed and smoldered and gripped him with an icy clutch that left him stupefied. He tried to raise his gun but his right arm seemed paralyzed. It was like a nightmare. As if in a dream, he saw Santine's gun rise slowly.

"Between the eyes, *amigo!*" called Santine in a droning, faraway voice. "Squarely between the . . ."

The *crack* of a .45! The dizzy, sinking sensation left Tom with the abruptness of a sleepwalker being suddenly awakened. He saw Santine's face, cold, sneering, merciless, take on a blank, puzzled expression. The scar, like a chalk mark, seemed to grow whiter. A rattling, hideous laugh came from the bared lips. Then Santine pitched forward on his face to lie still.

"Lun! Lun like helly!" shrilled the voice of Ling Sing from behind the crates. For a moment the Chinaman was exposed to view. A thin spiral of white smoke curled upward from the long-barreled gun in his yellow hand.

Before Santine's men had recovered their wits, Tom was crouched beside Ling Sing.

Santine's men dodged back in the brush. With their leader dead, they had no desire to linger. The crashing sounds told Tom of their flight.

In the doorway of the barn stood Bill, swaying like a drunken man, his face covered with blood that oozed sluggishly from the cut above his temple.

"'Lo, Billy!" called Ling Sing, grinning widely.

"You shot Santine, Ling Sing?" asked Tom as he and the Chinaman rose to their feet.

The yellow, wrinkled face was mask-like in its serenity. He nodded briefly. The long-barreled gun had disappeared and the yellow hands were hidden in the wide sleeves of his blouse.

"Santine one devil. Ketchum bad eye, alle same cat eye. Alle same snake eye. Kill bossy man, Joe. One time live in China, Santine. Cavalry. Makee soldier outta

China boy, savvy? One day get mad. Takee whip. Whip one China boy. China boy hit back with sword. Makee cut along cheek. Santine whip him till he die. That China boy my son."

Ling Sing's eyes met Tom's for the fraction of a second and in that brief moment Tom had a glimpse of the human heart that lay beneath that enigmatic stoicism of the Oriental. Then the old Chinaman shuffled off toward his kitchen.

Just as Tom reached Bill, Tuttle and Barney Nolan rounded the corner of the barn.

At first Tom did not recognize Barney. His eyes were fixed on Tuttle. It suddenly dawned on him that he was still a fugitive. He held up his hands.

"I quit, Tuttle. The only man that can prove me innocent of that train robbery is layin' yonder, deader'n a rock."

"I reckon not the *only* one," put in Bill. "I happened to be there myse'f. Rawlins was on top of the mail car, Sheriff. He done his best to stop Santine and his men. I know because I was one of them."

Then Barney took the center of the stage and for some time held it. Tom welcomed him with a heartiness that caused the sheriff to grin appreciatively.

"Bill stood by me when it shore took a man with nerve to stand his ground, Sheriff. Couldn't you kinda forgit the past and let him make a new start here at the ranch with me and Barney?"

"*Humm*. Reckon we kin manage it, somehow. There's some gents in the Crazies that I want bad. Reckon you could kinda come along as deputy, Bill?

113

You kin? Good. And now, Tom Rawlins, we'd best be hittin' the trail fer town. There's a young lady that's waitin' fer us to show up."

Tom flushed as he met Tuttle's level gaze. The old sheriff chuckled softly.

"Yeah," he mused half aloud, "I done read the sign right. Read it in her eyes when she kissed me good bye. And it's that same kinda far-away, foolish look that's in your eyes, son. It's plumb fatal to the freedom of single life, this love disease."

"Dinnah!" called a voice from the open door of the cook house. "Come ketchum or I thlow him out!"

THE SUN DANCE KID

"The Sun Dance Kid" first appeared in *Action Stories* (6/25). Jack Kelly, who was in charge of editing the Fiction House magazines, died in 1932 and Fiction House went into a period of re-organization. For a time in 1933 all publication ceased. Walt Coburn was released by Fiction House and he had to expand his markets elsewhere. He wrote again for *Adventure* and *Western Story Magazine*, and became a regular contributor to Popular Publications pulps such as *Dime Western* and *Star Western*. Fiction House resumed publication only slowly. *Action Stories* became bi-monthly, then quarterly. *Lariat Story Magazine* became bi-monthly. *Frontier Stories*, which had the longest hiatus from September, 1934 until Spring, 1937, returned as a quarterly. All the Coburn stories appearing in these magazines henceforth for their duration consisted of reprints of stories he had written from 1924 to 1932, usually with new titles. "The Sun Dance Kid" was reprinted under the title "Captain Gringo" in *Frontier Stories* (Fall, 1940). This short novel was filmed as *The Fightin' Comeback* (Pathé, 1927) directed by Tenny Wright and starring Buddy Roosevelt and Clara Horton.

CHAPTER
ONE

Any gambling man worth his salt in that border country would put up a fight for the *dinero* he'd won honestly from any cowboy. Occasionally one of them would risk the short end of gun play even when he'd taken that cowboy over dishonestly. After all, it wasn't his fault when the cowboy wanted to play his luck against familiarity with the pasteboards and a "system".

Three Card Spencer had been known to drill a man with his sleeve hide-out, even though he was covered when he started to spring it. And yet, he sat there with his white cuffs at the level of his ears and let the Sun Dance Kid sweep the Casino's bank roll into his shirt front. The Kid backed away from the table, his gun swinging in a short arc that covered every fighting man in the saloon. When his back touched the swing doors, he paused. A one-sided grin twisted his mouth sardonically. Specks of cold light flickered in his blue eyes.

"Three Card," he announced gravely, "you're so damned crooked you can't play solitaire without cheatin'. You won my six months' wages by cold-deckin' me. I'm usin' a straight shootin', honest six-gun to get back my money. I ain't travelin' on no rep as a gun scrapper. If I was, I'd shoot you where you set an' watch you kick. Howsomeever, I aim to take my own part if ary of you *hombres* trail me. Gents, I bid you a pleasant good night. I'm eatin' my breakfast south of the border."

At the hitch rack, reins dropped on the ground, a cactus-scarred grulla-colored pony stood sleeping on three legs. A hammer-headed, undersize animal was the grulla. The color of a Maltese cat, save for the black head and legs and the black line down his back. As the Sun Dance Kid hit the saddle, the grulla stiffened, kicked wickedly at the Kid's off stirrup, and sank his head in a short fit of bucking. The Kid fired over his shoulder at the front window of the Casino, jerked the grulla's head up, and disappeared down the street into the star-filled Arizona night.

Daylight found the Kid eating chili and jerked goat meat at a Mexican woodchopper's camp. Nearby, the grulla, rid of saddle and bridle, made a breakfast of grass, mesquite beans, and pieces of tortilla thrown him by his master. The wiry little animal ate ravenously, never raising his head from the ground except to snap at mesquite beans. Once he stood, head erect, whistling softly through his nose.

From where he squatted by the campfire, the Kid followed the pony's gaze and thought he saw a slight movement in the manzanita thicket beyond. He carelessly hitched his gun forward and helped himself to more brown beans. The woodchopper seemed nervous.

Suddenly the grulla lashed out into the brush with both hind hoofs, squealing. Out of the brush, groaning and writhing with pain, rolled a ragged peon, his rawhide reata still clutched in a grimy paw.

Without moving from his seat on the ground, the Kid shot at another spot in the brush where the limbs shook slightly. A yelp of pain followed.

The grizzled old woodchopper was, in loud accents, imploring the *Señor Dios* to look down from heaven and witness the sad plight of one who called no man his enemy and was but a hard-toiling chopper of cursed wood that was of extreme hardness and brought but a few *centavos* from the proud and thrice-cursed tyrant who was a second cousin of *el diablo* himself and . . .

In backing away from the Kid who had now slid in behind a stack of wood, the old Mexican came too near the grulla who promptly kicked him into a clump of cholla cactus.

The brush now swarmed with creeping, brown-skinned, rag-clad Mexicans who fired shot after shot into the wood pile until their rifle barrels grew hot.

"Hell," grunted the Kid disgustedly as he searched his pockets in vain for cartridges. "I must've jumped out the hull entire rebel army by the shootin' they're doin'. This wood's so full of lead it'll take twenty burros to pack a cord of it. Nary a shell left."

Further search of his pockets produced what had, at one time, been a white handkerchief. This he stuck to the end of a mesquite twig and waved until the firing ceased.

"¡*Amigos!*" called the Kid, careful not to show himself.

"*Amigos*, hell!" came the reply in English. "Only when the bullets for your gun are gone do you say *amigo*. Ees not so damn' extreme nice when the gun don't shoot no more, no? Better that you come from behind those wood, *gringo*, and make the complete surrender. Queeck, *hombre*, the absolute surrender. General Torres ees not to be made the monkey weeth!"

Hands elevated, a cold cigarette drooping sadly from the corner of his mouth, the Sun Dance Kid stepped into the open. Immediately the little clearing filled to overflowing with the sorriest-looking crew of cutthroats the Kid had ever laid eyes on.

He felt himself go down fighting under a bad-smelling, grunting avalanche of brown men. He got to his knees, shook off a half dozen of his assailants, and with uncanny precision floored four of the enemy with that many blows. Then a carbine caught him behind the ear and he went down to stay, a scrambling, cursing peon clutched in each hand.

"Take the great care not to tear the shirt on him," cautioned a corpulent man who sat a roan mule and whose fierce mustache, military bearing, and better pants marked him as General Torres. "Eet ees per'aps, weeth the neck button set over, my size." With pudgy fingers, he twisted the ends of his mustache and jingled his huge, rowelled spurs.

"Ah!"

He had caught a glimpse of the roll of greenbacks that a peon had dragged from the Kid's pocket. He

120

spurred the roan mule into the crowd, scattering them. Leaning from the low-cantled, dish-horned Mexican saddle, he grabbed the money from the finder and felled the man with an open-hand blow that held the speed and strength of a grizzly's slap.

A minute later the Kid blinked his eyes open, shook his head in a vain effort to rid himself of the throbbing pain behind his ear, then gasped in dismay as he looked himself over. Bound hand and foot, he was stark naked save for the underdrawers that no member of the band had taken a fancy to. He recognized his hat and shirt that now adorned the person of General Torres.

"Thees damn' hat, she don' fit so with the perfection like she might," grumbled the rebel leader, tearing out the sweatband and jamming the hat on his head again.

"Careful, Captain, that hat set me back twenty bucks," groaned the Kid. "Git a hair cut and it'll fit."

"The 'air cut? You are, per'aps, a student of this barber business?"

"Yeah. Clipped a mule's tail oncet. Say, that sun's plumb hot. Loan me the use of a shirt or some shade."

"*Si, Señor Gringo*. When you 'ave compose the note."

"What note?"

"For thees feefty thousand dollar United States money the frien's of yours weel pay."

The Kid grinned mirthlessly. "You read my brand all wrong. I'm a forty a month trail hand."

"A *vaquero* weeth the fat roll of money like thees?" Torres held up the roll that had once belonged to Three

Card Spencer. Unsnapping the rubber band, his fat fingers counted off the bills. $10s, $20s, $100s. Crisp and new-looking, the finest product of the U.S. Mint in Washington.

"I stuck up the Casino at Los Gatos," explained the Kid. "The job netted me that bank roll. I ain't got a friend in the world that'd ante six-bits to keep me from hangin'."

General Torres turned a deaf ear. This to the discomfort of the Sun Dance Kid.

Several times each day, for three successive days, the Kid was led under a hackberry tree. Around his neck was a noose and the rope thrown over a limb. The rope was tightened until the Kid was lifted to his tiptoes. Then Torres would, between drafts of cigarette smoke, talk of ransom. Talk until the Kid fainted and his sunburned body was dropped roughly to the ground.

The third day a Mexican *vaquero* who had stuck a knife into the ribs of a Los Gatos bartender drifted into camp. He had witnessed the hold-up of the Casino and vouched for the Kid's story.

"A thousand pardons, *señor*." Torres chuckled. "The extreme, but natural mistake have been made. I weel see that the pants and boots which are of good make but devilish small in the size are with the duest promptness returned to your body. The shirt and hat are now so stretched that they will not fit you . . . therefore, what is the use in returning them, eh? I recommend to you myself as a gentleman, and a soldier. Rafael, cut you the ropes that hold the *Americano*, and find you the miserable burro brains

122

who by the natural mistake have taken from him the most necessary pants and the boots."

Water and beans and a cigarette were given the Kid who now engaged himself in rubbing his sunburned body with melted goat grease. Painfully he picked cactus spines from his limbs and took his food standing.

"You are, so that new man tell me, no longer welcome in Los Gatos, señor?" Fat General Torres volunteered.

The Kid nodded.

"You have shown it to me that you are one who has it in him to be brave. Me, I admire with the great extremeness such attitudes in a man. That, señor, is why I offer to you, personal, thees honor about being from now on a soldier in the revolutionary army of the most victorious General Torres."

The heavy frame of General Torres shook with mirth. A pudgy hand of good fellowship banged the Sun Dance Kid between the shoulder blades where the blisters were largest.

"What the Billy hell you tryin' to do? Kill a man?" The Kid, goaded to the point of desperation by hours of torture, forgot the fact that he was still virtually a prisoner of this swaggering braggart. Blue fires of hot rage dancing in his blood-shot eyes, the Kid was atop the rebel leader with the speed and ferocity of a mountain lion.

With a bellow of astonished rage, Torres reached for his .45. The Kid's hard fist crashed into the flat-featured face. A deft kick tore the gun from Torres's hand. The next instant the weapon was the property of the Kid. A machete lay on the ground and the Kid now commandeered it. Thus armed, he waded into the bellowing rebel leader with gusto.

Spat! Crack! The broad blade of the machete swung in flat, convincing slaps against those portions of General Torres's anatomy where the punishment would be effective. For a moment, the fat leader of the ragged army held his ground. Then, unable longer to endure the stinging blows, he fled ignominiously with the Kid in hot pursuit.

The peons, stunned to the point of stupidity by this unheard-of conduct, stared wide-eyed, then burst into half-hearted cheering as they watched their corpulent general hurdle kyack boxes, saddles, and brush.

When a man whose height is but five feet five in his bare feet carries 200 pounds of weight, he cannot run fast or far. Thus it was with General Torres. Gasping, sobbing, he fell on the ground too winded to beg for mercy. The two-inch heel of the Kid's boot sank into grimy fat of Torres's neck where it wrinkled to meet the skull. The point of the machete prodded the spot below the ribs where the flesh is soft and there are no annoying ribs to deflect the blade. The Kid's boot ground the face beneath it in the sand burrs.

"Got aplenty, you hog-hocked hunk of dirty taller?" panted the Kid.

"*Si, si,* I make the surrender!"

"Then git on your laigs and shed the shirt of mine. From now on, you're the cook for the grand army of the republic of which the Kid from Sun Dance, Wyoming is the big boss. How about you yaller bellies? I got six bullets in the gun that's rarin' to puncture the hides of as many peon chili-eaters. Am I boss here?"

"*¡Si! ¡Si! ¡Viva el Americano!*"

"That's showin' sense. Git up, taller-head, and start dinner. *Pronto*, damn you. General, eh? Well, I'm goin' you one better. I nominate myself as Lootenant Colonel of this two-bit army. Colonel for short. Step sudden, *hombre*, or I begin the day right by shootin' you where you lay. And fork over that dough you took out of my jeans. I need it to buy pants fer my army. Hey, boys?"

"*¡Viva! ¡Viva!*"

Swinging machete and gun, the Kid swaggered to where the grulla pony stood nibbling at the end of a long mesquite bean. The little animal whirled, squealed, kicked, and snapped with one movement.

"Quit it, dang you," grunted the Kid who had dodged the hoofs and teeth. "I know I smell like a greaser and look like a boiled buzzard, but it's me jest the same. Say howdy."

Nickering softly, the grulla recognized the voice of his owner and friend, shoved a soft muzzle into the Kid's face, and nibbled at the sunburned nose. The Kid's arm went across the mouse-colored neck and rubbed a black, furry ear. There was a suspicious mist in the Kid's eye as he laid his unshaven cheek against the neck of the grulla.

"Son," he said softly, "me 'n' you has done grabbed ourselves a rebel army. The question is, what in hell we gonna do with it?"

CHAPTER
TWO

There was but one excuse for the existence of San Pablo. Water. That, in as arid a land as the endless desert country, was reason enough for the *padres* to build a mission there. Built in the early part of the 18th Century, its four-foot walls still stood. Repaired from time to time, it weathered the hot blasts of the countless sandstorms. Sandaled *padres*, browner than the sun-baked walls, with trowel and spade and infinite patience worked in the garden inside the outer wall. In the space of 200 years, with the aid of water, much can be done, even in such a blistered sand waste as San Pablo. Palm trees, fruits, flowers. An oasis that seemed paradise itself to the traveler.

Like chicks about the mother hen, squat adobes came into existence. Crooked streets. Hitch racks. A plaza where one could partake of a *siesta* under the feathery shade of giant pepper trees. Beyond, a *cantina* where the strumming of guitars and the *clink* of glasses filled with fiery mescal and tequila might be heard in the soft, gray-black night. San Pablo Mission, in the course of 200 years, had become San Pablo, the town.

"Modern? *Si, señor*. Does not the mail from Yuma, on the border, come once each week? And look you, señor, at the magnificent sign yonder! American Grub Café. Hipolito Quijada, Prop. 'Sta bueno, no? And the striped pole of the shop of the barber! Closed, to be sure, and some of the paint is, from the sandstorms, vanished as you see. All because of these many times cursed rebels. Eh? The barber hombre killed? Ah, no. He rides the hills at the head of his army, that one. The General Torres, señor. You have heard of him, no? That Torres is a man who can talk, I tell you. Like Hipolito, he has traveled far. To Phoenix, where he learn the haircut and shave and the striped pole. Mark you my words, señor, that same Torres will some day return to San Pablo at the head of his army."

Across from the deserted barbershop, Hipolito Quijada, tall, slender, handsome, twisted a slender mustache to needlepoints, stroked his shiny black hair, sleek and glistening from recent oiling, and surveyed his clean-shaven, heavily powdered jaw in the cracked mirror behind the lunch counter. From his resplendent checked suit wafted the aroma of perfume that made up in strength what it lacked in quality.

At the far end of the counter a blonde girl in waitress uniform wrinkled a small nose and sniffed audibly.

"Who shoved your face in the flour bin, Hippy?" she inquired. "And what peddler hung that musk on your lapel?" She faced him, arms akimbo.

Hipolito smiled complacently. "You like that perfume, no?"

"Decidedly no. You'll drive away trade. The joint'll be a total eclipse unless you bury them rags, Romeo."

"Eclipse?"

"A flop. And that ain't the half of it. You lose the other half of your act if you don't quit the perfume, hair tonic, slick-'em-down treatment you're treatin' your person to. I'm leavin' you flat if you don't use more washin' water and less face powder. For Pete's sake, go home and wash your neck."

Goldie LaRitz, formerly second from the end of the pony ballet of what had been Foley's "Golden Dreams" until the show flopped in San Pablo, held two manicured fingers to her nose and with the other hand pointed to the door.

"Be a good boy and air yourself, dearie," she suggested. "For more reasons than one, I'd hate to walk out on you, but, honest now, no lady could stand that perfume."

From behind the counter, she watched the departure of her employer. When he was out of sight, she dropped on the end stool and enjoyed the luxury of a quiet cry. This over, she tossed her blonde head that was too corn-colored and alive to be anything but real, and lit a cigarette. From little old New York to San Pablo, Mexico is a long walk. Alone, broke, without a friend save the solemn-visaged *padre* who was secretly putting aside the few *centavos* that came his way. Putting them away until they totaled the sum that would take this girl to the United States where she belonged. Meanwhile, Goldie hid the ache in her heart behind a smile.

Just let me see one plain, homely, unpowdered U.S. American face, and that bird's mine, she told herself. *And it ain't the restaurant that's wearin' me to a mere whisper. It's the hours I spend with the dear-heart attentions of every male human in San Pablo. I've bin sung at, knelt at, guitared at till I jump every time I hear the twang of a guitar string. All for a dollar a day and beans. Beans! May I never see another . . . now what?*

The staccato bark of 100 carbines shattered San Pablo's quiet. Running feet, shouts, the *thud* of racing hoofs.

"*¡Los insurrectos! ¡Por Dios!*" Then, imploring, placating: "*¡Viva el* Torres! *¡Viva el* Torres!*" This from the throats of the nimble-witted who from long habit in the rebel-infested San Pablo were eager to side with the temporary conqueror of the town.

Goldie LaRitz had never participated in a rebel invasion. Yet she lost no time in idle speculation. Quickly slamming the door, she took her stand behind the high counter, a heavy porcelain cup in either hand. White as chalk save for the rouge on her cheeks, she bit her lips to keep from screaming and prepared to go out fighting. What a fight it would be, too! Through the flimsy iron bars on the tiny window she saw a swirl of dust choke the street and made out shadowy forms of shooting, yellow horsemen.

"*¡Viva el* Sun Dance Keed!*" roared the riders.

"Shoot in the air, army!" bellowed a voice that rose above the popping of guns. "There ain't a gun in the damned town!"

"A Yankee," breathed Goldie. "My Gawd, d'you suppose the United States has took Mexico? They must've! Hooray!"

Still holding her impromptu weapons, she quit her barricade and jerked open the door. Dust choked her nostrils. The street seemed swarming with half-hidden riders and horses. Then out of that chaos shaped a mouse-colored pony that carried a dust-caked, sweat-stained rider. In one hand he held a blue-barreled .45. The other held a horsehair rope that was fastened to the neck of a disheveled fat man astride a roan mule.

"Back home, and broke, eh, Torres?" The Kid grinned as the grulla slid to a halt in front of Hipolito Quijada's American Grub Café. "This your joint?" The Kid, reading the sign, had not seen the girl.

"No, no *Señor* Colonel. Ees 'cross the street."

"We'll wait till the parade goes by then. The barberin' trade orter be plumb good by now. You kin . . . sufferin' snakes!"

The Kid had seen Goldie. The grulla, whistling gently through dilated nostrils, stepped closer and nibbled softly at the shock of blonde curls.

"Lady," said the Kid solemnly, "only for the grulla spottin' you for homefolks, I'd swear I was goin' loco. A United States lady in San Pablo? Tell me quick that I ain't sunstruck."

"Is this your show, cowboy?" asked Goldie, a little disappointed at not seeing a khaki-clad army officer.

"It shore is. Mine and Torres's. General, you're in the presence of a lady. Take off my twenty-dollar hat that you done ruined. Now bow purty." He gave the rope a jerk and General Torres, perforce, bowed suddenly.

130

"Ma'am, you ain't Hipolito Quijada, prop. Kin I ask how come you're hangin' out at this chili joint?"

"You *kin*," said Goldie tartly. "But who are you to be puttin' *me* on the witness stand? You got a nerve, you, with your last year's shirt on. Say, does this beast bite?"

"No'm. Not if he takes a likin' to you, which he done has."

"Cute, ain't he? Would you mind explainin' to a lady the big idea of the show you're treatin' us to?"

Goldie waved a hand toward the throng of Mexicans who had, upon locating the *cantina*, dismounted and were squeezing into the adobe where liquor might be had.

"Show?"

"Yes," explained Goldie. "When do the tents go up?"

"There ain't no tents, ma'am. We ain't got enough pants to go 'round, to say nothin' of tents. They had pants oncet but they wore 'em out follerin' Torres here through the catclaw bushes. Say, General, you better be shakin' a leg. If your shop ain't open in five minutes, I'm hangin' your fat hide on the fence."

The Kid tossed free the end of the hair rope and General Torres slid to the ground and waddled across the street. At the door, he hesitated. Slouching sidewise in the saddle, the Kid's right forefinger tightened on the trigger of his .45. A puff of yellow dust rose between Torres's bare feet and the general popped inside his former barbershop like a prairie dog seeking its hole. The Kid turned to the girl once more.

"If ary of your friends wants a free haircut or shave, send 'em across the street to the general. He'll fix 'em

131

up. He's goin' to shave and haircut the hull town of San Pablo. *Free*."

"Publicity stunt? Not bad, cowboy. Where's the rest of your white act?"

"White act?"

"Sure. Don't tell me you're the only paleface that's troupin' with these black and tan scarecrows."

"I'm the only white hand in the spread, lady, if that's what you mean."

Goldie stepped back, eyeing the Kid with suspicion. He was not altogether prepossessing in appearance. His clothes were ragged, his face covered with bristly stubble. Bareheaded, his hair powdered with yellow dust, he sat carelessly in the saddle, ejecting empty shells from a big six-shooter with an air of preoccupation.

Goldie opened her mouth to speak, but before she could find words, interruption came in the form of a brown-cloaked, leather-skinned *padre* from the mission. In his wake were a group of frightened-looking women, children, and old men. The *padre* addressed the Kid in the Mexican tongue.

"San Pablo, *Señor* Colonel, is at your mercy. These poor people have suffered much at the hands of the revolutionaries. We are but peaceful folks, *señor*, at war with no one. They beg protection."

"Say it again, *padre*." The Kid frowned. His knowledge of the language was limited. "Slower."

The *padre* repeated his message, wording it in simpler phraseology. The Kid nodded gravely.

"*Si*, pardner. Shore thing. And if you or ary of your friends needs a haircut, have at it."

The Kid nodded toward the barbershop that was now open for business. In the window was a hastily scrawled placard that stated that at the order of Colonel Sun Dance Kid barbering would be free of charge.

"Torres?" gasped the *padre*. "Back in his shop?"

"He done made a misdeal of the general job. I brung him and his army back home. They got a belly full of soldierin' and are rarin' to go back to their petty larceny, thievin', rooster fightin', bean raisin', and so on. For them, the war's over. Kin a man buy a pair of overalls in this town?"

The Kid produced a roll of bills. He peeled off several and handed them to the *padre*.

"To square any damage we done, pardner. Mebbyso some of the boys done tromped down some of your forgit-me-nots. Now about these overalls, I . . ."

Hipolito Quijada, the widely traveled one, had squirmed through the crowd. Hipolito had weathered more than one rebel invasion and was by no means a novice at the gentle art of handshaking. Back in his room was a checked suit, gloriously perfumed that he had reluctantly shelved at the whim of a woman whose love he hoped to win. Here was a chance to reimburse himself, make a profit, and put himself in the good graces of the conqueror. With a stiff bow, he faced the Kid.

"You see before you, *Señor* Colonel, one who, to the utmost perfection, speaks the language of the *Americano*. Shake the limb, *señor*, by the side of

133

Hipolito Quijada, and be clothed in that which the book calls the neat but not so gaudy suit. Then, *señor*, we return to my up-to-the-date restaurant and consume the steak which, personal, I shall smother under an onion."

A bit dazed, Goldie watched the Kid and Hipolito round the corner and turn into the trail that led to Hipolito's adobe. The *padre* and his flock made their way back up the street.

"I ask you," Goldie addressed the empty street, "Colonel Sun Dance Kid? Who'd take him for a dance act and what kind of a clog is a sun dance? Seedy-lookin' bird but packs a roll that'd choke the well-known elephant. If his show does as good as Foley's 'Golden Dreams,' he'll need that jack to take his show back home. Colonel, my eye. I bet he ain't even a buck private in the rear rank. Say, where d'you get that yoo-hoo stuff, Fatty?"

For Torres, taking courage now that the Kid was out of sight, was making clumsy but unmistakable efforts at flirtation. Clad in the soiled white uniform of his calling, he leaned against the striped pole.

Goldie still held the two cups of heavy porcelain. Now, with more or less accuracy, they sped, one after the other, in the general direction of the ogling barber. Torres, with due haste, sought sanctuary inside his shop and in no uncertain terms gave vent to his outraged feelings. A groan of abject misery escaped him as he espied the unshaven throng that was filing from the *cantina*, heading his way. With a gusty sigh he slid a

134

dirty towel under the chin of his first free customer and reached for a shaving mug.

Across the street, Goldie stood behind the counter, face cupped in her hands, and gazed broodingly into space.

The only white man I seen since Foley's left me flat, she mused. *Me, Goldie LaRitz, who needs a boyfriend more than a goldfish needs water. I ain't mercenary, that's it. Wait'll he shows again. Mebby I'll join his show. Sun Dance. Sounds Oriental. That's me. Bill me as Cleopatra and with a black wig . . . we'll turn 'em away in hundreds.*

Gliding from behind the counter, humming a number that had been one of Foley's best acts, Goldie's supple figure gyrated across the adobe floor. For the moment the stranded show girl forgot the ache in her heart and lost herself in her act. For, first and last, Goldie LaRitz was a trouper from the thin soles of her slippers to the tip of her tossing curls.

The Sun Dance Kid, resplendent in his newly acquired checked raiment, silk-shirted, brown-derbied, stood on the threshold of the American Grub Café and gazed with dumb astonishment. Behind him, Hipolito shifted from one squeaky yellow shoe to the other in an effort to see past the broad shoulders of the American into the little restaurant.

Goldie, lost in her dance and totally unaware of an audience, sank to the acrobatic and wholly unwaitress-like posture of the finale, golden curls at rest on the knee that showed the top of a sheer silk stocking. Then, for the first time, she saw the Kid.

"So it's you?" She smiled, scrambling to her feet. "Will I do, cowboy?"

"Do?" muttered the Kid whose sunburn hid his flush of embarrassment.

"For the frail end of your sun dance?"

"Ma'am," said the Kid, removing the derby and tearing his eyes from the tips of his boots, "I'm axin' your pardon, plumb. I never meant to horn into no place when a lady's doin' her settin'-up exercises. You'd orter've of shut the door. So far's I'm concerned, I never seen nothin'. The same goes for the Hipolito gent."

The Kid's right hand dropped to the butt of his gun and the smile vanished from Hipolito's face.

"Now ain't you the spoofer," said Goldie indignantly. "Listen, dearie, I ain't tryin' to butt into nobody's act. Either I'm good enough to do my stuff, or I ain't. You won't hurt nobody's feel-in's by refusin' to book me with your show. But when you call my Cleopatra's Dream a settin'-up exercise, you're storin' up grief for yourself, see?"

The Kid's astonished blue eyes looked into a pair of hazel ones that blazed with anger. He had understood less than nothing of her speech but he knew that somehow he had offended this girl who was about the loveliest bit of feminine humanity he had ever seen. He sensed that this girl from his country was in trouble. With all his heart, he wished to help her. Now, as she looked at him with mingled scorn and anger, he was gripped with the agony of self-consciousness. He'd make amends if it cost his life. The question was, what had he done and how could he redeem himself in her eyes?

He did not realize that his clothes looked ludicrous. Somehow the brown derby had got back on his head where it reposed at a rakish angle. The tight-fitting, loud-patterned suit, the striped shirt, and red tie. The worn boots with their large-rowelled spurs.

"That hat!" gasped Goldie, and flopped down on a stool, shrieking with laughter. Laughter that became wild sobbing. The spirit of Goldie LaRitz, trouper, broke and hysteria took its place.

For a moment the Sun Dance Kid stood petrified. Then he stepped inside and slammed the door in the face of Hipolito Quijada.

"I'll kill the first damned greaser that opens that door!" called the Kid, and took the sobbing girl in his arms.

CHAPTER
THREE

"Now," said the Kid firmly, when the sobbing ceased and the blonde curls lay quietly against his shoulder, "let's have it, both barrels. What kind of a jam are you in, lady?"

Goldie LaRitz made no effort to free herself from those strong arms that hinted of brotherly protection, rather than ardent wooing. Briefly she told of the failure of Foley's "Golden Dreams". How she alone had been unable to get out of town and back to the States. The Kid listened in silence.

"Quit worryin', ma'am. You'll be on the road home, come mornin'. Here." He shoved the roll of banknotes into her hand.

"Why . . . why, say, cowboy, that's sweet of you. After me laughin' at your derby. Honest, now you make me feel low. I could go to gay Paree on this roll. But . . ." She shook her head, smiled, and shoved the money into his pocket. "I can dance, Colonel. Honest. And if I gotta, I'll ride a horse. Just bill me any place on the program that you want to and I'll work my passage home. And, listen, cowboy, don't go throwin' your bank roll at every blonde that busts into tears. I know many a gal that calls theirselves ladies, that'd bury that kale and

138

walk out on you without so much as a farewell peck on the fatherly forehead. I didn't know that guardian angels lived outside of books. You're a sweet boy and I like you."

Her hands went up to his cheeks, pulled his head down, and, before the Kid realized what had happened, he had been kissed.

"And that's that." Goldie laughed. "Bill me as Goldie LaRitz, Colonel. If my act doesn't go over, put me on as cook. The great Wild West, where men are men and women are worms, has taught its great and everlasting lesson. If you know of any good cooking, nurse, maid, *et cetera* jobs north of the line that divides our land of the free from this perfectly all right but flea-infested country, put in a word for me. I'm through trouping, Colonel, if you know what I mean. I want to be domesticated. Do we play matinees?"

The Kid, slowly recovering from the effects of that kiss, now painstakingly explained that he was not the manager of any show, wild or otherwise. Once he had the floor, he held it. The only detail he omitted was the manner in which he had separated Three Card Spencer from the Casino's bank roll.

"So, you see ma'am, you better take this money, climb into that stage, and hit the trail for home in the mornin'. San Pablo's no place for a lady."

"A hundred dollars, then, cowboy, as a loan. I got a sister in San Francisco and she'll be tickled green to see me. I'll mail you the money back the minute I get it from Sis. San Pablo'll catch you as an address? Say, what's the name?"

"Jones. Jimmy Jones. They call me the Sun Dance Kid, bein' that Sun Dance, Wyoming's my home town. What you laughin' at?"

"Nothing, Jimmy. Jarred my funny bone on the milk pitcher. Jones, did you say? Jimmy Jones it is. How about the title? The colonel do-dad?"

"Forgit it." The Kid grinned.

"Say" — Goldie laid her hands on his shoulders and looked frankly into his eyes — "Jimmy, what brings you into Mexico?"

The Kid's eyes dropped. He had been thinking how pleasant it would be to escort this girl back to the States. The States! Home! Orphaned at the age of twelve, the Kid had never, in his drifting, experienced the pull of home ties. When Goldie had spoken of her sister, he had seen the look in her eyes and wondered. Now he understood. Home! Her longing had awakened a responsive chord in the heart of the Kid. In his dream of home, however, there figured a golden haired, frank-eyed girl. Home? Came the vision of Three Card Spencer and the law.

"How come I'm in Mexico?" He smiled crookedly. "Travelin' for my health."

"Oh." There was a hurt look in her eyes as she walked to the window and looked out at the cloudless sky. "I read a lot about the West," she said without looking at him. "Where the hero or the heavy or somebody says it's bad manners to ask a cowboy where he's from, what his name is, or why he's wherever he is. I thought it was bunk. If I've been fresh and nosey, I'm sorry. Why should you trust a girl you never laid eyes on before?"

"It ain't that, ma'am," muttered the Kid. "Hell, I'd trust *you* anywhere, beggin' your pardon for cussin' thataway. The grulla trusted you and I've never knowed that pony to make a wrong guess. It ain't that. Didn't you ever do somethin' plumb ornery that you was ashamed of?"

"Only about a million times." Goldie smiled, turning from the window and laying a hand on his sleeve. "If you're in a jam with the lawmen, Jimmy, tell mama. I hate lawmen, but I never seen the one yet that wouldn't fall for my stuff. I bet I can square things."

"You've never seen the sheriff of Los Gatos." The Kid grinned. "He's plumb woman proof. You'd *sabe* if you ever seen his wife."

"The more married they are, the harder they fall, dearie. However, my affairs are yours and yours are your own. It's a man's world, ain't it? Los Gatos, did you say? Somewhere I heard that name before. Foley's must've played it. Sounds like Hippy is getting restless outside."

The Kid had not seen the hurt look in her eyes. He saw only the smile on her lips as she tripped to the door and opened it. Taking off the apron she had been wearing, she thrust it into the hands of Hipolito Quijada as that gentleman stepped inside.

"I'm through, Hippy," she told him. "The hash-juggling act is over. No curtain calls. I'm leavin' you flat, if you know what I mean. The colonel will collect my pay and slip you the low-down on it."

Hipolito, loath to let this fair-haired lady of his dreams so easily depart, blocked the doorway, scowling.

"You're blockin' the unloadin' chute, *hombre*," drawled the Kid in whose hand a .45 had appeared. "One side or an arm off."

"*Si, si, Señor Coronel.*" Hipolito turned to the crowd of peons behind him. "*¡Vámonos, hombres!*"

"Suppose you come around this evenin'?" Goldie smiled over her shoulder. "There's gonna be a moon, Jimmy. But if you bring a guitar, I'll sic the dog on you. The little house just inside the mission wall."

Left alone with Hipolito, the Kid sheathed his gun and kicked thoughtfully at the counter. "She's goin' home," he explained, his voice lifeless as if he were thinking aloud. "Home to the good old United States."

"*Si, si.* Look you across the street. That Torres 'ave vamoose with the absolute completeness."

"Uh? Oh, well, let 'em go." Then: "Say, can't you dig me up some kind of a hat besides this hard 'un? She don't like it."

CHAPTER
FOUR

Meanwhile Torres, riding a fresh mule, pushed the animal at a stiff trot across the desert toward the Federal barracks, fifty miles distant. Hunger and fatigue were forgotten as the ex-general twisted his mustache and conjured up visions of the revenge that would overtake the Sun Dance Kid when the Federal troops rode into San Pablo. The punishment for revolt in Mexico is an adobe wall at one's back and a firing squad in front. As informer, Torres would be treated with due respect and perhaps given a commission in the Federal army. He pictured himself arrayed in gay uniform, drinking tequila and chatting with fellow officers while he listened to the volley that should tell the end of the Kid.

Back in San Pablo, the Kid smoked innumerable cigarettes until dusk, then bent his way toward the little adobe inside the mission wall. Much to his disgust, he found Goldie in the garden, talking earnestly to Hipolito Quijada.

"Remember, Hippy, not a word to *anyone*," she was saying as the Kid came up.

"*Si, si, señorita*. I recommend to you myself as a gentleman who can the secrets keep ontil that hell become like the ice cake, no? *Adiós*." He bowed low, hat in hand.

Goldie winked, blew him a kiss, and turned to the Kid who was frowning.

"Secrets, mister," she explained. "*Shhh* stuff between me and Hippy. Where's the derby? And the swell elegant suit?"

"Throwed 'em away. Swapped them store clothes for a flannel shirt and some overalls."

"That was sweet of you, Jimmy. Why, you're real handsome. Careful now, don't park yourself on that cactus. Did you bring the cute pony?"

"The grulla's grazin' somewheres." The Kid grinned. "Plumb handy in case he's wanted."

"Say, you made a hit with the *padre*, gettin' them rebel boys to stack their guns in the plaza and go back to the plow share. He all but wept when he told me. I bet you could run for mayor here and win in a walk, you're that popular. Even Hippy likes you, for all that you blighted his life by getting me outta hock at the American Grub Café. Now, after all them bouquets, it's up to you to open the floodgates of the pulsating heart and tell me how you like me in pink? Hippy put in twenty-eight minutes, time out for gestures, telling me about my hair."

"I . . . you . . ."

"You're all right, Jimmy. If you was to pull a line, I'd make you take your doll rags and go home. I can stand that bunk from Hippy's kind, but if a Yank went soft on me, I'd feel crawly, if you know what I mean."

"But, ma'am, that is a right purty dress and you shore look plumb grand in 'er."

"Glad you like it, Jimmy. Now, give me that hat before you pull it apart. If you don't know where to park your hands, roll a smoke with 'em. And quit ma'aming me. I'm not your mother."

"No'm. Yes'm. Yeah," he said.

"You can call me Mary."

"But I thought your name was . . ."

"Goldie LaRitz? Stage name. Mary Jones don't look ritzy on the bill. Plain Mary Jones. And yours is Jimmy Jones. That's why you gave me a laugh when you told me your name." She looked up at the stars, a whimsical smile on her lips. Then she turned to Jimmy. "Until today, I was always ashamed of my name. Since I was a kid, I hated it. Thought it was too plain."

The Kid nodded. So overcome was he by the sheer loveliness of this girl he seemed tongue-tied. In the daylight she had seemed wonderful enough. Tonight, there in the moonlight, she was the embodiment of all his dreams. Somehow she seemed changed. Younger and more girlish.

He did not know that Goldie LaRitz had thrown away her make-up box, several packages of cheap cigarettes, and most of her stage clothes. He did not know that she had made this simple pink dress that afternoon. Yet, somehow, he sensed that Goldie LaRitz was dead and Mary Jones had taken her place for always.

As they sat side-by-side on an old adobe bench, a silence fell over them. A silence that was, at first, uncomfortable to the Kid until he found himself carried away by the spell of the desert night and lost himself in the realm of dreams. Never had he been so happy, or so sad. Happy because of the nearness of this girl, sad because in the morning she would go out of his life. Out of his life — for good.

Something stirred in the grass near the girl's feet. With a gasp of fright, she shrank from the Kid. The next moment his arms were around her. The lizard that had stirred the grass moved on.

"Oh," whispered the girl as she felt the pressure of his arms about her. Then she felt his lips touch her hair. Like a tired child, she laid her head on his shoulder.

She could feel the rapid beating of his heart, feel the tremble in his arms that were unused to lovemaking. Then she felt him straighten up with a sharp intake of breath. Jimmy, the Sun Dance Kid, had suddenly recalled that he was a fugitive from the law.

Mary's arms went up around his neck with soft pressure. "Jimmy," she whispered, and there was a sob in her voice, "if you don't tell me you love me, I'll die."

Jimmy told her, over and over, and, although the lizard came back four separate times in his hunt for sleepy flies, not once did he attract the notice of the girl.

"I know it sounds like a comical remark for a chorus girl to make, but I've never been willingly kissed in my life till tonight. Gee, but I'm so happy I could weep buckets. Tell me some more, Jimmy dear, that you love me."

146

It was late when the Kid left the garden. For a long time they stood in the shadow of the wall where the giant palms grew.

"You get outta here, come mornin', *sabe?*" the Kid explained. "And travel in a high lope till you hit San Francisco. Me 'n' the grulla'll stay here in Mexico for a spell, makin' medicine. It'll take some time to square up a deal back at Los Gatos, but I'll do 'er some way. Then I'm comin' to where you are. *¿Sabe?*"

"Yes, dear." Her tone was meek. Too meek, if the Kid but knew it. Many a fellow trouper who knew Goldie LaRitz could tell the world that when she seemed meekest watch out.

The following morning, he kissed her goodbye. For one who was saying farewell to the man she loved, Mary Jones seemed quite gay. She wept a bit on his shoulder, to be sure, sniffed once or twice, then made him kiss the tears away. This to the great amusement of the crowd of grinning peons who witnessed the parting.

Mary, the sole passenger in the stage, sat on the front seat with the driver. When they had gone as far as the point where the road forked, Mary bade the Mexican youth stop while she searched in her bag for a hat that would shade her eyes from the sun. The business of changing the hat took her some minutes. She had got out of the coach and stood beside it, head cocked sideways as she gazed at the right rear wheel.

"The rim is coming off that wheel, sonny," she chirped.

The boy, with an exclamation of disgust, swung over the side onto the ground. As he started around, Goldie

147

hopped into his place, grabbed the reins, and with a thunder of hoofs left him standing in the dust, open-mouthed with astonishment.

"Hol' on! *Por Dios*, wait! Dat road ees go to Los Gatos!"

"Kiddo," she called, "Los Gatos is the burg where I'm billed to show next! Stick around here, sonny, till the rescue party comes. Hippy's sending you a swell mule to ride home on."

"You steal the stage!" yelled the excited youth, swearing grandly as he waved his arms. "The mail sack! You shall be keel!"

"Here's your silly mail sack." She tossed the canvas pouch onto the ground. "Now, go sit on a cactus and count your fleas till the mule comes. Bye bye!"

A wave of the hand and she used her whip.

"*¡Loco!*" shrieked the youth. "*¡Muy loco!*"

Seventy-five miles of twisting, sandy road. A journey that would try the mettle of a strong man. It was long past sunup the next morning when the girl and the rattling, bucking stage rolled down the only street in Los Gatos, and, wreathed in a cloud of dust, she jerked to a halt in front of the Casino.

The lanky, overall-clad individual who was nailing a plank across the closed doors of the gambling house paused in his task long enough to look at her wonderingly.

The girl threw down the whip, passed a grimy hand across a sunburned, dusty face, and vaulted to the ground. Her white flannel skirt was streaked with dirt and grease. Her sweater was a torn and soiled bit of cloth wreckage. The man tossed aside his hammer, bit a corner from a large plug, and eyed her with hearty disapproval.

Pete Slade, sheriff of Los Gatos, had fallen into the habit of looking with suspicious eyes upon each and every person who crossed his line of vision. He snapped his galluses, spat, and opened his thin lips in speech.

"Loco. Plumb loco, dang it all. Kin you tell me, lady, what in tarnation brings you into Los Gatos?"

"This." Goldie indicated the battered, brush-scarred stage, smiling up into the soured features of the man in the faded overalls. "And, listen, if you're tryin' to put over a comedy act, your jokes are a flop. I admit, baby, that I'm the living image of something that the cat dragged home, but you're supposed to be gentleman enough not to make funny cracks about me. I ain't said a word about that big wart on the end of your nose or the funny way your Adam's apple wiggles when you spit. Lay off me, Old Hickory, and we'll call it a day. I'm lookin' for a gent that comes to the call of Three Card Spencer. Don't get it mixed with Three Star Hennessy. Know the party?"

Pete Slade's eyes became slits of suspicious light. "I shore do, lady. Jest what is your business with Spencer, if I may ask?"

"That, dearie, concerns the Three Card party and me."

"And me," added Pete, stepping to the ground from the raised boardwalk. He turned back the lapel of a faded vest, displaying his sheriff's badge.

"So" — Goldie smiled sweetly — "what a pretty badge. Goes good with your eyes. Here I been dreamin' since I was a kid of meetin' up with a real, honest to gosh sheriff. Where's your other gun and the other fancy trimmings? Not that I'm disappointed, understand. Somehow, it don't seem like we're strangers. Hippy was tellin' me what a grand big man you were. Hipolito Quijada, remember him?"

"Tended bar fer Spencer. I recollect him. But look here . . ."

"It was Hippy that told me of the jam that Jimmy got into. He was on duty the night Jimmy eloped with the Three Card baby's life's plunder that I've brung back. All of it, see. Includin' the several hundred smackers Jimmy gave the *padre* and the fifty he wasted on that suit with the atmosphere. The heavy end of the roll I lifted from Jimmy's pocket when he was star-gazin'. Here it is, mister, read 'em and take your pick. And don't try to pull the old salve that you can't be thus approached. Hold out all you feel like on this Spencer burglar and I'm Missus Sphinx, see? All I ask is that you let Jimmy come back and make me Missus Jones insteada Miss Jones, then go our way without doin' a sprint every time we see a law badge. Do we meet on common ground, Adonis?"

Pete Slade slipped a circlet of pink elastic, beribboned and sacheted, from the thick roll of bills.

"You may need this," he said dryly, handing it toward her.

"Use it for a sleeve holder, Sheriff." She smiled. "Memento of the occasion, as it were."

Pete shook his head. "The missus," he explained.

"My mistake, mister. Nobody hurt. Only I could name off a dozen family men who'd . . . but no matter. The conscience is the guide." The pink garter spun about on her slender finger, then flipped into the dust.

Pete Slade did not notice. He was examining the bills with minute care. When he looked up, his face was as mask-like as ever but there was a triumphant light in his eyes.

"We'll be goin' along now, lady," he said, his tone lacking the note of cordiality that the girl hoped for.

"To fix it with Three Card?"

"Fix it?" Slade laughed gratingly. "Oh, yeah."

"But ain't this his joint?" She waved toward the Casino.

"Was . . . lady. Do you come peaceful or do I cuff you?"

"Peaceful? Cuff me? Say, where we goin', mister?"

"To jail, lady, to fix it with Three Card Spencer. You'll be in the cell next to his."

"You mean . . . I'm pinched?"

"Jest that. I warn you that whatever you say will be used ag'in' you. I done told Ma, I bet there was a woman at the bottom of this."

"Say" — Goldie swung out from under the hand he had laid on her shoulder — "how d'you get that way? I warn you, mister, if you treat me rough, Jimmy'll come back here and pick you to bits and feed the bits to the birds. So I'm the blonde hussy at the bottom of it, eh? You're one of these 'find the woman' sleuths, are you? Well, let me tell you somethin' while I got my mouth open. Lay off or you'll be yellin' for the police to pull my boyfriend off ye, see? And that ain't the half of it, dearie. I got friends at headquarters. Ever hear of *habeas corpus*, Happy Face? I gotta friend that knows the steno in a law office and she'll have her boss beat it out here and you'll get the axe. I know my rights and . . . say, mister, you're just spoofin' about the jail, ain't you?"

"I ain't never pinched no woman afore," said Pete. "And I'd plumb hate to handcuff you. But I'll do it, if I gotta. Comin' peaceable?"

"Start pawing me and I'll scratch you bald," snapped the girl on the verge of tears. "You'd oughta be ashamed of yourself. Lead on, but you're putting bruises in your hope chest, I'm tellin' you. Jimmy'll twist that wart off your nose and poke it in your eye. Let's go to the hoosegow, where I'll be in good company."

Brushing away the tears of chagrin that welled to her eyes, she followed him to the adobe jail. She made no comment until he had locked her in a cell and turned to go.

"I warned you," she said, her eyes blazing hotly through her tears. "The Sun Dance Kid will pull this shack down and throw it in your face. He's a man! Not a woman bullier."

"Did I hear you say the Sun Dance Kid?" said Slade huskily.

"You did. Who'd you think I was doin' this Paul Revere for, anyhow? He'll find out I'm here, and, when he does, the record between here and San Pablo's gonna be lowered about ten hours. All that cute pony'll need, to be flyin', is a feather in his tail. Say, what's bitin' you? Where you goin'?"

"To San Pablo!" shouted Slade over his shoulder. "After the Kid!" The door slammed.

"Now I have balled things up," groaned Goldie.

"You said it, lady!" called Three Card Spencer. "You sure played hell. And I'd've been out in a week for lack of evidence. I hope he's spent the roll he took off me, that's all."

Goldie said hollowly: "If you're Spencer, and you're referrin' to the Kid, you're wrong. I just handed over the funds to the funny man."

"I'm as good as hung. Damn women, anyhow."

CHAPTER
FIVE

Back at San Pablo, things were happening. In the American Grub Café the Sun Dance Kid was, with the feeble aid of Hipolito, standing off some 150 Federal soldiers.

"Lemme just line my sights on Torres, and I'll die happy," grunted the Kid as he shot a hole through the high crown of a sergeant's hat. "Hand me the other rifle, Hip. The barrel of this 'un's gettin' hot."

"May the *Señor Dios* come to our aid," groaned Hipolito. "Better to make the surrender, *Señor* Keed."

"Not while the terbaccer and ca'tridges hold out. I kin stand off the hull of Mexico from this place. We got 'em dodgin *poco* plenty. Roll me another smoke, will you?"

"That *caballo, señor*, that grulla *caballo*. Ees stand there where the tobacco ees on the shelf. Each time I make the approach to heem, he's keeck at the head of me."

"Then hold the window down while I git it." The Kid grinned. "The grulla ain't certain that you're friends with me. Hang the luck, I might buy that Federal general off if I hadn't lost my bank roll. Wonder how it got outta my pocket?"

Hipolito's lips clamped tightly. A promise was a promise. Especially when made to a lady.

The Kid rubbed the grulla's nose, fed him some sugar, and got the tobacco. Then he again took his stand at the window. Suddenly he sniffed.

"Seems like I smell smoke, Hip."

"*Si*. Those powder smokes ees make one choke, ees so bad."

"Not powder smoke, damn it. Smells like hay burnin'. It is!"

Hipolito, following the Kid's gaze, saw a dull red glow that was spreading over a spot in the straw-thatched roof. The Federals had set fire to the tinder-dry mat of brush and straw that formed the roof of the old adobe.

"Looks like I gotta run for it," muttered the Kid. "That roof'll be cavin' in no time. Stand by the door. When I give the word, sling 'er wide open. Me 'n' the pony's gonna make a run of it."

He led the grulla from the corner, loaded his .45, and swung into the saddle.

"Ready?" he called in a low tone. "Let 'er go."

Standing to one side, Hipolito jerked open the door. The next instant the grulla and the Kid shot past him. A dull, sickening *thud*. The Kid quit his saddle and flopped limply to the ground, just outside the door. Across the Kid's head was a deep gash that now oozed blood. In passing through the doorway, he had not lain low enough on the pony's neck and his head had caught with terrific force on the low doorway. A

155

moment and he was hidden by the swarm of Federal soldiers.

"He ees, per'aps, dead?" inquired Torres, pushing through the crowd.

"No, no. Ees get the bad bomp on the 'ead," replied the suave leader of the Federals. "When is the best hour, think you, for the execution, *amigo*?" he finished in Spanish.

"The sooner, the more sudden, no? At the hour of the sunset?"

"'*Sta bueno*."

Hipolito, taking advantage of the confusion, slipped down the street to the mission in search of the *padre*.

"Ah, *Señor Padre*," he panted, "the great calamity has fallen upon that *gringo*. What weel the *Señorita* of the hair of gold say to this miserable and wretched Hipolito when she find out that I 'ave allow that Keed to get shot to the bits? Look you upon my miserable plight and implore the *Señor Dios* to change the rotten luck."

The *padre*, insofar as he was able, did his best to avert the execution. He laid great stress upon the fact that this prisoner was a citizen of the United States. Aye, more than a mere citizen, he lied desperately. "A *Tejano*. A Texan."

More than the combined Army, Navy, and Marines of the United States, this Federal officer feared the dreaded Texan. He rubbed his chin thoughtfully, shifted his *cigarro* to the other corner of his mouth, and turned to Torres. His right eyelid lowered in a meaning wink.

"You hear, Torres? A *Tejano*. That being the case, he shall, with honor of an armed escort, be conducted to the border. A prisoner of war, you shall understand, *Señor Padre*."

The *padre* bowed, his tanned face grave, his dark eyes filled with sorrow. He had done his utmost — and failed. All too well did this Spanish *padre* know the law of the bush, the dread *ley de fuga*, the law of fire as some called it. Somewhere on the lonely desert, where none could see, the prisoner would be shot down without warning. The man in charge of the escort detail would report, with much regret, that the prisoner had attempted to escape.

"You, *Señor* Torres, shall have charge of the escort." The officer who called himself general but was, in reality, only an officer of mean rank smiled.

"*Gracias, Señor* General." The fat one smirked.

Hipolito and the *padre*, their hearts heavy with bitterness, made their way back to the mission. From there they saw the little cavalcade trail down the dusty street.

Four soldiers, all heavily armed, the Kid, feet lashed under the grulla's belly, hands lashed to the saddle horn. Torres himself led the grulla, sitting erect in the saddle, a broad smile on his thick lips.

"Good bye!" called the Kid as they passed the gate where the *padre* and Hipolito stood watching. "You'll get word to . . . her?"

"*Si*," returned Hipolito. "And the *padre* shall pray for the repose of your soul, *señor*."

The *padre* made the sign of the cross. Hipolito bared his head. Puffs of sluggish yellow dust marked the wake of the party's departure.

"I myself shall see personal to your death, *gringo*." Torres smiled.

"Now, ain't that kind of you?" replied the Kid. "For downright sweetness of disposition, you got the world cheated, tallow face."

Torres and the soldiers had brought along a lunch and a plentiful supply of mescal. As they rode, they drank freely, exchanged crude repartée at the *gringo's* expense, and sang many songs. The sun seemed to grow hotter each hour but still they kept on.

"To make longer the suffering of the *gringo*," Torres explained.

The *siesta* hour was approaching. Torres mentioned a mesquite thicket some miles away where they might rest in the shade.

The sun grew yet hotter. Torres dozed in the saddle.

Then the Kid's heels jabbed the ribs of the grulla. A streak of gray shot past the sleepy Torres, jerking the rope from his hand.

"After him!" bawled Torres. "Shoot to kill!"

Two hundred yards away, the Kid worked his hands free and picked up the dragging hackamore rope.

"Come on, you yellow bellies!" he called over his shoulder.

CHAPTER
SIX

Pete Slade showered a centipede with tobacco juice, and cursed in weary, monotonous tones. "Stall, you dad-gummed gray hellion," he grunted. "Stall! You don't git ary drop of water outta me till you pull outta this hole. Quit a man in a tight, will you? Lay down on me when I need you most, eh? You danged fleabit, bogged-down, sidewindin' . . ."

Ping! A bullet buried itself in the nearby sand.

Pete Slade dived out of the car and grabbed at his gun. He knew the meaning of that whining *ping*. Still swearing methodically, he wriggled into a hollow and spat disgustedly while he blew sand from the mechanism of his .45. *Whining, buzzing* sounds, like the drone of hornets, then a *spat*, where bullets struck the sand.

Under the battered brim of his high-crowned hat, Pete Slade squinted at the man on the mouse-colored horse, tearing at a run toward him. Behind, shouting and shooting, came Torres and the four half-drunk soldiers. Most of their shots were going high, finding the vicinity of the sheriff beyond.

"I'd know that grulla in hell," Slade told himself as he took shelter and held his fire. "And it's the Kid hisse'f a-settin' him. Luck's a-comin' my way."

"*Santa Maria*," roared Torres, "keel heem! *Por Dios*, what rotten shots!"

He stood in his stirrups and emptied a smoking carbine at the Kid's back.

The Kid felt a burning pain in his left arm, then forgot the sting of the flesh wound as he sighted the man in the sand wash beyond. The grulla, neck outstretched, ears flat, fairly flew over the hot sand. The kid leaned low on the pony's neck and talked softly to the grulla and knew that the wicked little animal understood. "We're leavin' them greasers behind like they was hobbled, li'l old pardner," confided the Kid to the mouse-colored ear. "We got 'em faded, grulla hoss."

The grulla dodged a catclaw bush, jumped a soapweed, and slid to a halt behind the sheriff.

"Light and make youse'f to home, Kid," invited Slade. "Don't set there like a big-billed bird, gittin' shot up. I need you to hep me git this iron-bellied cayuse a-goin' directly we've shooed off them greasers."

"My feet's tied under the grulla's belly, Slade. Cut me loose. I ain't settin' here in the sun for the fun of it."

Slade got to his feet and opened a pocket knife. A few slashes and the Kid's feet were free.

"Now grab that Winchester an' . . ."

The sentence died in a grunt of surprise. The grulla, whirling, had kicked the sheriff with both hind hoofs.

The hoofs *thudded* into the sheriff's abdomen and he doubled up.

"You'd oughtn't've gone behind him thataway, Slade," said the Kid apologetically, swinging to the ground.

As Slade, writhing with pain, gasped for breath, the Kid grabbed up the Winchester.

"You'll be all right directly, Pete. You were too close to git the full force of the kick. Take 'er easy fer a spell while I talk to them gents in their own language."

He lined the sights of the carbine, squinted, and pressed the trigger. One of the soldiers dropped his gun and grabbed at his broken shoulder.

"Git your wind, grulla," he told the pony. "You and me're gonna go from here directly." Again he fired and another soldier felt the tearing slug.

"Thank your Maker that I ain't mad an' shootin' to kill, brown boys," grunted the Kid as he wounded his third soldier, and then held his fire.

Torres, re-loading his empty gun, saw with a quick, horrified glance that the battle was now going against him. With a groan of mingled rage and fright, he swung on the bridle reins in an effort to whirl his running mule for a hasty retreat. But the mule was not to be thus easily swerved. Excited by the chase, the racing animal came on, straight for the Kid.

"I'm dyin'," groaned Slade. "Hurt internal. Damn that hoss. Consarn the . . . !" A wave of nausea laid hold of him and for the time being his speech was obliterated by other sounds.

"Heave 'er, Sheriff." The Kid grinned. "You must've swallered your terbaccer. Now, who'd've thunk that Torres had the nerve to come on like that? Well, *hombre*, if you're that game, so'm I."

Stepping into full view, gun ready, the Kid waited the coming of the Mexican.

Torres saw the move and caught the significance of it. Meeting this fighting American on equal terms was little to the ex-barber's liking. With a loud cry, he threw away his gun and elevated his hands.

"Don't shoot! *Por Dios*, don't shoot!" he bellowed in agonized fright.

The Kid grinned and lowered his gun. The mule came on in his wild stampede. The Kid grabbed a reata from the grulla's saddle, flipped a loop, and waited. As the mule charged past in his mad race, the noose went out, caught Torres, and the corpulent Mexican hit the sand in a cloud of dust.

"If you need a barber in Los Gatos, here's your man, Sheriff." The Kid reached for tobacco and papers. "He works free, too. I'll leave him tied here to your car."

"Leave him? Where you goin'?" gasped Slade.

"I'm goin' anywhere except two places. One of them towns is San Pablo, Mexico. T'other is Los Gatos, Arizony. So long." He moved toward the grulla, carrying Slade's Winchester and .45.

"Hold on," groaned Slade. "I'm dyin'."

"No, you ain't dyin', Pete. Nary bit. Half an hour from now you'll be fit to dance a jig. I'm goin' back to Los Gatos when I got enough coin to square what I took off Three Card Spencer. Then we'll shake hands all 'round and call it off."

"Wait! I want you!"

"Exactly, Pete. But the feelin' ain't what a man might call unanimous, *sabe?* I like my freedom plenty." He swung into the saddle.

"But the gal!" protested Slade, trying to rise but subsiding with a groan. "And the reward. Stand by me, Kid, and I'll split it with you fifty-fifty."

"Gal? Reward?"

"Spencer's wife, I reckon. Leastways she had the roll you took off him. She must've got word I had Spencer jugged and come to buy him out . . . *with that same money.* She looks like she had more sense, too. Purty as a pitcher with that yaller hair and them big eyes that ain't neither gray ner brown. It was her as told me you was in San Pablo. Spunkly li'l devil. Thought she was gonna scratch my eyes out when I throwed her in jail. I . . ."

"Say!" The Kid was on the ground beside the sheriff. "Say it over in words that mean somethin', Slade. What's this about a yellow-haired girl? And jail?"

Slade, recovering from the kick and the swallowed tobacco, lay on his side and told of the coming of Goldie. The Kid was white about the lips when the sheriff finished.

"I'm goin' back with you, Sheriff. It's Mary, all right. Only lady of that description in the hull world." He paused, fixing Slade with a chilling stare. "If she's hurt, Slade, in ary way, I'm goin' to kill you. Git on your laigs."

"But . . ."

"I may kill you anyhow, right here. You got it comin'. *Her* in jail. If you was half a man, I'd whop you with my hands, then shoot you. Git up!"

Pete Slade, seeing the look in the eyes of the Sun Dance Kid, needed no further urging.

"What of me, *señor*?" whined Torres.

"Hit the trail to San Pablo. *¡Pronto!*"

"No, no! I beg of you, *Señor Americano!* That Federal weel 'ave me shot against that wall because you 'ave escape!"

"That's why I'm sendin' you back. Pull out! If you ain't under way in one minute, I'll shoot you in the belly and let you lay here."

Torres read in the Kid's eyes much the same warning that Slade had seen.

CHAPTER
SEVEN

On the verandah of Pete Slade's house, two women sat side-by-side and watched the road from San Pablo. One of these was a tall, flat-chested, angular woman in calico. Years of desert existence had parched her skin and shriveled what beauty had been hers in youth. Only her eyes remained as they had been twenty years ago. Eyes of deep blue that grew bright when they dwelt on the girl beside her.

"My name is Mary, too," she said, and her smile was motherly in its affection.

"Now, ain't that nice, Missus Slade. You think your husband'll bring Jimmy back to me?"

"He'd better. The idea of him puttin' you in that hole of a jail with that low-lived gambler. Takin' along the keys, too. Lucky I came by there and heard you call me."

"He'll throw a fit when he sees where you sawed the bars and let me out."

"Let him," snapped Mrs. Slade. Then she put an arm about Mary Jones's shoulder. "The fust white woman I've seen in months."

"Me, too, Missus Slade. Ain't it a treat to rest the eyes? Say, Mary Slade, I'm gonna make you over into a new girl. You'll do a beauty comeback that'll make the other half of your act throw away them suspenders and wear a belt. And when Jimmy and I moves into that house next door, and we get to loaning one another dabs of sugar and shortenin' and do-dads . . . I'm too happy to live long!"

With a jump and laugh, she was hugging the older woman.

At that juncture, Pete Slade, traveling on foot and followed by the Kid astride the grulla, halted at the gate.

Not until the grulla whirled and kicked at the picket fence, did they take heed of the presence of the two men at the gate.

"Jimmy!"

"Mary!"

Slade and his wife watched the meeting of the young couple. Tears of joy glistened in Mary Slade's blue eyes. Pete spat methodically and scratched his head.

"Jimmy, you're hurt!"

"Scratch, that's all. You're all right?"

"Of course."

"Then here's your guns, Pete. Bein' as things're how they are, I might as well lay down my hand. I'm your pris'ner."

"Pris'ner, hell! Nobody wants you fer no pris'ner. I bin tryin' to tell you that all I want you to do is testify that you took that roll of money off Spencer."

"All right. I'm guilty. I done it and I'll take my medicine."

"You'll take five hundred dollars, half the reward."

"What reward?"

"For ketchin' Spencer with bad money. Counterfeit, *sabe?* He's bin makin' the stuff an' passin' it. When I pinched him, all I found was one five spot on him. You'd done lifted the bulk of it when you flew off the handle and stuck him up. I bin huntin' you and that there evidence ever since. We splits the thousand dollars reward on him, Kid. Hey, lady, watch out fer that grulla hoss! Don't git clost to his heels thataway!"

But Mary only laughed.

"There's men, Sheriff," said the Kid, grinning, "that knows a heap less than that grulla hoss. I've never knowed that pony to make a wrong guess."

Pete Slade's hand caressed the sore spot below his ribs. Then he grinned. "You win, Kid. Plumb." He looked at his wife, who nodded and smiled.

"I could use a deputy," he went on. "Want the job, Kid?"

"Reckon so, Pete." He turned to Mary. "How about it? Shall I take the job?"

"Why not?" Then she burst out laughing. "All my life," she explained, "I've hated sheriffs. Now I'm marryin' one named Jones! Ain't it a scream? Jimmy, ain't you *ever* gonna kiss me?"

RIDERS OF FORTUNE

"Riders of Fortune" first appeared in *Action Stories* (9/28). It was later reprinted under this same title in *Lariat Story Magazine* (8/36). As with the other short novels in this collection, this marks its first appearance in book form.

CHAPTER ONE

Because his hair was as white as alkali and his face so badly scarred, your first glance at Crill Sadler told you he was an old man. Then you saw that his muscles were the lean, hard meat of youth and his puckered gray eyes were bright and youthful and sometimes cold and full of suspicion. Then you knew that he was under forty and you wondered what made his hair white and how his face got so badly scarred up.

Crill Sadler had a peculiar way of talking without much movement of his lips. Men who have served a long prison term talk like that. Crill's ranch lay south of the Mexican border, near the abandoned Mormon village on Pulpit Creek. He got along with the Mexicans and what few white men he met.

Now and then he came across the border at Nogales or Columbus, for reasons of his own. He gambled a little, drank a little, and kept out of quarrels. He seemed a little amused and almost bored when questioned by the men of the U.S. Border Patrol. Those government men always were a trifle disappointed when they could hang nothing on Crill Sadler.

The men of the Border Patrol will agree that the strip along Devil's Bend is hard to cover. The hills might have been piled there for the sole purpose of defeating the law. And if the hills of Devil's Bend were laid level tomorrow, they would already have served well their evil purpose. Mexicans shunned the place as being haunted. Even the Yaquis rode around it, muttering darkly at the campfires that spotted its ragged ridges and dry washes. Now and then, at the edge of the bend, where those who rode the trail toward Pulpit Creek might see, there would be the dead body of a man hung from the limb of a scrawny juniper or hackberry tree — hung there, no doubt, in a sinister spirit of deviltry by the nameless dwellers of the bend, thus warning off trespassers.

Any one of the harassed men of the Border Patrol would have risked his life to probe those hills. They're a hard-bitten lot, picked because of their ability to face danger. But save for the northern fringe of sandy dunes, drifted washes, and lava ridges, the Devil's Bend was on Mexican soil and beyond the reach of Uncle Sam.

Water drenched the hills for a brief week or two during the season of the rains. The rest of the year it was baked by the merciless sun and hidden at times in the terrible sandstorms, storms that uncovered whitened bones of men and horses picked clean by the buzzards that dwelt in its cañons. There was said to be water there — water, and nuggets of pure gold as big as a man's fist. Perhaps, or perhaps it was only the weird fancy of desert rats, although few of their mysterious clan ever had the temerity to penetrate the hills. Those

172

who tried returned empty-handed with maybe a bullet hole or two in the crowns of their hats.

Because Devil's Bend was within a day's ride of Pulpit Creek and because Crill Sadler was a man of mystery, rumor claimed that he spent much of his time in those ragged hills in company with the nameless men who dwelt there. But perhaps that was only fabrication, like the gold and the fresh-water springs surrounded by tall palm trees.

No man could swear that he had ever seen Crill Sadler ride into the hills of Devil's Bend. He had never been caught coming out. But he might have hidden his comings and goings under the cover of night.

Some had tried to check his movements at his home ranch. The ten or twelve Mexican *vaqueros* there seemed willing enough to be bribed. That is, they took the money offered by way of inducement to talk.

Chuck Lannigan of the Border Patrol had tried it twice. And twice, when Crill Sadler came across the border, he had personally returned Chuck's bribe money with a frosty smile of ridicule.

"I'll hang that *hombre's* scarred hide on the fence yet," vowed Lannigan, who was inspector of the district. "He'll get over-confident and careless. They all do."

Because Lannigan had made the remark in the Oasis bar in Nogales, and because Crill Sadler was wont to sit at a table playing fan-tan with the bartender sometimes, this threat of Chuck's reached the suntanned ears of the man with the scarred hide. Crill had grinned.

"Lannigan'd ought to know better than to make a crack like that," he said in his soft, drawling voice, coming from lips that did not move. "Talk like that only gits a man into trouble. You owe me two-bits, pardner. You should have played that ten spot on the nine. Seen Crockett lately?" Big Bob Crockett was the chief inspector of the Border Patrol.

"Last night."

"When'll he be back this way?"

"Not for two weeks."

"Thanks." Crill Sadler nodded. An hour after dark he rode out of town in company with a Mexican *vaquero* who worked for him. The two conversed in the Mexican tongue, their voices lowered to almost a whisper.

Presently Crill Sadler seemed to vanish as if by magic. The Mexican kept on alone.

Crill had ridden off the trail and now sat his horse behind a thick brush patch, twenty feet from the trail.

Half an hour passed. The man with the scarred face still sat his horse. Although a high-spirited animal, the big roan horse stood with a patience that was almost human. Now and then Crill patted the sleek neck, leaning across his saddle horn to rub the furry ears.

The *thud* of hoofs sounded in the still night. Five men, riding in single file, came at a trot along the trail. The night was moonless but the five sombreros showed dimly against the starry sky. When they had passed, Crill rode back to town, halting at a Mexican adobe that showed the thread of lamplight behind a tightly drawn window shade.

Hiding his horse in a brush-sheltered corral, Crill slipped off his spurs and chaps. He loosened a big Colt that he carried in a scabbard on a sagging cartridge belt. Then he unbuttoned his shirt so that a second gun under his right armpit beneath his flannel shirt was more easily reached. He tiptoed to the curtained window and stood in the shadow, listening to the murmur of voices inside — the voices of men and one woman.

At first the voices were indistinct. Then a heavy voice, that of an American, rose in sullen anger.

"You'll tell where Sadler's map is, you little hellcat of a chili eater, or we'll toast them purty feet of your'n. Tighten that hammer-lock on 'er, Jockey. Spit 'er out, you she-devil."

"I do not spit notheeng, *gringo*. I am not the spitter. *Ouch!* You peeg! You are 'urt my arm!"

"Then talk!"

"I make the talk only weeth frien's."

"Pull off her slippers and stick her feet in the fire, Larson. No use bustin' 'er arm. She's got me all bit and scratched now. Toast her feet. Crill Sadler has a map and us boys is gonna git it, lady, if we have to cut on you with a dull butcher knife. Him and you is plenty good *amigos* and you savvy where his cache is. How's them fer hot coals? Talk, you . . ."

Crill Sadler's left hand lifted a short club. Even as it smashed the windowpane, his hand reached through and ripped away the shade. Two men were struggling with a Mexican girl dressed in a short skirt after the manner of the dance-hall girls uptown. One of these

175

men was a burly fellow with black whiskers that hid his features. The other was a rat-eyed runt whose face was tinged yellow from habitual opium smoking.

With an oath, the big man threw aside the girl and jerked an automatic. But even as its blue barrel slid from the scabbard, Crill Sadler shot. The rat-eyed man leaped for the door. Sadler met him as his wiry little form shot through the doorway. The barrel of Crill Sadler's Colt knocked the opium smoker cold.

Inside, the big, bearded man, his chest smeared red with blood, groped feebly for the automatic that the girl had knocked from his hand with a chair. She stood, the chair poised over his black head, ready to strike if his hand closed over the weapon. The girl, oddly, strikingly beautiful, was white as the white-washed adobe wall. Her silk stockings were burned. There were ugly bruises and welts on her bare arms and shoulders. Like some tigress, she stood there.

Then, as Crill dragged the unconscious hophead into the room, she gave a glad cry and wilted in a dead faint. Crill kicked the automatic out of the wounded man's reach. The big fellow cursed in a thick voice, then sat up unsteadily, his big, hairy paw trying to stop the spurting blood that gushed from the wound below his shoulder.

From outside came the sound of running feet. A Mexican sergeant of police and one of his men burst into the room.

"Two prisoners, Sergeant," said Crill Sadler in a brittle voice. "The big one may die off but the little one will spill his guts if you keep his hop away from him.

They were mistreating the *señorita*. See where they mauled her arms? They were burning her feet when I came in."

"Who are they?" asked the sergeant, his gun covering Sadler.

"The big one is Black Gus Larson, hop-runner and hijacker. He's wanted across the line for bank robbery in Los Angeles and Chicago. The runt is Jockey Slicer, from Tíajuana, Juárez, and all points south. Dope peddler. Joe, at the Oasis, will give you their number. Nice bounty on both of 'em, Sergeant. Hand 'em over to Chief Inspector Crockett of the Border Patrol. He'll see you get your jack. *You* shot this black bird and sapped Slicer. I wasn't within a hundred miles of here. Get that right, Sergeant. These gents are from the Devil's Bend. If it gets out that I had a hand in it, I won't enjoy a long life. You and your man keep your traps shut. Your chief *sabes* what I mean. Send over a doctor for the *Señorita* Lopez. And for God's sake, put up those guns. I'm not your prisoner, Sergeant."

"*¡Si, si!*" The sharp, almost military crack of Crill Sadler's voice held unmistakable authority. The sergeant and his man slid their guns back.

"Damn your double-crossin' heart, Sadler," gritted the burly Larson. "The boys'll string you for this."

"The boys" — Crill smiled frostily — "won't learn the details, you hound. You knew better than to pull this. You may croak if you don't get a doctor soon. I hope the doc is late."

The girl moaned a little. Crill picked her up and placed her on a serape-covered couch. Her feet were scorched a little, no more. She woke with a start, her eyes wide with fright until she recognized Sadler.

"Easy, Chiquita," he told her in a barely audible whisper. "And the tight lips, *sabe?* Manuel will be here soon."

"*Si, señor.*" She sat up, felt of her scorched feet, and made a ridiculous little face. "The stockeeng ees 'spoil, complete. Damn the luck!"

"Manuel will buy you a dozen pair." Crill smiled. "*Buenas noches, Señorita* Chiquita Lopez. *Buenas noches*, Sergeant. So long, Larson. Think of me when they lock you in San Quentin." He paused at the doorway. "When your five men return, Sergeant, tell them they should look sharper as they ride these dark trails. A snake might bite 'em."

He chuckled dryly, bowed formally to the Mexican girl, and was gone.

CHAPTER
TWO

Chief Inspector Crockett was a large man with curly, thick hair the color of silver. Ruddy of cheek, hearty of voice, he looked more like a prosperous banker than a government officer. But there was a grim set to his mouth and his blue eyes were keen and shrewd and seemed to look clean into a man's soul.

Chuck Lannigan, whose uniform hung on his lean, spare frame, looked like a man turned to leather. Even his hair and mustache and eyebrows were the color of new saddle leather. But he could wear out ten men on the trail and his nerve was cold and tempered. Lean-faced, ferret-eyed, he had won fame in the Rangers long before he joined the Border Patrol. It was said that he knew every foot of the country by night or by storm, that he knew the name and record of every border outlaw, and that, once he went after a man, nothing kept him from bringing in that man, dead or alive. He might have whittled a dozen notches into his gun butt and not lied about the score. But if you wished to hear his jaws snap like the jaws of a wolf, the mention of Crill Sadler's name would do the trick.

They snapped now as Chief Crockett spoke of Crill Sadler. Lannigan's eyes became green slits. Crockett chuckled.

"Gets your goat, eh, Chuck? Just the same, it was Sadler that did the job. I got it from the sergeant. Now what I want to find out is this . . . did Crill Sadler turn in those two out of jealousy over that Lopez woman, or was it the outcome of a hijacker's feud? They were chumps enough to put Larson and Slicer in the same cell. Of course, Larson killed the rat. And all hell can't make Gus Larson open up, even if he dies, which he may. Have you a man that can make love to the Lopez woman?"

"Have I?" One of Chuck Lannigan's rare smiles cracked his leathery face into a thousand wrinkles. "Every man in our bunch would give a month's pay for the job. I'd take it myself if I wasn't such a homely devil. Sure, I can detail a man to make love to Chiquita Lopez. But you're loco, Chief, if you think the girl will talk."

"Close-mouthed, eh?"

"Yeah. And brainy. She's no part-Injun greaser, Chief. She don't any more belong down there than Crill Sadler belongs. Check up and you'll learn that they landed here about the same date, three years or more ago. She works at the Oasis as a singer. Ever hear her? Then you've missed something worth twice any price. Old Manuel Ramirez and his wife never leave her alone. Manuel stays there within call at the Oasis. He's knifed half a dozen that got fresh with her. Didn't kill 'em. Just marked 'em up. He's an old hellion with a pig-sticker. Every boy on the job has called at her home. And the old lady Ramirez never leaves them out of her sight. The boys call her the Oasis Icicle and such names. Get her mad and she swears cuter'n a green parrot. But she's straighter than an arrow weed for all her silk legs and cute cussin'."

Chief Inspector Crockett took the cigar from his mouth and scowled hard at its short ash. The muscles of his heavy jaw tightened into hard knots. Then he smiled into Chuck Lannigan's ferret eyes.

"I'll send a man down from El Paso, Lannigan, that should be able to get behind this Lopez woman's guard. She knows all your boys. My man will be out of uniform. When he reports, give him what aid you can without arousing suspicion and let him go at it in his own way. He's clever and a scrappin' fool, and he has a way with the ladies."

Lannigan, for all his chief's recommendation of this man, smiled thinly and did not seem much impressed. Crockett laid a big hand on his shoulder.

"I don't mean to throw mud at your boys, Chuck. But this is a tricky job that needs special treatment. I'm going to find out who Crill Sadler is and what his racket is. And mark me, Chuck, I'll get the dope through this Chiquita Lopez. Now let's stroll over to the Oasis and hear this paragon of yours sing."

Together they wandered into the Oasis and sat down at a far table. The Oasis boasted of an American bar and a Mexican patio where the entertainment was worth hearing. The tables were scattered about the tiled patio.

One sat in the shadow of an arcade, at the edge of the moonlit tiles. A sandaled peon served drinks and food. A Mexican string quartet played and sang.

Here gathered the *dons* from nearby *haciendas*, an army officer or two, visiting Mexican officials, and a sprinkling of tourists whose bad manners should have been a disgrace to the white race. Even the uncouth peon is better mannered than the average American who crosses the border to swill down liquor that is forbidden in the States.

A group of these thirsty citizens now occupied two tables at the edge of the patio. Some vendor had sold them straw sombreros and black cigarettes that they warily inhaled, wondering if they were smoking the much talked-of marijuana weed mixed into tobacco. They wore badges that declared them to be delegates to some convention at Tucson or Phoenix. Even the two women with them were intoxicated to an extent that should, tomorrow, bring vows of everlasting sobriety. The voices of the visitors rasped loudly. Their laughter was inane and uproarious.

One of the women was flirting covertly with two well-dressed and apparently wealthy young Mexicans at a nearby table.

"Some of our big ribbon and button men seeing Mexico," grunted Chuck Lannigan, who detested the average tourist breed. "Just raisin' hell and puttin' props under it."

"Harmless idiots." The more tolerant Chief Crockett grinned.

"Not so harmless, Chief. Look at that woman in the short skirt and Mex hat. She thinks she's vamping those two Mexican gents. She don't know that her husband isn't too drunk to notice. He's getting sullen and ugly. He may jump the two Mexicans. Know 'em, don't you, Chief?"

"Sure. Mexicali gamblers. Nasty boys with a knife. They've come here to watch Chiquita Lopez, but they'll while away the interim with a flirtation."

"Look . . . coming in from the bar. Our friend, Crill Sadler. Watch old Manuel Ramirez yonder at his table. The old rascal looks at Sadler as a man looks at a tin god. Who's that with Crill Sadler, now?"

For the man with the scarred face was not alone. At his side strode a tall, spare-framed young man in white flannels and a sky-blue tie that matched a pair of dancing eyes set into a deeply tanned face. The man in white flannels removed an expensive panama and the sunburned hair was sleek and sun-bleached until it was the color of new buckskin.

"Who is he, Chief?"

"You mean you never met him, Chuck?" Chief Crockett half rose as Crill Sadler and his companion approached. Then the big chief sank back into his chair as neither of the two men was inclined to stop. Crill Sadler waved the two Border Patrol men a careless greeting, but the man with the blue tie merely eyed them with calm indifference, then directed the gaze of his blue eyes elsewhere.

"No, Chief, I never met him." Lannigan grinned. "I'd say you hadn't met the gentleman, either." He was looking curiously at Crockett who had colored a little at being ignored.

"I reckon," said Crockett, reaching for his drink, "that I've mixed the man up with someone else. For a moment I thought I knew him." He lifted his glass. "Here's how, Chuck."

"Here's luck, Chief." Chuck Lannigan was wondering why his boss was lying about that fellow. But Crockett never moved without reason. That was one of his characteristics. It was said of him that he was the model of efficiency because he always had a motive behind everything. Now, if Crockett did not choose to explain this fellow, there must be a good reason behind it.

Crill Sadler and his companion took a table just beyond that of the two Mexican gamblers. Crill nodded to the gamblers briefly as he and his friend sat down. The Mexican waiter had followed the two Americans with their drinks. The orchestra was playing "Chapultapec".

Crill Sadler's companion glanced about, smiling in a bored fashion. His eyes met those of Chief Crockett, not a flicker of recognition in their sky-blue depths. But he was twirling his wine glass between long, tanned fingers. Not even a close observer would have caught anything unusual about that twirling glass. But Crockett was watching it with careless scrutiny. Because the twirling glass was spelling out a code message. Left. Left. Left. Right. Right. Left. Right.

The left turns were dots, the right turns dashes. The blue eyes wandered with mild amusement about the place while he chatted idly with Crill Sadler. Then the man lifted his glass to touch Crill's glass.

"*Salud*," he said softly.

"*Salud*." Crill Sadler smiled, and from the shadow beyond the little patio gate came the voice of a woman singing, her voice throbbing from a soft whisper into full-throated melody. Then a figure in white took form in the moonlit gateway — a vision in white, with an elaborate Spanish shawl, the face of a red-lipped Madonna, and a red rose in the jet hair.

"Chiquita." The whispered name rippled across the moonlit patio. "Chiquita Lopez."

The two Mexican gamblers tried to catch the glance of the singer. The neglected tourist lady pouted and applied her lipstick. The men of her party became quiet, their liquor-loosened lips leering in grins. And in his secluded corner, old Manuel Ramirez, who was past master of knife fighting, watched Crill Sadler and the singer with dark eyes that burned like smoldering coals.

Because Chuck Lannigan was a man whose years had been spent along the border in manhunting, some sixth sense warned him of a subtle tension that filled the place, an indefinable tautness that might snap any second.

Chief Crockett was also sitting with his legs braced for instant action. He watched the man in white flannels, as if awaiting some cue.

The song ended. Chiquita's last notes had throbbed into silence. There was gay applause. Crill Sadler and his companion raised their glasses to salute her. She smiled at them, then acknowledged the other applause with a low curtsy. And for an encore she sang a brief little song, full of the fire and swing and poetry of her people. The orchestra joined in, their voices swelling the swinging chorus.

Then Chiquita Lopez was gone, as if she had evaporated into the very moonbeams. The little door of the patio closed. From beyond the wall came the echo of her voice. Then the music stopped.

"Encore!" called a tourist. "Bring on the li'l' lady shome more. Ain't had 'nough shingin'. Horray for li'l' gal with the red roshe."

Something small and red came over the wall and dropped near Crill Sadler's table. It was the red rose that had been tucked in the raven hair of Chiquita Lopez. Crill picked it up and handed it, with a quick smile, to the man in white flannels. He took it with an eager, pleased look on his tanned face and said something in a low tone that brought a little laugh from Crill.

He was putting it in the buttonhole of his immaculate white coat when one of the Mexican gamblers rose and came to stand by the table.

"The *Señor Americano* has made a very pardonable mistake. The *Señorita* Lopez meant the rose for me. I will trouble you, *señor*, to hand it over."

"There is only one way that any man can get the rose," said the American with a smile that carried a cold insult. "That way, *Señor* Liar, is to fight for it."

Lannigan, Crockett, Sadler, the two Mexicans, all grew tense, waiting with taut-muscled readiness for what the next moment would bring. For the American's voice, although quiet, had carried to the far corners of the moonlit patio.

There were several Mexicans at nearby tables. The American tourists were drunkenly frightened, as if they suddenly realized that they were in Mexico where it is bad taste and very bad luck to become involved in quarrels. It is hard to crash out of a Mexican jail, and even the muddled minds of the tourists grasped the danger of that tense silence that filled the patio with the heavy hush that precedes the crash of storm.

The American in flannels rose, tall, tanned, smiling, his blue eyes glinting like sunlight striking steel. The Mexican was white with fury as the two faced each other.

All eyes were on the two men who stood there like cougars about to spring. Nobody had time, in those split seconds, to notice the other Mexican gambler who still sat at his table. This fellow had moved his chair back a little into the shadows. Now a heavy automatic slid into view in his hand.

Then a swift sliver of light sped across the patio, like the *hiss* of some snake, and the keen-bladed knife of old Manuel Ramirez struck the arm that held the automatic, pinning it to the chair arm.

A startled yelp of pain came from the man. At that instant Crill Sadler's hard fist lifted the other gambler off his feet and sent him into a heap under a table. A gun dropped from the Mexican's hand as Crill's swing felled him.

Crill Sadler stepped swiftly to the man whose arm was pinned to the back of the heavy wooden chair. As he jerked the blade free, Crill's other hand deftly searched the man. Something like a small package of letters was transferred to Crill's pocket.

The American in white likewise searched the other Mexican gambler.

The proprietor of the place now came rushing in, followed by a policeman.

"Sit tight, Lannigan," warned Crockett. "We'll keep out of this."

The tourists were leaving in sober haste. Manuel Ramirez had vanished as if swallowed by the night. The American in white flannels lit a cigarette, then the flame of his match set fire to a tiny square of paper that he had taken from the heart of the red rose.

"These two Mexicali gamblers," explained Crill Sadler, "were insulting and annoying to the tourist ladies. My good friend here is a gentleman and resented the insult to a woman of his country. Neither of these two gambling men will wish to cause any more trouble. The affair is ended. *Señor* Crockett and *Señor* Lannigan will vouch for the truth of what I say."

"Quite so," said Crockett, smiling a little.

"Ask this Mexican with the scratch on his arm," suggested Crill, "if he wishes to make charges against anyone."

"*Dios*, no!" growled the fellow, knotting a handkerchief about his wound. His companion was still lying there, dazed by Crill's blow. "Did I not tell that fool lying there that we were making a mistake in coming here?

But he went loco over a pretty face and her singing, and so we . . ."

"So you made eyes at a tourist lady, thou donkey," snapped Crill.

"*Sí, sí.*"

"And now my good friend and I bid you good night." Crill smiled. And taking the tall man by the arm, he walked past the policeman and out of the place.

"Well, Lannigan," said Crockett, "thanks for a nice evening." He rose, Chuck Lannigan following suit.

"Now, Chief," grunted Lannigan, "tell me who's the bird in the white coat and pants."

"He happens to be Cato Morgan, the man I had in mind when I said I'd send a man to get in right with Crill Sadler and Chiquita Lopez. Looks like he's beat me to it."

"You mean Cato Morgan, the millionaire . . . sort of playboy of Palm Beach and Del Monte and always into some sort of mix-up with the police? Plays polo, owns a yacht, and so on? That the same Cato Morgan?"

"Same baby." Crockett nodded. "And pinned to his undershirt is a little gold badge, Chuck. He's one of the shrewdest men of the International Secret Service. He's one of half a dozen wearing that little gold badge. They're quite an organization, Chuck. Not many men even know of their existence. All millionaires, all men of the truest sort of courage, who pay their own way, can't be bribed, and whose hands are able to juggle kingdoms or an automatic, as the case may be." They had quit the place and were going to their office. "I'm wondering, Chuck, what in hell brings him here. And how does he happen to be on such easy terms with Crill Sadler?"

Chuck Lannigan's leathery face wrinkled in a mirthless grin. "Now *I'll* ask one, Chief."

CHAPTER
THREE

"Well, Cato?"

"Quite well, thanks, Crill." He took the package of letters that Crill Sadler passed him. He ran through them with swift precision.

"All there. Thanks to you and Yolanda."

"*Shhh*. Not Yolanda. Chiquita Lopez, you dumb egg. Now, you long-geared son-of-a-gun, let's split a bottle."

The two men were at Crill Sadler's *hacienda*. Save for a coating of dust and a trifle redness of eyes, neither man showed traces of a hard night's horseback ride. They could look out of Crill's living room window and watch the first red edge of sunrise on the desert. But neither man had taste for it. They had, perhaps, seen other dawns together, for theirs was that easy comradeship that comes only after two men have stood side-by-side and seen death about them. Unlike in appearance, still their manner with one another was much the same. Without backslapping or handshaking or wordy greetings, they made each other feel that each liked the other's company. Each was ready to face life or death for the other.

A servant brought a bottle of wine. From a bathroom came the delicious sound of a shower running, and the grunting and puffing of someone under the needle shower. Only a big man can make such sounds.

"We're splitting a bottle of good wine, Colonel!" Crill called to the man in the shower.

"Wine before breakfast!" boomed a voice. "Not for me, boys. I'm too old and too dang' sensible to take up with such la-de-da notions. I got a bottle of good whiskey in my bedroom. I taken a shot afore I clumb into this ice water. I'll need another when I get out. But I ain't so soft-minded as to swaller wine afore breakfast. Crill, don't let that danged millionaire contaminate your ideels. I'm plumb ashamed fer you."

A short, heavy man with thick gray mustache and a bald head now came into the living room. Still damp, with a huge bath towel about his middle and a pair of fancy-topped, high-heeled boots on his feet, Colonel White, cowman, soldier, and mining power of the Southwest, joined his two companions. He carried a whiskey glass in one hand, a bottle in the other. He was humming the doleful tune of "Sam Bass" as he stepped into the room.

"Welcome home, boys. Kill anybody much last night? No new notches on the smoke-poles? Gosh, this country's a-goin' to hell. When I was your age, I done things. And I never fooled with wine of a mornin'. Here's lookin' at your sweet, shinin' faces. Now let's look at some ham an' eggs."

In the long shed near the corrals was Colonel White's brush-scratched, dust-caked car. It was a car of the best American make with many special features that included everything from a thermos cabinet, well stocked with food and drink, to a machine-gun ingeniously mounted on a bolted tripod. The windshield and tonneau shield were of bulletproof glass. The car was painted the color of sand, thus lessening its visibility. For Colonel White was in the habit of touring sections infested by rebels and enemies.

He and his chauffeur and his big Texan bodyguard had rolled into Crill Sadler's ranch the previous evening. He was one of the few men who Crill welcomed unreservedly. It was apparent that theirs was a friendship of long and staunch standing, even as was the acquaintanceship of the colonel and Cato Morgan.

Now, in his boots and bath towel, he joined the two younger men, falling into their mood without effort, as if he expected to meet them under almost any circumstances.

"Got word that some letters were in the hands of the wrong people, Crill," grunted the colonel. "Then I heard that Cato's yacht was in the Gulf. Picked up his sign and hit a lope. Your majordomo said you two had lit out for Nogales. Get the letters?"

Cato Morgan nodded and handed over the package of letters. Colonel White looked through them.

"That's the works, Colonel."

"Means the firing squad for the gent that wrote 'em. The damn' fool! Who had 'em?"

"Two Mexicali gamblers. They came here to peddle the letters to a certain person."

"Yolanda, eh?" snapped the colonel. "What was their price?"

"What a beautiful girl prizes above all else," spoke Crill.

"*Hmmm*." The colonel looked from Crill to Cato Morgan, then back once more at the scarred face of the rancher. They looked at him as if waiting for him to speak. Instead, he took the package of letters and, crossing to the open fire that crackled in the fireplace, tossed them into the blaze.

"We all three know that a certain man needs killing," said Colonel White. "He's a menace to both governments as long as he's loping around free. How such a dirty scoundrel can have a daughter like Yolanda beats me. But because he has, I'll give him another chance."

"That's mighty white of you, Colonel," said Crill Sadler.

"Shut up, you gosh-darned sheepherder. What became of the two gamblers?"

"They'll get theirs," put in Cato Morgan. "Crockett will nab 'em. One of those two birds is head of a smuggling ring. I tipped Crockett off to their racket. He'll have both of 'em in his sack by now."

Crill Sadler gave the tall, suave Cato Morgan a swift look of inquiry. "When did you tip off Crockett? I didn't know you even knew him."

"Sure I know him, but I didn't want to upset anything last night by yapping to an officer. Crockett and I met a few years ago when I got in a tight jam at Juárez. He's all right. Appreciates a favor like I tipped him off to last night."

"There have been times, Cato," said Crill bluntly, "when you act for all the world like a fly cop."

"Nonsense," rumbled Colonel White, "I told you not to monkey with that wine in the mornin', Crill. Cato's no dick. If he was, you 'n' me would be behind bars right now. Either that or Cato would be dead and a long time buried. We're all blackened with the same brush, us three. Eh, Cato?"

"You should know, Colonel. Let's eat."

Cato Morgan tossed off the last of his wine and rose. Crill and the colonel also got to their feet. Together they walked to the breakfast set on a linen-covered table in the patio, the colonel's short frame now wrapped in a bathrobe, his boot heels *clicking*.

"Men," said Cato Morgan solemnly as they sat down, "may God, man, or devil never smash the friendship of Crill Sadler, Colonel White, and Cato Morgan."

There was a quiet, somber fervor to his tone that made the two other men wonder. Later they were to understand. But this morning they sat as three comrades, breaking bread. Their tomorrows had not yet come.

CHAPTER
FOUR

"I wish, Crill," said Cato Morgan, late that afternoon as he watched Crill saddle his horse, "that I could go along with you into that Devil's Bend country."

Crill did not reply immediately. He jerked his saddle cinch tight and shoved a Winchester carbine into the saddle boot. The faint glint that might have been suspicion was gone from his eyes as he looked into the eyes of Morgan, who had changed from flannels to riding breeches and a pair of shabby polo boots.

"Those Devil's Bend rannihans would shoot you just for luck, Cato, for wearing such dude clothes. They're hard babies."

"*Hmmm*. So were the Germans at Verdun. So were the Russians in Siberia and the Chinese rebels at Nang Ping. So was Pancho Villa, as we both have cause to remember. Tough! I'll risk their ridicule, buddy."

"Sure you would, brainless. But I won't let you. You wouldn't want to get me killed, would you, Cato? Well, that's what would happen to me if I let you come with me into those hills. They're a hard lot. Not a man there but has a price on his head. When I say price, I mean better than cigarette money. Savvy? Big game. They won't stand any monkey work." Crill swung up into his saddle and grinned frankly at his friend. "I'm playing too dangerous a game, old pardner, to take any risks. Getting those letters for the colonel won't help my standing one bit. And a few days ago I had to shoot one of their bunch. I'm just going back to see how hard the boys took the news of Larson's capture."

"If they kick up a fuss, what then, Crill?"

Crill patted the butt of his gun. "Fight it out, that's all."

"Wish I could help. Could you signal the ranch from there?"

"Whatever starts would be over in a few seconds, I reckon. I'm afraid a signal wouldn't help. But in case it should, the boys here savvy. I have rockets cached in the hills."

Colonel White had left for Nogales or Douglas. Crill and Cato Morgan were alone at the ranch.

"Make yourself at home, Cato. I'll be back by sunrise. That *siesta* made me feel fresh as a daisy."

He rode away with a careless wave of his hand, a tall, graceful rider in overalls, jumper, and chaps. He needed a shave and more sleep, but he set out eagerly on his ride that would not bring him home again until the next morning.

Cato Morgan watched him out of sight. Then, scowling a little, he strolled into the house. As he hunted in his pocket for a cigar, his fingers touched the small gold badge pinned to his undershirt. His eyes hardened a little as they stared out across the desert that was graying now in the brief afterglow of sunset. He poured a stiff drink of whiskey and gulped it down.

For Cato Morgan was about to violate the code of comradeship. He smiled disarmingly at the Mexican, who was clearing away the dishes that had held his and Crill's supper.

"It's too nice to sit around the house. Will you ask the stable man to saddle me a horse?"

"*Si, señor.*"

Cato Morgan buckled on a cartridge belt that held a Colt. Over his whipcord breeches he wore a pair of lightweight chaps. A tall, smiling *vaquero* rode from the barn, leading a horse. Cato Morgan knew that Crill had left orders that the visiting *Americano* was not to ride forth alone. So Cato made the best of it. They rode together into the dusk. Cato took a silver flask from his pocket.

"Drink, old chap?" he invited.

"After you, *señor.*"

The American drank, then passed over the flask. The *vaquero* took a hearty pull at the liquor and passed back the flask. Again they rode along, side-by-side, and Cato Morgan kept up a running fire of gay talk. The *vaquero's* replies became a little thick and drowsy.

Presently he swayed sleepily in his saddle and might have fallen had not the American caught him and lowered his limp form to the ground. For that flask was the handiwork of a clever craftsman who had divided its interior in two sections. By pressing a hidden spring the contents of one section was corked. The drinker who was aware of the hidden spring had the option of either section. Cato Morgan had put a small white capsule in

198

the section from which the Mexican had unwittingly drunk.

Alone, Cato Morgan swung from the main trail and headed across for the hills of the Devil's Bend, pushing his horse to a long trot.

He had been traveling for an hour when the topography of the desert roughened into narrow draws and razor-back ridges, black as agate, the giant boulders, fantastically shaped, taking on the aspect of colossal tombstones, silent, grotesque, sinister. Cato Morgan rode with his right hand near his gun.

"¿Quién es?" ripped the challenge of a hidden sentinel. Cato Morgan stiffened, his senses quivering. That voice might have come from any angle.

"¡Amigo! Friend!" His voice was calm and cold. His slitted eyes peered about him, searching for some human shape

"Amigo, eh? Friend, eh? Like hell. And damn' your pitcher, keep them hands high or I'll gut-shoot you. Hey, Joe, kin you make this gent out?"

"He's ridin' one of Crill's hosses. Might as well kill the fool, eh?"

"Might as well," came the grim reply. "You shoot 'im, Joe, you're closter."

"If I were you boys," said Cato Morgan without a trace of fear in his voice, "I'd wait till I knew who I was shooting. Maybe you'd change your mind and let me live."

"Most mebby not, mister. We never sent out no engraved invites to nobody to pay moonlight calls. Where you think you are, anyhow?"

"Frankly, old warrior, I haven't the slightest idea. I've been lost for half an hour. I wanted to get into the hills of Devil's Bend."

"Hear the crazy fool, Joe? And once you got to them hills of Devil's Bend, *hombre*, just how did you figger you was gonna do yourse'f much good, hey? You better pot 'im while he's skylighted so purty, Joe."

"I'd hate to spile his white shirt, Bill. I bin achin' fer a white shirt. If I hit 'im in the belly, it'll be spoilt fer shore."

"You don't need no white shirt, Joe. You ain't goin' no place where you need no white shirt. What you want of a white shirt?"

"What size is that shirt, mister?" asked Joe.

"Fifteen, I suppose. I had it made. It's a good shirt. Cost fifteen bucks."

"Per dozen?"

"Per one. It's silk."

"Gosh, Bill, a silk shirt. Hey, you, skin 'er off. Silk! He must be a damn' duke, Bill."

"I told you boys to go slow," warned Cato Morgan. "How can I pull off a shirt while both hands are reaching for the moon?"

"That's somethin' you'll have to figger out fer yourse'f, mister," came Bill's harsh voice. "Joe 'lows he wants that there shirt. But if you lower a finger, I'll throw hot lead into your brisket."

"How about it, Joe?" Cato's voice held a bit of a chuckle. "Got any rules in your I.D.R. to cover the situation?"

"Jest you go easy for a second, Bill," said Joe, whose voice never seemed to come twice from the same place. "That's a silk shirt. Hey, feller, you spoke of the I.D.R. What you know about Infantry Drill Regulations, huh?"

"I know enough, Joe," said Cato Morgan.

"A second looie, mebby? If you are, we'll hang you instead of bein' merciful and shootin' you, humane and quick. Was you a shavetail in the big push?"

"Nope. Only a lousy major."

"Now I know he's lyin'," said Bill. "He ain't got no potbelly. Ever seen a major, Joe, without a potbelly?"

"Yeah. One. Me 'n' him got decorated in the same town."

"Decorated!" snorted Bill. "You?"

"Me," came the haughty reply, "me 'n' this long drink of a major . . . together . . . at a château. He knowed his wine, that dude. And fight? A Eyetalian and a Frog staff officer tried to take away this staff car we swiped. Fight? And sing? He had a barbershop tenor that'd carry sweet no matter how plastered we gits. He laid it to that *vino*. Not a sour note in a case of the stuff, says this major."

"White seal," said Cato Morgan, "is sweet-drinking liquor. Better than tequila. Still, Joe, if you'll lead off with 'Sweet Adeline,' I'll try to catch the tenor something like that night we raided that château near Chambray. By the way, did they take away those corporal stripes next day, Joe?"

"It's *him*, Bill! It's the same bird! I knowed that voice. Never seen him after. But his sign showed plain when that M.P. officer turned me outta the guardhouse. And my C.O. says I'm sergeant because a certain major from headquarters says we done somethin' brave. What was it we done, anyhow? I never knowed."

"Well," said Cato Morgan, risking a bullet as he lit a cigarette, "that Italian officer and the French colonel we took into Chambray were Hun spies. And they had a lot of maps and code documents hidden in that car we hooked. If you still want this shirt, you yellow-legged cavalry sergeant, I'll shed it."

"Naw," said Joe's voice almost within reaching distance of Cato Morgan, "keep 'er, Major. Bill, kin we rustle a drink fer my friend here? I'll say he's right. Right as hell! I dunno what he's doin' here, but he's a right *hombre*."

"I've got some of Crill Sadler's best bourbon here, boys," said Cato as two shadowy forms took shape alongside him. "Only it has a pill in it that'll put a man to sleep for a few hours."

"A friend of Joe's must be OK, mister," said the rather dubious voice of Bill, who loomed up like a huge grizzly, "but we got orders. What you doin' here?"

"Well, boys," answered Cato Morgan, wondering how far he could impose on the chance and sketchy friendship of the man Joe, "it's like this. I was paying a visit to . . ."

A sharp ejaculation from the two men interrupted. They all three stared at a rocket that shot up into the purple night.

Cato Morgan's blue eyes narrowed. That rocket — what did it mean? Was it Crill Sadler's signal of distress? Faintly, borne from a long distance on the breathless desert air, came sounds of rifle fire.

Cato Morgan leaned low on the neck of his horse and jabbed the spurs to his flanks. The animal leaped straight at the bulky Bill, who tried to dodge and fell headlong. Joe was shooting, but Cato knew that the ex-cavalryman was aiming high. Excitement or memory of a past A.E.F. friendship was lifting his gun barrel.

As Cato's horse tore along a narrow draw at breakneck speed, he heard Bill and Joe swearing lustily.

CHAPTER
FIVE

It was Crill Sadler who had set off the rocket. He lay behind the dead carcass of his horse, cursing the pain of a badly twisted leg, squinting along the blue barrel of his carbine and lining dim sights as a score of riders tore past, emptying their guns at the pile of granite rocks where Crill fought for his life. Despite the pain of his bruised leg and that death now stacked the odds against him twenty to one, the scarred face twisted in a semblance of a smile. For if death came now, it would be as Crill wished it to come — swiftly, with a fighting chance, with a gun in his hand and a white moon hanging above the broken hills. Crill Sadler wished no quiet bed and drawn blinds. For him it would be like this, the smell of burned powder tingling his nostrils, the thrill of danger, the chance of cheating death's hand, and the open sky. If he could have confided such a wish to some learned doctor or psychologist, he would have been told that such a wish, akin to an obsession, dated back to a time when stone walls closed out that open sky, back to a time before his handsome face had not been so scarred, when his hair had been black instead of snowy white.

That rocket was but a forlorn hope. The ranch was miles away. There was but a slim chance that anyone would see the rocket. And if one of his *vaqueros* did see it, could help reach him before these riders closed in? He grinned sardonically as he set off the rocket and watched it thread a crimson trail against the star-filled sky.

A mile or two away were men whose ears would hear the sound of rifle fire, whose eyes would follow the rocket's passage across the sky. But those men would not come to his aid. Those were the nameless men who dwelt here in the hills of Devil's Bend.

But a brief hour ago Crill Sadler had stood before these bearded, cold-eyed derelicts. They had listened in silence as Crill talked. There was the mockery of death itself in their heavy silence. And when he had done talking, one of their number had stepped up to him and, without a word, had handed Crill a bit of folded, black cloth. This black cloth, which Crill Sadler had unfolded before them, was a hangman's cap. Crill had looked from it up into the dozen pairs of cold eyes.

"You squealed on Larson, Crill Sadler," said their spokesman. "From what we learned, you bin double-crossin' us. We give you a week's time to save your neck from stretchin' rope. Fetch us Chiquita Lopez and Colonel White. Fetch 'em here, into the council of the black cap."

"If I don't?" said Crill Sadler in a brittle voice. "If I don't bring Chiquita Lopez and Colonel White here, what then?"

The spokesman laughed gratingly. "What then? You know damn' well what then! You'll hang by the neck until dead. We give you one week."

For answer Crill Sadler took the black hangman's cap and, balling it in his hands, tossed it contemptuously into the fire. His scarred face looked white and terrible as the flickering firelight played on it. He stood there facing the row of men, his hands on his guns, his slitted eyes blazing with deadly anger.

"That's what I think of you and your hangman's cap, you and your council. If there's anyone in this pack that has guts, let him stand up on his feet. I'll kill him like a dog. Larson and Jockey Slicer never belonged here. They framed a little game and they lost. They got what they needed. You want me to bring you Chiquita Lopez so that you can learn something, eh? Something about a map of a place. And you want me to trick Colonel White into coming here because he also has knowledge of that same map. And you give me a week, do you, you fools? I don't want it. Before I'd see you lay your filthy paws on that girl, I'd kill the whole jackal pack of you. Hear that? And no scurvy rat nest will ever see Colonel White where he has to weaken. He's a man. He's my friend. And I'll see the lot of you rot in these hills before I turn on him. Hang me, will you? Come on. Now! I'm waiting. And my guns are waiting. And let me tell you, *hombres*, I'll send a few of you along ahead of me before you slip the rope over my neck. I'll be back in a week. I'm coming back to rid these hills of their vermin. I'll teach you, you rats, to turn on Crill Sadler.

I'm going now. Lift a gun barrel to stop me and some of you will eat breakfast in hell."

And when Crill Sadler, a gun in each hand, had backed out of the rim of firelight, no man of them had made the move to stay his departure. So he had swung up on his horse and ridden away.

A scant three miles from there he had been attacked. The first volley that came out of the night had killed Crill's horse. Now he lay there, counting his shots, as the shadowy horsemen charged in an ever-narrowing circle. The riders were not members of the outlaw band. Nor were they Mexicans. Crill knew them by their tactics to be Yaquis. Better by far to die fighting than to endure the tortures of this merciless band of Yaquis who had turned renegade against Mexico and preyed on all who they found, white or Mexican.

Not daring to brave the superstitious menace that shrouded Devil's Bend, they had hidden along the trail where the hills flattened out into mesquite desert. They had seen Crill ride from the hills and had shot at him for no other reason than that of cruel hatred against the men who lived in those dreaded hills. For their habits were as those of a wandering wolf pack that preys on the weak. Fired by the tequila they made from cactus, half crazed by marijuana, they were bold and cunning and more to be feared than were the roving bands of half-starved rebels who made futile attempts to gain power in that country.

Back in the hills, those men who had passed the sentence of the black cap heard the firing and chuckled. And not one among them had any intention of riding out of the safety of the hills to aid him who needed help so badly.

Bill and Joe, when their erstwhile prisoner had given them the slip, railed at one another for lengthy minutes. They finally brought forth a bottle of tequila and drank.

"May git a idee of some kind, Bill."

"Fer instance?" growled the dubious Bill. "Collectin' another white shirt, mebby?"

"Not another shirt, Bill. Same shirt."

"Why didn't you drop him, hey? You was so clost to him you could've spit on him. And you missed 'im clean. On purpose, if you ask me. Just because him an' you oncet drunk up a case of wine. The boys'd tip you the black cap fer this, Joe, if they found out."

"How they gonna find out? I tell you, Bill, that major is a right guy." Joe took another drink. "How they gonna find out?"

"I'll tell 'em, that's how," growled Bill.

"I've bin kickin' around this old world with you fer twenty years and you never told nothin' on nobody yet. I ain't worryin'. Who you reckon is doin' that shootin'?"

"Must be the gang is sendin' Crill Sadler along the way. And Crill sent up a rocket. Let 'em fight, says I. Me 'n' you is on guard. A guard with two-bits' worth of sense never quits his post. Ain't that what we learnt in the Army?" Bill reached for the bottle.

"We'd orter hunt up the major, just the same, Bill."

"To hell with the major. I'm thinkin' about another party. Joe, I never liked that damned Larson Swede. Never taken to him a-tall."

"Ner Jockey Slicer?"

"Nope. Ner Slicer."

"Crill Sadler's a white gent."

"None whiter, boy."

"You thinkin' what I'm thinkin', kid?"

"Wouldn't be no ways su'prised if our thoughts fits into the same hole."

"It means hangin' fer us if we lose."

"Hangin's better'n bein' yaller to a friend."

"Then lemme have that bottle oncet before we start."

Joe held the bottle to his ear and shook it. Then he sighted its contents against the white moon.

"One apiece, Bill. May be our last. Here's how, boy!"

Bill took the bottle with its last shot. He held it up in way of a toast.

"To us! Me 'n' you, Joe. May we live to drink all the tequila in Mexico." And when he had drained the bottle, he smashed it against the rock. "Come on, Joe."

"Right with you, Bill. Wisht you could sing. That major has a hell of a swell singin' voice. Lemme have some Thirty-Forty shells."

Thus did Bill and Joe, with a carelessness that was sublime, cast their lot against the band of nameless men to serve Crill Sadler in the simple name of friendship. Better to hang than quit a friend! History gives to posterity the names of heroes made of no better stuff.

CHAPTER
SIX

It was plain that Bill and Joe were men of fighting experience. They parted, each creeping toward a different flank of the Yaquis who had quit their horses and were advancing, deployed, toward the lone man who was putting up such a desperate and crafty fight.

Another figure also dodged among the boulders. Cato Morgan, no less versed in guerrilla warfare, was slipping through the Yaqui line and toward his friend. He saw the yellow spew of Crill's gun. A bullet whined like a hornet past his ear.

"Lay off me, big boy!" he called. "Hold 'er, Crill!"

"Great gosh, Cato! You long-complected idiot!"

Cato slid in among the boulders beside Crill, followed by a spattering hail of bullets.

"Hot, what?" He grinned, taking a snap shot at a Yaqui who had showed himself. The range was long for a six-shooter but the Indian's yelp told a hit.

"Got an extra Winchester, Crill?"

"You mean you broke into this game with only that Colt?"

"An oversight," grunted Cato. "Didn't expect a war."

"Well, here comes a war, right now!"

For with a yell, the Yaquis charged. The following seconds seemed hours to the two white men who crouched, back to back, their guns belching death at shadows that rose and fell and were replaced by other shadows. Then, from beyond the Yaquis, came a yell that sent the blood of the two besieged men pulsing.

"Powder River!" A wailing, long-drawn coyote howl of a shout. None other than big Bill.

"A mile wide and a foot deep!" bawled Joe. "*Whoopee!*"

From different points came the two outlawed cowboys at a jog trot, crouching, firing Winchesters from the hip.

"Powder River!" yelled Crill exultantly.

"Let 'er buck, you hellions!" added Cato.

Four men fighting twenty or more. But their aim was deadly and their courage that of chilled steel. And if the gait of the two outlaws was a trifle unsteady, the wavering was due to raw tequila on empty stomachs.

"If a bullet hits me, that licker'll leak out all over hell," grunted Joe as he shoved fresh shells in his gun and forged ahead again.

Bill plowed through a nest of fighting Yaquis, clubbing, shooting, one man among half a dozen. Then Cato Morgan leaped into the dog fight, his Colt rattling like a machine-gun. He and Bill faced each other across dead men, grimy, blood-spattered, their faces white and ugly with the smear of desperation stamped there, like a mask, teeth bared, eyes glinting like red slits, brutal, uncompromising: war faces!

"Joe'll shore feel bad," panted Bill, his huge chest heaving from exertion. "You've done ruined that there nice shirt, feller."

"Damned if not, Bill. Let's go. Crill's down." Cato swung back, jamming shells in a hot-barreled gun.

"Hey, bonehead!" bawled Joe from somewhere. "Hey, Bill!"

"Hey yourse'f, homely!"

"How're ya, an' where?"

"OK, noisy, an' right here!"

"Where the hell's here?"

"Dry up and go to fightin'!"

But the fighting was about over. Bill, Cato, and Joe found Crill trying to stand up. His scarred face was twisted with pain but he greeted them with a grin.

"I bet me 'n' Joe su'prised you, Crill."

"Not so much, boys." His eyes silenced the two outlaws.

Cato was unbuttoning his shirt. "What's left is yours, Joe."

"Keep 'er, Major. What's a shirt, anyhow, between old college mates? You must be that guy that they talk about. The guy that'll give you the shirt off his back. What you limpin' fer, Crill?"

"He's got corns, fool," said Bill.

"I bet they're plumb painful, them corns. I got dandruff, myse'f."

"That's his side of it. Dandruff, nothin'. He taken a hat off a dead Mex. That there hat was inhabited. It'll learn 'im. He's bin usin' tequila fer shampoo . . . tequila mixed with cattle dip. Then we run outta nourishment an' we drunk the hair stuff. Joe's dandruff taken a new start. Sort of volunteer crop. But I bet a horse that there ain't none of them Mexican dandruff nits in his stummick."

"Boys," said Crill earnestly, "I don't quite savvy how you three gents met or why you're here. But here you are. And I'm sure obliged. I want to . . ."

"Ain't we got another bottle somewheres, Bill? Crill's bunions is achin' so that he's kinda outta his head. Comes from wearin' tight boots."

"Yeah. Mind them number five boots I taken off that corpse down on the San Pablo, Joe? Too tight, but too purty to th'ow away. I wore 'em till I was gaited like a box-ankled cow with spikes driv into her hoofs. Rustle Crill a hoss. We better be slidin'. I don't feel like bein' hung yet."

Joe and Bill got their horses and rode back, leading Cato's mount and a Yaqui horse for Crill.

"Cato," asked Crill while the two were waiting, "how did you get here anyhow?"

"Followed you, old son. Had a craving to get a squint at these tough hill babies."

"*Hmmm.* What did you do with the Mexican *vaquero* that I gave orders to stick to you?"

"Gave him a drink with a sleeping dose in it."

"Oh." Crill said no more. When Bill brought the horses, the four men set out at a brisk gait for the Sadler Ranch. Crill's swollen leg pained horribly but he gave no complaint. Sometimes his eyes clouded

213

with a look of brooding. Cato Morgan knew that Crill was wondering a lot, his thought stained with suspicion.

The Yaquis had vanished. They had tasted the bitter medicine of the white men's guns and they were content to gather their dead and wounded and seek safety.

Bill and Joe rode behind, keeping up a line of banter. Silence separated Crill and Cato Morgan like some wall. Despite the fact that Cato had aided in saving Crill's life, he had committed an unforgivable sin in violating Crill's hospitality. Crill knew that no mere curiosity had sent Cato Morgan into the hills of Devil's Bend. He wondered just how much Cato knew or guessed concerning the secret of those hills — a secret known to Crill and Colonel White and the girl Yolanda, who danced and sang under another name — Yolanda, whose father was a traitor.

Cato Morgan was in Mexico on a secret mission. That much Crill knew. That the mission had to do with Yolanda's father, Cato had told him. The two had recovered letters written by Yolanda's father. Those letters, if made public, would cause international trouble between certain powers.

So much Cato Morgan knew of the girl Yolanda and the part Crill played in the scheme of things. But did he know of that other thing, that thing for which men would do murder, that thing that had to do with a map — a map divided into five parts, which had no value until those five parts were pieced together?

That was Crill's secret. Not even the nameless men of Devil's Bend knew the value, the origin, or the intrigue behind that divided map. They guessed and speculated and plotted and sometimes killed men in vain hopes of solving its mystery. This much they knew. It told of the hiding place of gold and jewels valued beyond several millions.

This is what they did not know — of the five parts of the map, three were accounted for. Yolanda, White, and Crill Sadler each owned a part. Two parts were missing. Somewhere in Mexico or the United States or in Europe, two men lived who each owned a part of the map — that was the heritage of bitterness and jealousy and hatred and intrigue, a heritage handed down by a man raised from peonage to power. That man's very name sent cold chills down the spines of kings and czars and presidents. He was dead now, but his power lived on and his skeleton hand seemed to push aside the mold of a hidden grave and move pawns in endless maneuvering across the deserts and hills of Mexico. And his dead face rode of nights into silent reaches where bleached skeletons guard buried treasure; his dead voice must mock those living men who claimed victory in that man's death.

This man had left behind him a tremendous fortune in gold and jewels, the loot of palace and cathedral, of gambling resort and mining office, crowns and crosses encrusted with jewels, sheafs of banknotes taken from the shattered safes of the border gambling houses, raw gold in bricks. He had hidden his treasure with the skill of a pirate burying loot. His last act had been to make a map of the place. And it was typical of him and his grisly, grim-lipped humor that he should divide the map into five parts. Each part had gone to a different compass point. Each of the five persons receiving a portion of the map was a deadly enemy of the four others. Therein lay the ghastly humor of that dead man. He left behind him a vast treasure. And he left his five worst enemies to fight over it. His final gesture had been one that was wholly in keeping with the man's nature — this man who, once upon a time, had halted in the midst of a banquet to pass sentence on an officer who had violated a rule of that rebel army.

"Take him out and shoot him," said the great rebel chieftain, and, turning to the waiter, added: "Bring on the salad, *hombre*."

So he had left his treasure and his divided map. As Crill Sadler rode homeward, he wondered if Cato Morgan knew of the map. If so, would Cato Morgan be traitor to a comradeship to fight for that gold?

CHAPTER
SEVEN

Again Crill Sadler and Cato Morgan sprawled in easy chairs in the living room of Crill's house. Neither man had spoken for an hour. The silence was not an easy one. Each seemed loath to meet the eyes of his companion. Neither man had the temerity to break the silence.

Crill's scarred face was shadowed with some brooding thought. Now and then he stared at his bandaged leg as if he blamed his injury for his present mood. But Cato Morgan knew that Crill was fighting down his suspicion of a friend. Cato was almost on the verge of unpinning that small gold badge and handing it over to Crill. He wanted to make a clean breast of it, tell Crill that he'd rather die than mar the splendid unity of their comradeship. But he could not find the courage to say what he wished. "I say, Crill," Cato broke that silence at last, "is there any need of Yolanda Bertoncini staying on at the Oasis?"

"Uh? Yolanda? No, she's all washed up there. She's due here this evening. I thought I'd told you."

"Yolanda coming here?" Cato was on his feet, a scowl knitting his sun-bleached brows.

"Yep. Here. Why not? Her scoundrel of a father is due to pay me a visit. Wouldn't surprise me if the colonel also dropped in. Sort of a family reunion." Crill grinned mirthlessly.

"That being the case, old man," said Cato, "I'll be trotting along. I don't want to outstay my welcome."

"Cato," said Crill earnestly, "my home is always open to my friends."

"You still believe I'm your friend, Crill?"

"I'm trying to, old-timer. I've so damned few friends. I'd sure hate to lose one. We've seen a lot together, you and I. I don't reckon there are many men that have faced death together as we have."

"Yet" — Cato smiled wistfully — "we've been sitting here for an hour thinking a lot of rot. I'm coming clean now, as clean as a man can come. I'm down here for a purpose, Crill. That purpose is to check a revolt that is about to break. General Adolfo Bertoncini is at the head of it. I was informed that his stronghold was Devil's Bend." Cato unpinned the badge and held it out in his right hand.

"That's why you followed me, Cato?" Crill had taken the badge. He examined it with a crooked little smile, then returned it.

"That's the reason, Crill, that I violated our friendship and trailed you. That revolt of Bertoncini's is doomed even before it starts. If you or Colonel White happens to be mixed up in it, for heaven's sake, draw out. You know what that badge means. You know, old buddy, that I'm violating orders by telling you this or revealing my identity. Pull out of the damn' thing,

Crill!" He crossed over and put an arm across Crill's shoulder.

Crill's eyes looked into Cato Morgan's blue ones. Then Crill broke into a hearty laugh. Cato drew back, brows quirking in puzzled inquiry.

"So that's why you trailed me, eh? No other reason, old son?"

"None other. Ain't that enough?" He shoved his badge into a pocket. "I'm nothing but a fly cop, a dick."

"No. That badge is one to be proud of. I knew you wore it."

"What?"

"You had it on, that night you were wounded at the Marne. I saw it when I was bandaging you."

"You never mentioned it, Crill."

"No need to yippy-yap about it. I know it's a badge worn by few men, that it's given for life, that the men who wear it don't mix in anything but big games, and that you don't know what other men wear a similar badge. I know that much about it. And if you're worrying about me being mixed up with Bertoncini, forget it. If you stick around, you'll learn something about that foxy cuss."

"How's that?" asked Cato Morgan.

"I don't want to spoil the surprise, old-timer. But I'll guarantee to put on a show worth watching. Not only that, but I'll send you back with more secret information regarding this Bertoncini revolt than you ever hoped to get, even by tracking me into Devil's Bend. You'll carry back a contour map of their stronghold, an exact list of personnel, both officers and adobe soldiers, guns, field pieces, machine-guns, ammunition caches, or what have you."

"You're kiddin' me, Crill."

"Nope."

"Then you must be in with Bertoncini."

"On the contrary, old war boss, Bertoncini plans to capture my ranch and use it for his rebel headquarters. He hates me so hard that I'm flattered. Those Italians know how to hate."

"Odd that Yolanda doesn't share that hatred of her father's."

Crill nodded, smiling oddly. Then he poured two drinks. When he had set down the bottle, Crill took a pencil and a pad. On a blank sheet he drew a circle. Then he divided the circle into five segments. Cato Morgan watched him with tense interest.

"That mean anything to you, Cato?" asked Crill.

For reply Cato took the pencil and wrote five names, one in each segment of the circle. They were Spanish names. In the order of their listing, they read as follows: Diego, Emanuel, Arnaldo, Tomás, and Hermano.

"Those are the names that belong there, Cato. Any number of Diegos and Emanuels and so on, here in Mexico, though. Do you happen to know the history of that divided circle and what those names mean?"

"I've seen the circle divided like that, Crill," said Cato Morgan, "with these names written in the segments. But beyond that and the fact that it is the symbol of a secret order, I'm ignorant."

"Then I'll enlighten you enough to grab your attention. One night, 'way back, the greatest man in all

Mexico called a conference of his five field chiefs. Usually informal, the leader, who I'll call *Don* Francisco, could be military when he set his mind to it. And so could these five men. For all of them were veterans of foreign wars, all soldiers of fortune, and in spite of their ragtag uniforms they looked somehow splendid as they stood there at attention, the American, the Russian, the German, the Italian, and the Frenchman. Some mixture, eh? And let me tell you, Cato, they were soldiers. *Don* Francisco stood them there at attention while he called the roll. It was a whim of his to call each of them by a Mexican name. Diego was Pierre La Porte, Emanuel none other than our friend Bertoncini, Arnaldo was that Cossack butcher Blotski . . . damn his memory! . . . Tomás was Colonel Tom White himself, and Hermano was Herman Blucher, who had been in the Prussian Guards."

"As *Don* Francisco called the roll, he wrote each name down on a blackboard he'd found somewhere. Then he drew a circle and divided it, marking each segment with a name. And all the while that merciless smile of his worked about his thick-lipped mouth. There was a joke coming, one of his jokes that so often was spattered with blood. Every man there knew it. For all their reckless nerve each of them was uneasy. Because, Cato, no man of them but had a guilty conscience. Well, there were the five names there on the blackboard, one below the other . . . Diego, Emanuel, Arnaldo, Tomás, Hermano. Then *Don* Francisco took an eraser in his hand. Slowly, carefully, with five pairs of eyes watching, he wiped that eraser through the names, leaving only the first letter of each name. They stood, those five letters in a row . . . D-E-A-T-H."

Crill Sadler's scarred face was tense and grimly tragic. It suddenly struck Cato Morgan that this graphic tale must have been gained first-hand. Crill Sadler must have been there at that rebel camp, and must have seen it with his own eyes. Yet Cato Morgan knew that no man of Crill Sadler's name or description had been with *Don* Francisco at that time. He waited for Crill to continue.

"The circle with the five segments," Crill said finally, "is a circle of death. No man of those five liked the others. Their hate for one another was as strong as was their loyalty to *Don* Francisco. He and his power kept those five men from tearing at one another like five wild beasts. *Don* Francisco got a lot of amusement from their hatred of one another. He could savvy hatred, could the *don*, even as he could savvy the meaning of loyalty, once a man proved faith. And each of these fighting men of his had more than once proved his loyalty, even Bertoncini and that damned Cossack Blotski. Now they stood there, stiff-backed, and waited for *Don* Francisco to explain . . . which he did."

" 'My wolves,' he said, twirling an end of his mustache, 'so long as I live, you five will run in one pack. Eh? Five wolves. And together you are strong, the strongest men in Mexico. That is why I keep you. I need you while I live. I pay you each well to run together in one wolf pack. 'Sta bueno. But, *hombrecitos*, someday I shall die. A knife. A bullet. And *pouf* . . . I am gone. And my power over you will be gone. And you will fight among yourselves, like five wolves until you are all dead. And, damn you, you fools, your fighting will undo what good I have done here in my beloved Mexico. Hear that? All I have done will be wiped away. Your *gringo* newspapers call me a bandit, an outlaw, a man who kills and rapes and robs for gold. *Nombre de Dios*, what do they know of what is in my heart? What do they know, eh? Nothing! And yet, *hombrecitos*, my wolves, I would die by torture tonight with a smile, if I could die knowing I have helped poor Mexico. For *Dios*, I do not lie.

" 'And what of you my wolves, eh? What do you care for Mexico? Nothing. You fight for money and because the *Señor Dios* made you of fighting material. But for Mexico you care not so much as one *peso*. And when I am gone, you will be a pack of snarling, snapping wolves fighting over a bone. A bone of gold, set in jewels, eh? Your eyes shine now at the mention of gold and your hands itch to feel of a gun or knife.

" 'You, my Diego, with your Frenchman's mustache and your sword, ready to stick it into the guts of them that stand in your way! You, Emanuel, with your stiletto! Arnaldo, ready for the chance to slice a man's head off with one swing of your Cossack saber! Tomás, my *Tejano*, who makes me laugh when my heart is heavy! You and I, we understand each other because we were born within the day's ride of each other. You in Texas, I in my Mexico. May the *Señor Dios* always keep your guns so quick, *Tejano*, my *amigo*. I could not love a brother better, even though you also are a wolf, a wolf like Hermano with his saber cut across the jaw and his beer and his cheese that smells like the animal that is dead . . . my big German wolf!

" 'So, *hombrecitos*, I make the joke. There will be much gold and many jewels buried at a place. There will be a map cut like that circle into five parts. Each of you will give me the name of a friend in your own country. To that friend I will send your part. Diego's part goes to France, Emanuel's to Italy, Arnaldo's to Russia, Tomás's to Texas, Hermano's to Germany. And, *señores*, by the time you are again gathered with your bits of the map and must sit down together and piece together the bits, that will be time enough for my work here to be rooted beyond all pulling up. My job will be well done. Peace will make happiness here where we are spilling blood. There will be schools and colleges started. My people will forget how to shoot and turn their efforts to works of peace. And no man of you will retain the power to start a successful revolt. My wolves will be like wolves in a pen. Your teeth will be too old and broken and rotten to bite. No man of you can raise a revolution so that you will get more gold.

" 'You will meet again in a few years with your bits of map. And you will fight like wolves over your golden bone. But you will fight only among yourselves, *señores*. And you will kill each other. And perhaps my Tomás, my *Tejano*, will remember that sometimes I like the little joke.

" 'So, *hombrecitos*, my wolves, I called you those names that, when the letters are spelled, make the *gringo* word "Death". There is your circle, your circle of death. *¡Adiós, señores!*' "

224

Crill Sadler leaned back in his chair, his face flushed and his gray eyes glistening with memories. He lifted his drink, rising.

"A toast, Cato," he said huskily. "To the greatest man of them all! To him I call *Don* Francisco. *Salud*."

"*Salud*." And when they had drunk, each broke his glass.

"One of those five men is dead," said Crill. "Diego, the Frenchman, whose real name was Pierre La Porte. He was a gentleman and a soldier. He died well, serving his France. I was with him when he went West. And he gave me his bit of map. It was his wish that the map be given to the daughter of Bertoncini. La Porte had met Yolanda when she was doing war work. It was love at first sight. Odd, but he never knew she was old Bertoncini's girl. He died with her name on his lips. I never let him know he died loving the daughter of his enemy. Those Latins are so darned touchy. I didn't want to spoil his romance."

"She has La Porte's portion of the map, then?" asked Cato.

"Yes. Colonel White has his portion." Crill grinned as if recalling something humorous.

"And I suppose Bertoncini has his?" asked Cato.

"No. I have it. That's one reason he hates me so much. He doesn't suspect, however, that I know the history of the map. He has never recognized me as a man he knew once. He believes that man to be dead. For that matter, so does Colonel White. No man living today knows who I am." Crill Sadler held out a pair of blunt-fingered hands that were criss-crossed with scars.

"Even my fingerprints are gone. The man I was is dead. I am Crill Sadler. I won Bertoncini's map in a gambling game. When he came to redeem it, I told him I'd lost the thing. The old rascal was upset. He suspects I have it and he's going to make a try for it . . . tomorrow night, I think. He doesn't know I'm wise. Yes, Cato, old trapper, I promise you a show worth the seeing."

"Ever hear of the rest of the map, Crill?" asked Cato.

"I have reason to know that both Blotski and Herman Blucher are in Mexico. So I've set my trap for them and baited it well. If things break right, buddy, you'll have the doubtful pleasure of seeing *Don Francisco's* wolf pack fight over their golden bone."

"The devil!" gasped Cato.

"Exactly. The devil." Crill crumpled the paper with its drawing, and tossed it into the fire. He took a pipe from his pocket and shoved it between his teeth. Then he fumbled for tobacco. Cato Morgan's glance shifted to a door that was open an inch or so. He filled another glass with liquor and was moving it in circles. Left. Right. Right. Left. Left. He glanced back at Crill, who had quit hunting tobacco.

For Crill Sadler's right hand held a heavy Colt. The gun was pointed squarely at Cato Morgan.

"I don't want to use this gat" — Crill's voice bit like a sharp knife into the pregnant silence — "so call in your friend Crockett and tell him to keep his hands away from his gun."

"Come on in, Chief," called Cato Morgan, "and better do as Crill says! He never pulled a gun yet that he wouldn't use."

The door opened wider. Into the living room stepped Crockett of the Border Patrol. But the big chief's arms were bound to his sides and there was an ingenious gag in his mouth. Behind him marched the old Mexican Manuel Ramirez, an evil grin on his wrinkled face, a long knife in his hand.

"The *Señor* Chuck Lannigan ees tie up to the tree outside, *señor*."

"*Bueno*, Manuel. And the *Señorita* Chiquita?"

"Ees een the kitchen getting a cup of coffee."

"*Bueno* again, Manuel. Where's the colonel?"

"The *Señor Coronel* ees also een the kitchen for that coffee."

"Untie the *Señor* Crockett's arms and take that wire loop off his tongue. Then bring in the *Señor* Lannigan." Crill hadn't let Cato Morgan outside the radius of his gaze. He now addressed him personally. "Frisk yourself, Cato. Lay your guns on the table. Under the circumstances, I think you're safer without a rod on you."

CHAPTER
EIGHT

Crockett, his arms free once more, felt gingerly of his tongue. "Some gag, Sadler. Wire, and a copper bar."

"Regular Spanish bit." Crill nodded. "Have a drink. There's cigars and cigarettes. I hope Lannigan didn't force us to muss him up."

"Chuck laid 'em down when Colonel White threw down on him. The colonel has a convincing way of handling a shootin' iron." Crockett poured himself a stiff drink and downed it. "How the devil did you get wise, Sadler?"

"Intercepted Cato's messages and substituted mine. You're really here at my invitation, Crockett. You and Lannigan. He's been so damned anxious to hang something on me that I couldn't bear to leave him out of this. Cato bribed my *mozos*, and, of course, they told me what he wanted. I carried out the game. Let the cards fall as he expected. Only he didn't know you'd be a prisoner when you got here, Crockett. You gents mean well but you're all wet. Sit down, Cato. You won't grow any taller standing. Ah, Lannigan!"

Chuck Lannigan stood in the doorway, his leathery face drawn in lines of disgust and anger. Lannigan was not a man to conceal his feelings behind a poker face.

228

"Well, Sadler, what's the game? You're damned high-handed, eh? Lemme tell you, though, if you try any rough stuff, the U.S. government will hang you for the black crook you are. You and White, both. You damn' filibusters. I got the goods on you now. Gun-running and smuggling. I'll see both of you in the Big House before I'm done."

"Pass Lannigan the bottle, Crockett," suggested Crill. "He has a bad taste in his mouth."

Crockett, with a faint smile, handed Lannigan the bottle. But Chuck Lannigan ignored it.

"Don't be such a rotten loser," said Crill. "You bet and you lost your socks on the deal."

"Oh, go to the devil!" Lannigan's thin-lipped mouth twisted in a snarl.

"If I do go, my *amigo*, I'll take along an escort. Don't make a play for Cato Morgan's guns, there on the table. If you do, I'll break both your arms before you can thumb a hammer. If you think I'm bluffing, try your luck. You're among gentlemen. Try to profit by their manners. You'll learn a lot before long. Sit down. Don't drink unless you want it, nor smoke. And for that matter, we can get by without your conversation. There's a lady in the house, so keep a tail holt on your adjectives."

Again Crockett smiled faintly and selected a cigar from Crill's humidor. Cato Morgan had dropped into a chair and reached for his drink. Save for the vitriolic Lannigan, these men played this game of wits and guns as gamblers play poker. Their faces were pokerfaces. And now another pokerface was added to the group.

Colonel White, munching a roast beef sandwich heavily upholstered with sliced onion and catsup, strode into the room. His ruddy face beamed with bluff good humor and his keen eyes twinkled. His overalls and flannel shirt were powdered with dust. He wore two low-tied, white-handled guns. This was the old war horse of Mexico who had followed the fortunes of that war-torn country for the past thirty years. Some called him the most dangerous factor in Mexico. This was *Don* Francisco's *Tejano*.

"Howdy, boys? Still drinking wine before breakfast? Cato, my son, don't say I didn't warn you. Well, Crill, looks like things are movin' right along, eh? Regular family party. Hungry, Crockett?"

"I could eat." Crockett met the colonel's grin with one that was its equal in grim mirth.

"Lope out to the kitchen. Chiquita will fix you up. Her and a pair of birds called Bill and Joe who are on K.P., so they tell me. Bill is showin' her and Joe how to tie a hangman's knot. They're a great pair of joshers, them two. They'd make even Lannigan crack a grin. Cato looks like he needed some comedy, too. And Chiquita was askin' about him."

Cato colored a little. "I'm in disgrace, Colonel. I'm the traitor of this war, the fly cop . . . the spy."

"Don't take it so hard, boy. Trot out there, now, and let Chiquita feed you. And you might pick up somethin' from Bill and Joe, if you ain't run outta twenty-dollar bills. Them two is always open to persuasion."

"So I've learned." Cato grinned crookedly and rose. "I paid each of 'em a hundred bucks for information."

"You might git it back with a good pair of dice," suggested Colonel White, his mouth full of food. "There's enough of us here fer a good poker game. I bet Lannigan is a sea-goin' hound at stud."

"Oh, go to hell!" Lannigan bit off a chew of plug and spat into the open fire.

"Lannigan is shore good at them snappy comebacks, Crill." The colonel chuckled. "Wait till he takes us back to the States. Gosh. Enjoy life while you kin, Crill. You ain't got many days of freedom left. Lannigan told me so with his own mouth. Shore enough."

"Oh, dry up!"

"That's his other hot 'un, Crill. Ain't he good? Ain't he the comical jasper, though?"

Crill grinned wryly. In spite of all evidence to the contrary, he wanted to think well of Cato Morgan. Whenever his eyes met those of Cato, the latter sent him a message of mute appeal. Cato now rose and stood there with his gaze fastened on Crill.

"Better mosey out to the kitchen, Cato," said Crill. "My house is yours, even if there is a guard all around it."

Cato Morgan nodded and obeyed. When he had left the room, old Manuel Ramirez closed the door and stood there on guard. Crill picked Cato's two guns off the table and pocketed them. Crockett's faint smile died. Lannigan sat in his chair, muscles taut, ready to fight hard for his life. But Crill shook his head.

"Now," said Colonel White, "we'll get down to cases. Make yourse'ves comfortable, gents. Crill, you do the gabbin'."

Crill nodded as he limped about on his injured leg. He did not seem to know just how to begin. He looked from the enigmatic Crockett to the sullen Lannigan, and then a slow smile spread over his face. He took from his pocket a small notebook, its pages filled with jotted notations. Skimming through its pages, he found one that held a list of names and dates. This he tore from the book. With a pencil he drew that circle and its five segments while Lannigan and Crockett watched. Then he passed the list to Crockett.

"Recognize those birds, Crockett?"

The Border Patrol chief scanned the list, his face a study in changing expression. There were thirty names listed, each with a date beside it. The last two names were those of Jockey Slicer and Black Gus Larson.

"It's a list of men captured by the us the past three years," said Crockett.

"Let Lannigan check the list and dates," suggested Crill. This was done.

"In each instance," said Crill, "you men were tipped off by someone who signed the tip with that divided circle. Am I right, Lannigan?"

"Right as hell."

"And I'm the man that signed the tip," said Crill. "Lannigan, before you accuse me of too many crimes, think that over. I've delivered men to you that no man or no ten men of your patrol could have nabbed. I've another list, not quite so long. It's a list of men you want. You can scratch 'em because they're dead, as dead as rope or bullet can kill a man. I sent Crockett a copy of that list. Did you get it, Chief?"

"I did. And I'll say this much, Sadler. I've always had a hunch it was you that was cleaning up Devil's Bend."

"But you've always questioned my motives in turning in those yeggs?"

"Frankly, yes. I've wondered a lot, a devilish lot. You're a mysterious sort of man, you'll admit that. While you were accomplishing the impossible by cleaning up Devil's Bend, still I suspected a selfish motive behind it. I've sometimes thought you wanted those hills to yourself. That's the one spot along the border that cannot be patrolled. I've wondered what your game was."

"Spoken like a man, Crockett," boomed Colonel White. "And bless me for a monk if you ain't about hit the nail on the old head. Excuse me, Crill, fer hornin' in. You're the mouthpiece."

"I had a reason," Crill went on, "in fact, several reasons. But we won't go into that. What I want to get at is this. There is still a nest of snakes in Devil's Bend. So I sent for you two men to make a dicker. Cato's message to you said to keep out, that he could swing it alone. He was trying to be loyal, perhaps, to both his job and to his old friendship for me. Or maybe he saw the futility of any attempt to buck my game here. Anyhow, he sent word for you to stay out of here. I substituted another order asking your immediate help."

"You used our code," said Crockett. "Where did you get the key?"

"Figured it out. I've had some experience with codes, Crockett."

Crockett eyed Crill shrewdly. Crill returned his scrutiny with an enigmatic smile.

"Now for the proposition. You want Devil's Bend cleaned out for always?"

"Do I?" Crockett tapped the arm of his chair with a clenched fist. "I'd give a year's pay to wipe it clean."

"So we figured. You'd even put on civilian clothes and handle a gun to help do it?"

"What do you mean, Sadler?" Crockett's face was again the pokerface of a gambler.

"What I mean is this . . . there are enough of us in this house right now to clean up the hills of Devil's Bend. I'll vouch for the fact that the government of Mexico will not interfere. They'll shut their eyes and ears and mouths. And your leper spot along the border will be cleansed. There's the proposition. Want it?"

The face of Chuck Lannigan was a picture of bewilderment, but Crockett's expression was mask-like. The big chief leaned forward in his chair, his eyes glittering shrewdly.

"Where's the catch to it, Sadler? You're not doing this out of mere generosity of heart. What's your price?"

Crill Sadler and Colonel White traded a quick glance. There was a mute question in Crill's eyes. The colonel nodded.

"Inside of two weeks, gentlemen, if Colonel White and I are alive, we will wish to cross out of Mexico into the United States. We will be leaving Mexico forever, understand? We will have a pack train of twenty or thirty mules. Those mules will be loaded, but not with contraband. Their loads will represent the wages of thirty years of heat and thirst and hunger and firing squads and prison . . . thirty years of hell. Our wages for what we have done will be loaded on those mules. We ask free passage across the border and we ask our freedom until we can get to San Francisco. From there we sail to another country. Where we go doesn't matter. That, gentlemen, is our price."

Crill Sadler's face looked grim and hard and yet somehow wistfully sad as he faced the two patrol officers.

"It's an odd proposition," Crockett broke a heavy silence. "Give me a little time, will you, to consider it?"

"Time?" Crill Sadler sent a look of inquiry toward Colonel White.

"Until tomorrow mornin' at sunrise," said the colonel.

"And if we don't take you up on it, what then?" It was Chuck Lannigan who cannily voiced that question.

"That's bin boilin' inside of you fer some time, ain't it?" The colonel grinned. "If you'd bin a buck Injun, they'd call you 'Man-Afraid-Of-His-Hide'."

"Go to hell!"

"Alias 'Go-To-Hell Lannigan'," finished the chuckling colonel, and even Crockett grinned at Lannigan's sour expression.

"So"   Colonel White took the floor — "you'd like to know what'll become of you, eh? It's hard to say. That rests purty much with the big boss, the *Señor Dios*. As Herman Blucher used to say . . . '*Gott in Himmel* and Herman in Mexico is a long ways apart.'

And he'd unlimber his second gun. Mebbyso that's what'll happen. You'll have to fight."

"We can do that," grunted Crockett.

"No doubt about it," agreed the colonel, "and a sweet fight it'll be. Crill kinda fergot to tell you boys that we're expectin' an attack from General Bertoncini and his rebel army. Crill ain't used to makin' speeches and he must've got rattled. Have a drink, Go-To-Hell Lannigan. You look sick."

Chuck Lannigan was pasty white and his eyes were slits of glinting, baffled rage. With a rasping snarl, Lannigan leaped at White. But Crill's fist caught the officer flushly on the point of the jaw, flooring him. Crockett had not moved from his chair but his eyes watched Lannigan with an odd scrutiny.

From the gathering dusk outside came the sound of a shot, of quick feet running, and staccato orders. A muffled bugle called assembly. There was the rattle of gun bolts.

A Mexican burst into the room, his arms waving excitedly.

"What is it, *hombre*?"

"The rebels, *Señor Coronel*. Hundreds!"

"Go count 'em again. There's fifty thousand! Attention! Now, blast your measly hide, make a decent report. Get military or I'll take a machete and slice the lousy head off your humpbacked shoulders. And I'll cut off your toes and put 'em in your mouth. Straighten them shoulders. Now, then, report!"

The man saluted stiffly. "*Señor Coronel*, Private Pallacio reports the approach of the enemy."

236

"Good. Dismissed. Vamoose!"

"But I have not feenish, *señor*. Eees 'nother theeng."

"Spit 'er out."

"The *Señor* Cato Morgan 'ave escape!"

CHAPTER
NINE

Yolanda Bertoncini, known sometimes as the *Señorita* Chiquita Lopez, stood very white and wide-eyed before Crill Sadler and Colonel Tom White. There was no light in the room, save the flickering firelight that threw distorted shadows on the white walls. Save for these three, the room was empty.

"And so, Yolanda," said Crill sternly, "you got rid of Bill and Joe, then aided this *Señor* Cato Morgan to escape?"

"That is so," came the rich voice of the girl.

"You have known that the *Señor* Cato Morgan is perhaps a spy?"

"Whoever 'as tol' you that ees one damn' beeg lie!"

Colonel White was seized with a sudden fit of choking. Crill bit his lip.

"What makes you say that?" Crill asked.

"Well, this *Señor* Cato ees, weeth hees own face tell me so, all by heemself. Eef you are going to choke again, *Señor Coronel*, you 'ave better to take a dreenk of water."

"So Cato told you himself that he was not a spy, eh? And you believed him?"

"Why not?"

238

Crill turned to the colonel with a helpless sort of look. "You talk to her, Colonel. I don't seem to be making much headway."

"Why do you think Cato Morgan told the truth, young lady?" asked the Colonel.

"Well," said Yolanda, "ees like thees. I 'ave a very large love for thees *Señor* Cato. Almos' so moch as he 'as for Yolanda. And when two people get into love, *Señor Coronel*, those two do not make a lie at each other. Ees very damn' simple, no?"

Colonel White bowed and turned to Crill. "And there you are, Crill. As Yolanda says, it's very damn' simple. He's made love to her. Sheik stuff. The boy has a way with the wimmen."

"He'll have a knife in his gizzard when Manuel catches him," said Crill. "As we agreed, I came clean with him. Told him plenty. I'd counted on his loyalty to help handle Crockett. Now he's taken his knowledge and skipped. Hang the luck!"

"But down in your heart, Crill, you trust Cato as much, almost, as our little Yolanda trusts the young rascal. Eh? No hedgin', now."

"Well, it's hard to mistrust a man that's fought and starved with you, a man that's saved your life, and you've saved his. Things like that make for comradeship. If Cato proves rotten, he's killed my faith in that thing we call comradeship."

"Exactly, son." Colonel White put one arm around Yolanda's waist, the other arm across Crill's shoulders. "If Cato Morgan shows a rotten streak, he's losing two things . . . two things that any man would die rather than lose. He'll lose the love of our Yolanda and the comradeship of his best friend. Do you think, for one unholy second, Crill, that the boy will make a sacrifice like that? Not in a million years. Forget it. Forget Cato till he shows up again. You two kiss and make up."

"Yes, please." Yolanda smiled, and, holding up her face, she took Crill's scarred cheeks and pulled his head down until his lips touched hers. Then the girl suddenly drew back, a look akin to fright in her eyes as she looked at Crill. "Your lips," she whispered huskily, "they are cold like the lips of a dead man."

"Don't be foolish, Yolanda," said Crill, and, turning abruptly, he limped away with his cane. Yolanda, the color drained from her face, watched him with tortured eyes. Colonel White's lips pursed in a soundless whistle. Crill, leaning heavily on his stick, had passed into the next room where the two Border Patrol officers were under guard.

With a hurt little cry, Yolanda turned to the colonel. He put his arms around her, mumbling words meant to soothe her.

"Een hees eyes, I saw it. He loves me. *Madre de Dios*, and I 'ave hurt heem. He who has been so moch like the brother by me. So beeg, so kind, so brave, always since I 'ave known heem. Now I 'ave stab heem. May *Dios* forgive me!"

"Hush, honey. Don't go gittin' your nose all red. He'll git over it. They all do. Shucks, with a face that looks like he'd bin caught in a mowin' machine, how kin he expect a girl to fall fer him? How could any woman love a guy with a mug like that?"

"How?" cried Yolanda fiercely, slipping from his arms. "How? Weeth her heart, *Señor!* That ees how. He ees the fines', the 'andsomes' man een the worl'. And *Santa María*, I did not until this minute know about it. You say to me one small, even one very small word about heem, and I shall make the bum out of you! I weel scratch the eyes! I shall poke the beezer! *Dios*, what 'ave I done?"

"Search me, young lady. You win all bets. One minute it's Cato. Then it's Crill. Mebby it'll be me next. *¿Quién sabe?*" The colonel reached for the whiskey bottle. "I'll call him back, Yolanda."

"*Santa María*, no! Not now. Weeth my nose red, no! 'Ave you nevair become een love, *Señor?*"

"Sure. Plenty times."

"Een love weeth per'aps two at once?"

"As many as five, sure. Lady, in my day, I was a warthog, a curly wolf with the wimmen. This Don Juan bird was a piker alongside your Uncle Tom White." He blew a neat smoke ring. "The purtier they was, the harder they fell. White, tan, or black. From Singapore to Rio de Janeiro. From Nome to the City of Mexico. Yep, a howlin' wolf with a wavy tail, that was me."

"The 'ell of a fellow, no?"

"That's it in a nutshell."

"The original son-of-the-gon, no?"

"That's me." The colonel puffed out his chest.

"*Dios, señor,* you mus' 'ave change one hell of the lot since then." And with a quick little laugh she was gone. The colonel's booming laugh followed her. He was still chuckling when Crill came in with Lannigan and Crockett. From a distance came the sound of scattered rifle fire.

"Well, boys," questioned the colonel, "what'll it be?"

"Stake us to guns," said Crockett, "and we'll fight. How many men have you, Colonel?"

"Not so many, but every man of 'em is a fightin' fool. Even my cook has six notches on his gun. All Texans and all of 'em has sniffed powder smoke. The Mexicans belong to Crill, all hand-picked and tested. We're outnumbered twenty to one but we'll win. Bertoncini has men and guns aplenty but he's shy on ammunition." The colonel turned to Crill. "Take Crockett into the gun room and rig him out with what he wants."

The skirmish firing was growing louder. Yet Crill and the colonel seemed unperturbed. He motioned for Lannigan to stay there with him while Crill fitted Crockett out. When the two men were alone, Colonel White faced Chuck Lannigan coldly, all the bluff good nature gone from his face, leaving it square and grim and dangerous.

"It takes a thief, Lannigan, to ketch a thief. You know what I mean. I want that map you stole from Chiquita Lopez. I'll count five. Then my gun is gonna go off and I'll take the map off your dead carcass."

"You needn't count," snapped Lannigan, and jerked at the lacing of his field boot. With his pocket knife he ripped the stitching of the lining and produced the map, which was wrapped in oiled silk. With a wry smile he handed it to the colonel.

"You should have stuck to your knittin', Lannigan. I kin smash you fer this. Men of the Border Patrol ain't supposed to cut into Mex politics."

"Politics! The stuff belongs to nobody."

"It belongs to five men, Lannigan. I'm one of 'em. If it's ten million I get, I've earned every *peso*. So has Bertoncini, La Porte, Blucher, and even that Cossack butcher. Earned it by giving all we had to give and all we had was our services as soldiers. And you cut into the game with a piker ante. You don't know what it's all about. Who hired you, Lannigan, to steal that map?"

"Nobody." Lannigan stood with his hands clenched, his mouth drawn into a lipless, crooked line. Colonel White blew a smoke ring and watched it curl ceilingward.

"Crockett don't know a word about this business, Lannigan. But if you don't give me a truthful answer, he's gonna know the works. Once more, who hired you?"

"Nobody!"

"Hi, there, Crockett!" called the colonel. "Come in here a second!"

"I'll squeal," whispered Lannigan. "Bertoncini hired me."

"Yeah?" Colonel White stepped toward the closed door leading to the gun room. "I reckon Crockett's deaf."

"Hold on, White. Don't! All I want is my job on the border. I'll talk!" There is something pitiful in the breaking of a strong man. White's eyes held a look of pity rather than disgust as Lannigan, the ferret, the blood-hound, the crafty manhunter, now became the quarry and stood as if he had suddenly grown old and feeble.

"Who hired you, Lannigan?" he repeated almost gently.

"Bertoncini, Blotski, and Blucher. They're together now. I was to meet them and hand over the map. That's God's truth. I needed money bad. We don't get much in the way of wages. I've a wife and three kids to keep and two of 'em had pneumonia. There was the doctor and hospital to pay, and a special nurse. They caught me when I needed money and . . . well, that's that. I'm not whining. I want my job and that's all."

"You'll git it. Crockett'll never know. And if you and him agree to our proposition, you'll both be well taken care of. Tom White's no piker. And he's no crook. I'm askin' fer nothin' I ain't earned. Down in his soul, Crockett knows that. Or he'd've told me to go to hell." He smiled and shoved out his hand. "Want it, Chuck Lannigan?" he asked.

"You bet I do, Colonel." And Lannigan gripped the extended hand.

Colonel White said to Crill later that it was worth 100 *pesos* to see Lannigan smile.

"I'd've bet a man five hundred he didn't know how to grin."

244

That was after he led Lannigan to the gun room and the colonel and Crill were alone.

"Blotski and Blucher has pooled with Bertoncini to clean me out, Crill. That means that the Devil's Bend gang is with Bertoncini. This fight is anybody's fight till the last shot is fired."

CHAPTER
TEN

Night. A purple black night as soft as velvet spangled with stars. It was a night meant for lovers. In that lull before the firing broke could be heard the strumming of a guitar. Here and there cigarettes glowed. Men talked in low tones. Once a man laughed. And there was a constant undertone of *creaking* leather and *clicking* gun locks. The *hacienda* was in darkness. The odor of orange blossoms hung in the patio.

And out there, out beyond the picket lines, the corrals and stable, Bertoncini's rebels crept like shadows in an ever-narrowing circle that closed about the *hacienda*. The wily Italian had seen to it that there was a goodly ration of marijuana for every Mexican and plenty of tequila for the nameless white warriors from Devil's Bend.

Bertoncini himself moved among them, a tall, bony-faced man with fierce mustaches and a goatee, straight, military, black-eyed, treacherous. He wore the faded, tarnished uniform of an officer of the Italian cavalry. It must be said for him that he wore it well. Even his broken boots were polished. A handsome old hawk, Bertoncini, a man of many battles and many

246

mistresses, gambler, rake, but a soldier always — a soldier whose blade was for hire to the highest bidder.

"*Gott mit uns*," grunted the short-statured, blond Blucher who looked like a brewer but who was a tactician and as cold-blooded as a fish. "*Gott sei mit uns diese Nacht, mien Herr.*"

"If God's with you," sneered the tall, lithe, immaculate Blotski, whose handsome, dissipated features were a reflection of the dark sorrows and crimes of the Romanoffs, "then He's giving me an escort of guardian angels. Me *und Gott*, eh?" Blotski berated him in his own tongue, then fashioned a cigarette made of a mixture of Russian tobacco and marijuana.

The ugly saber scar across Herman Blucher's cheek grew livid in the light of the campfire. With all the stolid hate of his race, he detested this man who called himself Blotski. That hatred was based on envy. For the Russian was of noble blood and had been a high officer of the Cossack regiment before a duel with some Romanoff nobleman over a woman had exiled him.

"I'm just a damned blot on the name of my people," the Cossack had once said. "Therefore, 'Blotski'." He carried a small ivory miniature of the woman who had broken him. Not because he loved her, he explained once in a fit of morbid drunkenness, "but because she is the most beautiful creature I have ever laid eyes on . . . the most beautiful, the most passionate, the most coldly cruel woman God or devil ever made."

Blucher had seen the Russian kill a man for smiling. Yet the Teuton did not fear Blotski. Herman Blucher

247

was hard to scare. In his deliberate brain he conceived the idea of someday killing the Russian, even as he planned now with Blotski to kill Bertoncini.

"Let the *verdammter* wop push ahead *mit* his greasers. *Ja.* Like der steam roller, he crushes our Colonel White and dis *Dummkopf*, Sadler."

"Who the devil is this Crill Sadler, Herman?"

"Some fool that White hires . . . a convict."

"You underestimate him, Blucher. The man was a captain in the A.E.F. The United States isn't in the habit of commissioning convicts."

"Vell, I'm so dumb. Who is he?" But the abrupt appearance of Bertoncini cut the Russian's reply.

"My men are placed." The Italian gave the two a sharp look of suspicion. "Where are your men, Blotski?"

"Where they belong, my friend. In reserve. Throw your foot troops and cavalry in. My men will handle the machine-guns and mop up behind. Order deployed advance. Fire their buildings. My men will cover the road and trails with a machine-gun fire that will cut them down like wheat before a sickle."

Bertoncini consulted his watch. "In half an hour."

"Half an hour," agreed the other two. Bertoncini gave them another hard scrutiny, then saluted and moved off.

Blucher shivered and moved up to the fire. "*Gott*, he giffs me der creeps, Blotski." The Russian shrugged his splendid shoulders and lit a fresh cigarette. His swarthy face was the color of old ivory and his eyes were like red coals.

Herman Blucher got to his feet and moved off into the night like a man who is haunted by ghosts. The Russian squatted there, the firelight reflecting in his deep-set eyes, glittering on his saber scabbard, his red sash, and his cavalry boots. He wore a military tunic over his bare torso. As he smoked, a smile played about his face. It was a smile that might send a shudder over any who saw.

Crill Sadler, eh? he mused. *Name of a dog, who are you? Dead men cannot write. Yet* . . . He took a bit of paper from his pocket and scanned its penciled wording. Then he tossed it into the fire. He rose, drawing his saber. Tall, powerful, still smiling, he tested the blade, swinging it with swift slashes that whistled as the keen blade cut the air. There was something savage and barbaric in the dark face of this ex-Cossack of blood-soiled Russia. A harsh laugh rattled in his throat. "Man, devil, or ghost from the grave of the dead," he gritted through white teeth, "I'll cut you in two."

"If I had a temper like that," came a pleasant drawl from somewhere beyond the firelight, "I'd pickle it in brine . . . or vodka, my Cossack friend. Move the wrong way and I'll have the pleasure of shooting you square in the belly."

Cato Morgan, suave and smiling a little, stepped from the darkness, a blue-barreled Colt swinging in his hand.

"March, Blotski. I said march, blast your murdering heart." Cato Morgan's voice hissed like a powder fuse. His smile twisted into a snarl.

The Russian, after a tense moment of indecision, sheathed his saber and saluted.

"I'm only hoping you'll make a gun play, my vodka-drinking, hop-smoking *amigo*. Then I can kill you without a troubled conscience."

"Name of the devil's image, who are you?" The Russian's voice trembled with hate, but he marched ahead of the American, who watched his every move.

"Never mind who I am. My name would mean nothing. There's your horse. Mount."

A look of cunning flickered in the Cossack's eyes as he swung onto his horse. But the light died the next instant. From out of the dark came the quick, sure noose of a lariat. The rope fell about the Russian's middle, pinioning his arms. Two swiftly thrown hitches completed the tying job.

"That ties him, Major."

"Good work, Joe. Where's Bill?"

"He's tryin' on Blucher's pants," explained Joe. "But they won't fit. Dang the luck, this Rooshian ain't wearin' no shirt!" Joe spat disgustedly and flipped another hitch about the prisoner's neck. "The other end of this ketch rope is tied hard and fast to my saddle horn, Blotski, so if you kick that hoss into a runski, it's gonna be just too damn' badski for your neckski."

Bill loomed up with a grunting, sputtering Herman Blucher. A pair of thick, hairy legs showed below his shirt tail. Bill had tied the misfit breeches about the German's neck. Bill passed a bottle to Joe.

"The dang' stuff tastes like tequila mixed with caraway seed. What you call it, Herman?"

"I chust vish it vass poison," grunted Blucher. "Ha, Blotski, you too, eh? *Himmel!*"

"Let's go, boys. This spot is dangerous. God help you, Blotski, and you, too, Blucher, if you act up in case we're challenged. Tie Blotski's bridle reins to the tail of Blucher's mount, Joe. Bill, tie their feet under their horses' bellies. All set? Then forward. You know the idea of procedure, boys. Shoot if you have to."

Bill and Joe had disarmed the prisoners. They moved on now, Cato Morgan leading the way, Bill leading Blucher's horse, Joe bringing up the rear. Their way led back along the trail to Devil's Bend and away from the fighting forces that were closing in on Crill Sadler's *hacienda*. Now and then Joe took a pull at the bottle of *Kümmel*. *Kümmel* is as powerful as T.N.T., but the stuff was going into a stomach of rawhide. Joe's face fairly beamed as he nibbled at the liquor.

This stuff, he told himself, *is the shore enough fightin' hooch. Pore Bill.* For Joe did not know that Bill was likewise equipped with a quart of Herman Blucher's precious *Kümmel.*

Cato Morgan halted, holding up his hand for silence. Bill, ever generous, held the bottle to Blucher's mouth.

"Swaller, Herman. You'll need it afore we hang you."

Suddenly the still night was shattered by the crash of rifle fire. Bertoncini had begun his attack. Cato motioned for the others to stay halted. Alone and on foot, he slipped along the trail.

A sharp challenge. A shot. Then Cato returned and mounted. In his hand was a vital bit of gun mechanism, a small bit of tooled steel that, when taken from a Lewis gun, renders the gun useless. Again the cavalcade moved on. The horses shied at a motionless, huddled thing beside a gun mounted on a tripod.

"Good work, Major," grunted Bill. "That was Jimmy the Rat."

"Wanted fer triple murder," supplemented Joe in passing. "One was a woman. Here's hopin' hell ain't too crowded to hold you, Jimmy."

So they moved on, this oddly assorted company of men, toward the ragged peaks of Devil's Bend.

"Listen to them guns," complained Joe. "We're missin' all the excitement. Have a shot, Major. Then gimme the name of this brave-maker. When I git rich, I'm gonna get me a barrel. Ten barrels. And a gold cup that holds a pint. And a good saddle and a good hoss, and I'm gonna hire all the cow bosses I've worked under, and a couple of shavetail louts to fetch and carry fer me. And I'm gonna hang a top-kicker I had oncet. Then I'll . . . what's the name of it, Major?"

"*Kümmel*." Cato coughed and passed back the bottle. "Hit 'er light, boys. It's dynamite. A shot of that and one of the caviar's hopped cigarettes and you'd throw away your clothes and lick Mexico bare-handed. Let's go, cowboys. We're clear of the guards. We can make time."

"How about a li'l song, Major?"

"Later," promised Cato. "And I'll sing with you till sunup. You boys are the real goods."

"Crill'll hang us if you've given us a bum steer," groaned Bill.

"Didn't the major show us where he was jake, bonehead? Didn't that swell lady at Crill's tell us it was OK to faller him? Ain't we put four machine-guns outta commission, captured two generals, and ain't we got swell drinkin' licker? What more do you want fer two-bits?"

"You never led me into nothin' but misery," Bill came back at him. "I ain't got nothin' to go by but past performance."

"Hey, General Orderski" — Joe grinned — "have a shotski of hoochski, then tell a man how you make that moostache so sharp-pointed and what's the idee in wearin' no shirt?"

"He's tough," explained Bill. "Take a few more bites of that funny licker an' you'll start sheddin clothes just like him. Me, I already th'owed away my boots."

"Your boots?" growled Blucher. "My boots, *Dummkopf!*"

"Kin we scalp these birds afore we hang 'em, Major?"

But Cato had pushed on ahead. He was playing a dangerous game. One mistake might be fatal. It was not personal achievement that he wanted. Cato Morgan was thinking of Crill Sadler — Crill of the snowy hair and the scarred face, in whose eyes Cato had seen the fresh scar of a broken loyalty. And for what he had done tonight and what he hoped to accomplish, he was asking no finer reward than the clasp of a friend's hand — that, and a woman's smile.

CHAPTER
ELEVEN

"Not that I figger for a minute, you understand, that Bertoncini might lick us," Colonel White told Crockett, "but in case the worst gits to the worst, here's the getaway." He pointed to the high-powered car with its bulletproof windshields and its machine-gun. Two men sat in the car, kept in a garage that had been tunneled in under the house. You entered the garage by a trap door in a closet off the kitchen.

"Always like to have a back exit in case there's wimmen in the place, savvy? It'd take an army to stop that bus, once that driver of mine gives 'er the gun. Tex and that machine-gun has got us outta some tights, here and there." The colonel chuckled softly, then led the way up the tiny stairway and through the trap door to the floor above. "It may be, Crockett, that we'll want Chiquita to git back across the border. In that case, I'd like you to go along in the car with her . . . you and Lannigan."

"What about you, Colonel?"

"Me 'n' Crill will stick around here, win or lose." There was a note of grim finality to the old soldier's voice. He would fight to the end, whatever that end might be. Victory or defeat would find him there. And Crill Sadler would be with him, fighting at his side.

Crill and Lannigan were on top of the flat roof now. On the roof were mounted four machine-guns, the guns well sheltered behind sheets of steel shutters. The place was built after the manner of the early-day blockhouses. The surrounding wall of adobe was four feet thick and twelve feet high. Inside it were the barn, the corrals, and the house. It was a veritable stockade where a few good fighting men could hold off an enemy many times their number. And there was no doubt as to the ability of these men when it came to lining a pair of sights. Now, as they waited for the attack, they chatted with careless indifference.

Word had been passed around that the outlaws of the Devil's Bend were with Bertoncini. Lannigan's confession had confirmed certain rumors. Speculation ran high. Crill was like a man tipsy on champagne as he moved from post to post on a tour of final inspection.

"What does the girl think about her old man being in this scrap?" asked Lannigan of Crill.

"You couldn't have opened that oiled silk that held the stolen map, then?"

"No. No, I didn't open it."

"Then do so now." Crill grinned and passed him the packet. Chuck Lannigan ripped it open with his knife, then grunted with astonishment. For the carefully sewed oiled silk contained nothing but a thick sheet of notepaper across which, in a woman's handwriting, was written a short message.

255

To General Bertoncini:

A man may lose everything, even to his life, and still be rich if he still retains his honor. But you, my father, are a pauper even if you had all the gold in the world. For you have sold your honor. I find it hard to pity such a father.

Yolanda

P.S. You steal from me, eh? But you are not so smart, after all. The map is where you can never find it.

Lannigan grinned shamefacedly.

At that moment the world seemed to explode about them. Bertoncini had attacked. With wild yells and shots, they charged out of the night and were swarming over the wall.

Crill jerked a whistle from his pocket. At its first blast the guns went into action like riveting machines gone crazy, spitting streams of crimson flame.

Screams of the wounded. Yells of marijuana-mad Mexicans as they slid over the wall and into the red arms of death. Crill's men fought in silence, cigarettes, perhaps, hanging limply from tight-set lips. One fellow whose cheek bulged with natural leaf tobacco spat methodically as he worked his gun.

Colonel White was down in the yard. Those on the roof could hear his voice as he called orders in a large but unexcited voice.

"A leetle bit higher, boys. That's better. Hold 'er there. Save the bullets. Git 'em as they crawl over the wall. Sing 'em to sleep to the tune of a Forty-Five! Fight, *Tejanos!* Give 'em what they come fer!"

Up on the roof a ricochet bullet hit a gunner in the arm. Without a word, Chuck Lannigan squatted in his place. Crill grinned his approval. Crill's night glasses swept the wall. He was watching for a certain man. That man was the Cossack, Blotski.

Flares had been set off along the wall so that the invaders were fighting in a glaring light. Now a searchlight was turned on to take the place of the dying flares. The big searchlight was hidden along the wall and operated from the house.

Cries of dismay came from the rebels as the glaring light struck them. Beyond the wall the hawk-like face of old Bertoncini darkened with futile rage. He tried in vain, time and again, to get snipers into position to kill that light.

Heedless of danger, the old Italian rode around the wall. He pleaded with and bullied his troops. They charged and charged again, only to fall back, defeated. He had his bugler sound for the machine-gun squads. Then he cried out in futile fury when they did not heed his call. A runner was sent to each machine-gun nest. They came back, white-eyed with terror, to report the guns out of commission and four gunners dead.

Now Bertoncini himself led a concentrated charge over the wall.

"Up and over! Up and over, *hombres!*" And so they went, up and over that blood-smeared wall, and into a nest of bullets and sharp steel, up and over, then down to defeat.

"*¡Soccoro! ¡Soccoro!*" But there was none to heed their cries for help. Back they scrambled out of that patio where guns spewed death, out and over the wall, into headlong retreat. And Bertoncini, white with fury, watched them run like rabbits.

He cursed Blotski and Blucher, for he suspected treachery of some sort. Fear chilled his fighting heart, but he did not run. Tears of rage dripped down his cheeks as he raked his horse with the spurs and shot down his own Mexican officers when they would not rally their men. He charged here and there, a naked gun in his hand, his face gray with the nausea of defeat. And even when his last handful of Mexicans ran into the brush, throwing away the guns that had cost him good money, he sat his horse, his white mane bristling, snapping an empty gun at the backs of his cowardly troopers.

If he saw the patio gates swing open, he gave no sign. Only when Colonel White and Crill Sadler, riding at the head of their hard-bitten Texans, came at him did the old Italian show signs of any reaction to the situation. He took something from his pocket and hurled it into the brush. Then, erect and unafraid, he rode at the charging men. But if he expected a volley of death, he was wrong. Not a gun blazed at the lone man who had met their charge.

"Don't shoot, boys! We'll cage the old war hawk!" shouted Colonel White.

But even as they closed in on him, Bertoncini laughed into their faces. It was a terrible laugh that ended in a rattling cough. Then the old rebel leader pitched sideways out of his saddle and into Colonel White's arms. In the Italian's talon-like hand was clutched an empty vial. It had held enough cyanide to kill twenty men. Bertoncini had drunk it all.

Crill and the colonel covered the dead body with a serape. Then they rode on with their men. Lannigan rode on one flank, Crockett on the other. They were rounding up the frightened Mexicans like so many cattle.

Crill and the colonel kept together, their eyes searching the night for Blotski and Blucher.

The first inkling they gained of Cato Morgan's share of the night's action was when they came upon a Lewis gun with two dead men beside it.

"Here," said Crill grimly when Lannigan and Crockett came up, "are two of your Devil's Bend gents. There's been something doing out here." He examined each man in turn. "Each with a busted head. Not a bullet mark. A Mex would use a knife. Colonel, this job has the earmarks of two birds that once served their U.S. under alias names. Bill got one of these toughs, Joe crowned his mate."

"And Cato Morgan bossed the job," added Colonel White. "Listen!"

From the darkness ahead came the popping of guns, and above the scattered fire the battle cry of the fighters.

"Powder River!"

"A mile wide and a foot deep!"

"Let 'er buck!"

"Come on, boys! Double time!" roared the colonel. "Ride like hell! Bill and Joe are scrapping what's left of Bertoncini's men!"

"And by the noise they're makin'," said a lanky Texan, "they're drunker'n hoot owls!"

CHAPTER
TWELVE

To Cato Morgan it had seemed as if a dozen men or more had risen from the bowels of the earth; moreover, that each of these shadowy men was shooting at him. He had been riding ahead as a sort of scout while the garrulous Bill and Joe brought the prisoners.

In a flash Cato was off his horse, crawling on all fours in the brush, while Bill and Joe fought with a reckless desperation against the men who rode straight at them. It was no time to waste in vain regrets. Turning loose their prisoners, the two ex-soldiers of the A.E.F. sought a place of safety from which to resist the whirlwind attack.

The attacking party consisted of white men from the Devil's Bend. Chance had sent them along this trail. Chance now rescued Blotski and Blucher and turned the tide of Cato Morgan's raiding party. Cato met Bill and Joe near a nest of boulders.

"Hi, Major, here's your army."

Blucher's bellowing voice roared orders to this impromptu rescue party. Blotski, more silent of tongue but nonetheless deadly of purpose, flexed his freed arms and jerked out his saber.

"Get the three coyotes alive, men!" he snarled, his swarthy face distorted with hate. "I'll make hash out of them. Hunt 'em down, you devils from Devil's Bend!"

But Cato and Bill and Joe had no notion of being captured. Bunched there among the rocks, they fought off the men that came at them. And the men of Devil's Bend, paying no heed at all to Blotski or the roaring Blucher, emptied their guns in hopes of hitting those three men who were putting up so hard a fight.

Outnumbered, their ammunition limited, Cato and his two men were shooting only when a target appeared, making every shot tell. Cato, his blue eyes glittering, smiled bitterly at the ill luck that had stolen from him the chance to reclaim Crill's friendship.

If I get killed, he mused, *Crill will never know but what I was a traitor.*

"Got any stuff left in your bottle, Joe?" asked Bill.

"Are you hit, pardner?" asked Joe anxiously.

"Me? Naw. But the major's shirt is all blood. Where you hit, Major?"

"Just creased along a rib, Bill."

"Then here's your soothin' syrup." Joe grinned. "It taken more'n a few bums like them birds to separate Joe from his bottle. Drink hearty. Then pass 'er to Bill. Then we'll sing. Mebby we ain't got so dang' much singin' time left, savvy? So we better . . . we better . . . better . . ." Joe's voice trailed away into silence. With a sort of sob, Bill was kneeling beside his crumpled partner.

"Dead?" asked Cato huskily. "Let's have a look at the boy." He bent over Joe, who lay limp.

"Bullet clean through his shoulder, Bill. Tear up something for bandages. I'll keep off these coyotes. Then you stand guard while I get him tied up. He must have gotten this an hour or more ago. He's soaked with blood. Never whimpered . . . not once."

"That's Joe. Never whines. Damn 'em! I'll kill the pack of 'em if Joe croaks. You don't think he'll . . . ?"

"No, bonehead," said Joe, opening his eyes suddenly, "I ain't croakin'. But I'll take a shot of licker."

Joe, bandaged and pale, took a pull at the bottle. Then he raised his voice in that wild war whoop that had carried to Crill and Colonel White.

"Powder River!"

He yelled it again when, as in a dream, he saw Crill and Colonel White break through those warriors of Devil's Bend.

"Powder River!"

"A mile wide and a foot deep!" yelled Crill, standing in his stirrups as he charged into the midst of the men who were fighting like trapped wolves. "Here I am, you buzzards. Try and get me, you black caps! You whelps of inbred coyotes! Here's Crill Sadler."

He was fighting like a man gone mad when Lannigan and Crockett rode up. For Crill had heard a voice above that mêlée, a voice that belonged to a never-to-be-forgotten past — the voice of the Cossack, Blotski.

"Where are you, you Russian jackal?" he called.

"*Schweinhund!*" roared Herman Blucher as Colonel White rode at him.

"Howdy, you Prussian butcher!" chuckled the colonel, and loaded his empty gun.

"*Hi, hi, hi!*" The wild Cossack yell ripped the night like a sword rips silk. Blotski, his tunic off, his hairy torso spattered with blood and sweat, swung his saber in a wild challenge.

"Diego! Emanuel! Arnaldo! Tomás, my *Tejano!* Hermano!" Crill's voice rose above the tumult. "Death, *hombrecitos!* Fight, my wolves! Fight, my Arnaldo! Know me, you dog, before you die! I am the man who was *Don* Francisco's adopted son! I am he who made the map, the one who buried the treasure! I am *Don* Alvarado, who fought with my father until Arnaldo the Cossack murdered him. I am *Don* Alvarado Crillon, son of *Don* Francisco's saddler. I am the boy that Blotski the butcher captured and tortured because I would not tell where the treasure was buried. Ha, you Cossack! You cut me till my face was like raw beef. My hands burned with hot coals. My body was buried alive. But damn you, I didn't die. Fight, you Russian butcher. Fight! Out of my way, you dogs of Devil's Bend. It's your master that's talking!"

For the fighting had quit as if by some sign. Even the wounded quit moaning and sat their horses in silence. Blucher and Colonel White, riding toward each other with drawn guns, pulled up. It was as if they again obeyed the commands of that old *Don* Francisco. Blucher was white as chalk. For had he not drawn lots with Blotski and Bertoncini to see which would kill *Don* Alvarado, the adopted son of old *Don* Francisco? Only the Frenchman and White, the Texan, had refused to join that bloody conspiracy to torture the secret from young *Don* Alvarado and so cheat *Don* Francisco.

Colonel White cocked his .45 and waved Blucher aside.

"You later, Herman. If Blotski so much as scratches Crill's hide, he gets this slug between the eyes. Gangway, you Dutch Dachshund!"

He spurred to Crill's side. But Crill smiled and shook his head.

"He belongs to me, Colonel." Crill pulled an ugly, flat-bladed machete from a scabbard under his stirrup leather.

"He'll cut your head off, Crill!"

Crill, his scarred face set, gripped the machete and spurred his horse forward.

The moon had pushed over the hills, throwing a pale light on the weird scene. The men of both factions had parted, forming a wide lane. And at either end of this human lane the two combatants faced one another.

Colonel White groaned. What chance had Crill, with his mediocre Army training in saber, against this terrible Cossack? Less than no chance. It would be murder. Yet the colonel dreaded to interfere. Too late now. For the two horsemen, their blades flashing, were charging at a run toward each other.

The Cossack stood in his stirrups, bare-chested, powerful, without equal in this butcher's game. No man there but knew it. Even Crill must have felt his puny contrast as this yelling Cossack charged, the moonlight on his slithering blade.

Thundering hoofs. Two blades glittering. A leer of maniacal triumph on the Cossack's face. Only a scant ten feet separated the charging men.

The *ping* of a rifle shot was barely heard above the *thud* of hoofs. The Cossack's blade jerked, then swung at Crill's head. Crill's machete met its force. Crill felt his arm go numb. Dazedly he saw his broken machete flung high in the air. Something hot bit his shoulder. Empty-handed, he whirled his horse to face Blotski again.

But the Cossack, a widening crimson smear on his hairy, naked chest, pitched clear of his horse and lay in a misshapen heap on the ground.

Cato Morgan lowered the smoking rifle from his shoulder and grinned crookedly at his two white-faced companions.

"If either of you rum hounds ever tell who fired that shot, I'll hang you both, then scalp you. Get that?"

"Major," said Bill, wiping beads of cold sweat from his forehead, "me 'n' my pard here is deef, dumb, and blind. I wanted to pot-shoot that Rooshian myse'f but, so he'p me Hannah, I ain't got a shell left in my gun."

"Ner me," added Joe.

"For that matter," confessed Cato Morgan, reaching for the bottle, "that one was my last cartridge."

He swayed a little, his face drained of blood, then his knees buckled and he wilted. For that bullet which had creased a rib was only one of three that had found him. He had used his last cartridge and his final ounce of strength to pay off a debt of comradeship.

CHAPTER
THIRTEEN

Herman Blucher was no man's coward. He saw White's Texans close in on the men from the Devil's Bend. He shot at White as the big soldier of fortune came at him. Then the colonel's bullet knocked him from the saddle; he was dead before he struck the ground.

White cursed the Luger bullet in his arm as he rode toward Crill, who sat his horse as a man in a daze, staring at the dead Blotski. The Russian's saber had bit to Crill's shoulder blade but he did not feel any pain. He was trying to puzzle out how Blotski had died.

"You shot him, Colonel?"

"Not me, Crill."

"I swear I heard a shot, just as we met. And there's a bullet hole in his chest. I wanted to kill that buzzard myself."

"So I reckoned," came the dry reply, "but, man, you shore picked a fool way to go about it. Leave the knives, big or little, to the foreigners. There was a good Yank named Colt that makes weapons for us fellers. Now lemme have a look at that dent in your shoulder."

"How about that hole in your arm?" Crill managed to grin, then swung to the ground to search the Russian's clothes hastily for his part of the map. The colonel, with a grunt of remembrance, made his way back to where Herman Blucher's body lay.

Forgetful of wounds, they completed their search. The colonel handed Blucher's oilskin-sealed map to Crill, who displayed the one taken from Blotski.

"I saw Bertoncini throw something in the brush," said Crill. "I'm sure it was the map."

"Correct. Here it is. I had one of the boys hunt till he found it. Looks like we got the whole map, Crill. Dang me if I kin call you *Don* Alvarado Crillon. Man, you can't be him! I mind the young rascal well. Always with old *Don* Francisco. A good-lookin' young feller with black hair. He used to call me . . ."

"I used to call you Uncle Texas Sam."

"You did, fer a fact. But your hair was black."

"Ever been buried alive, Colonel" — Crill's voice was brittle with the memory of torture — "with only your head above ground, the buzzards sitting around watching, and you screaming till your throat was dry as dirt? Ever had your face cut to ribbons and the ants and flies crawling into your flesh? God knows how long I was like that. I'd passed out when a goat herder found me and nursed me back to life. Manuel Ramirez was that goat herder. Yes, my hair was black. And my face wasn't scarred. And my name was *Don* Alvarado. But I took the name of Crill Sadler and no man in Mexico or across the border ever knew me for *Don* Francisco's adopted son . . . not even Cato Morgan, who knows everything and everyone in Mexico, not even you, who taught me how to shoot. Speaking of Cato, where is he, I wonder?"

They found Cato and Joe lying in the rocks. Bill was dressing Cato's wounds. Cato, conscious and white as a sheet, greeted Crill with a one-sided smile. Joe proffered an empty bottle by way of greeting.

"Dang it," said Bill, "we had Blotski and Blucher captured oncet. The major here done the trick. Then these jaspers jumped us and the two sons-of-bitches got away. We didn't sneak off fer nothin'. The major taken us when he left the ranch. 'Lowed we'd be doin' our duty if we could glam them two furriners. Which we done. Then we spills 'em again."

Crill was kneeling beside Cato, wondering if the man were dying.

"I hope," said Cato, "that you won't go on thinking I'm a rotten bum, old man. I meant well. That yarn of yours clicked in with some bits of information I had. I wanted to pull a slick one and fetch your two shareholders of this subdivision into camp. I missed fire. Is the war over?"

"Never mind the war, pardner," said Crill. "How are you fixed?"

"I'll have some nice scars to show my grandchildren, old kid." He gripped Crill's hand, hard. "Bill and Joe are champs . . . the real goods, Crill. You'd ought to hear Joe and me sing 'Cross-Eyed Katy'."

It was a weary, bandaged, war-torn crowd that journeyed slowly back to the *hacienda*. But every man of them was happy in spite of the wounds that throbbed and ached.

270

"Crill," asked Colonel White as they approached the ranch, "did you say you drew the map and divided it, and even buried the stuff?"

"I drew the map from a sketch *Don* Francisco gave me . . . no names on it. And I was taken blindfolded by him on a long ride before we reached the spot. He was shrewd, that *Don* Francisco. The stuff is in the hills of Devil's Bend, I think."

"So I've always figured, Crill. That's why I let those men hang out there as sort of guard. They've kept the curious out. You've been enough in touch with them to know if they stumbled onto it. I never had an idee you buried the stuff. I'm right anxious to git this map together."

"All we need is Yolanda's section of it." As he spoke the girl's name, Crill's face settled into a sort of hopeless look. The colonel smiled but said nothing. Perhaps the girl had again changed her mind. Women were beyond all understanding.

But as they rode up to the gateway and old Manuel Ramirez let them in, the question in the colonel's mind was forever settled. For as they swung to the ground, Yolanda came running. With a sobbing, laughing cry, she threw her arms around Crill's neck. Her lips found his and told him, without words, where her heart lay.

Cato Morgan, on an improvised litter, grinned.

"I was afraid," he told himself and Colonel White later, "that I'd have to go through with a little cavaliering that I did in order to make an escape from the ranch. I was after Blotski and Blucher, not a wedding ceremony. Truth is, Colonel, I'm engaged to a girl in New York. Blonde. I've always liked blondes."

The colonel snorted. "I wouldn't trust you with no gal of mine, even if she was blacker'n a derby hat, cross-eyed, and bench-legged. Here's how!"

CHAPTER
FOURTEEN

Yolanda, Crill, and Colonel White sat about a carved mahogany table and pieced together the five segments of the circular map. Each segment was fitted in and pasted on a huge blotter. When the whole map was pieced together, the three bent over it.

"Stung!" Colonel White thudded a fist on the table. "By gosh, Crill, the danged thing don't make sense. Lot of fool lines meanin' nothin'. Lot of words strung together, 'round and 'round the circle. Looks like a roulette wheel with letters instead of numbers."

Crill nodded. "The letters spell out the instructions. Yolanda, take down the words as I read 'em."

Slowly, word by word, Crill called the words that he picked by means of a code key which he told the colonel was the only thing left him by *Don* Francisco in the old Mexican's will:

To my five wolves. From the grave, I salute you. Diego, Emanuel, Arnaldo, Tomás, Hermano. ¡*Salud!*

The *Señor Dios* alone knows who, if any of you, shall ever read this. Without the key that belongs to my adopted son, *Don* Alvarado, this map is without value.

Together *Don* Alvarado and I buried the treasure. We buried it in the Cave of Skulls in Devil's Bend. No man, save me, has ever explored the Cave of Skulls to its end. I found it by accident many years ago when the Indians chased me there. It took many hours to find its end. And at its end the treasure is buried, all of it.

All of it is gold, gold taken by peon toil from the earth. For five *centavos* per day the peons labored like slaves to make their masters rich, sweating under the hot sun, too tired to eat their beans at night, sleeping like dogs. I, *Don* Francisco, was one of those peons. I helped slave for the gold that went into the making of crowns and rings and cross and trinkets. It is stolen gold, all of it — stolen from the peons by the *jefes* and *dons* and men who rule with whip and gun. I, in turn, have again stolen it.

I have lived to make happy those peons. I have given them land and stock and food. I have killed with my own hand those men who drove me with the whip and the gun. And my country calls me a bandit and an evil man.

You, my wolves, have fought with me. But you did not fight for Mexico. You fought for gold. Except for Tomás, the *Tejano*, who has been my friend and has saved my life, you wolves would kill me for even the small portion of that gold. Someday one of you will kill your *Don* Francisco. That I know. An old woman who tells the future has spoken so to me. One of my wolves will kill me for gold. That is the way of things in this world.

274

So, because I do not know which one of you is to kill me, I reward you each alike. Whoever shall get this map may go to the Cave of Skulls and there this gold, enough to load many mules, is buried. It is yours, my wolves, for the digging. May you enjoy the fruits of that labor, my *hombrecitos*. Again, my wolves — *¡Salad! ¡Adiós!*

Crill looked up from the map at Colonel White, who sat puffing his cigar, his face like a mask, his grim mouth smiling faintly.

"Well, Crill," he said, "sounds simple enough, eh?"

"It does, Colonel." Crill also smiled. "Have you ever been in the Cave of Skulls?"

"I have," came the grim reply. "Devilish spooky hole, full of bones that's bin there hundreds of years. Yep, I've bin to the end. Have you?"

"*Don* Francisco himself took me once," said Crill. "Once was plenty."

"Don Francisco was my guide, too," said the colonel. "I wouldn't go in again fer ten million."

"Amen to that." Crill nodded.

"Then you weel not go for that gol'?" questioned Yolanda. "You weel not deeg up that millions?"

The two men exchanged a grimly humorous glance.

"Honey," said Crill, "*Don* Francisco had a purpose in taking the colonel and me there. There is only one month of the year you can get in there, and it's dangerous even then. The Cave of Skulls is pitted with quicksand spots. If that gold is buried there, no power on earth can ever raise it. *Don* Francisco knew that. He knew that if any man tried to find it, he would step into one of those quicksand sinks. He guided the colonel and me so that we would be warned and not go there."

"He was a visionary cuss," said the colonel, "a dreamer . . . ideals that was too fine to come true. He gave back to the earth what belonged to it. And he left this map as a death warrant for those he called his wolves. By the eternal, I'm for him. Crill, get on your laigs and drink to the old man. To *Don* Francisco!"

"To *Don* Francisco. *¡Salud!*"

When they resumed their seats, Crill again examined the map.

"Here's a few more words, Colonel. Get out your pencil, Yolanda. All set?" He again read the words from the code:

To Tomás, my *Tejano*, my friend, and to my son, *Don* Al-varado: in the Argentine Bank at Buenos Aires I have placed to your credit each one million dollars. May it bring happiness to you, the two who loved me. And when happiness has come, try to remember in your thoughts a man who died poor in all save love for his country and his friends. *Adiós*

A long silence held the three. The firelight threw dancing shadows on the white walls. At last Colonel Tom White got to his feet and, stepping to the door, called to Crockett and Cato Morgan. Crockett pushed Cato's wheelchair into the living room.

"Our medicine talk is over, gents. Crill's *mozo* will fetch cigars and what you boys want in the way of drinks. We won't be takin' that mule train across, Crockett. We done made other arrangements. Me and Crill is headin' fer the Argentine as soon as the *padre* marries him and this young lady. I don't reckon you'll have any more trouble with Devil's Bend. Cato's busted up his revolution. Looks to me like the party is about to all go home. Cato, you got a yacht layin' off the harbor, down yonder. Will the damn' thing run?"

"Anywhere except on dry land, you old pirate."

"*Hmmm. Bueno.* How's the leg and the rib and the arm?"

"Great, Colonel. Why?"

"You're not askin', jest answerin'. Now, if me 'n' Crill here deed over this cow land and minin' stuff to the *vaqueros* and peons, kin you fix it so they'll get it?"

"You bet. But what the dickens . . . ? Excuse me. My error. Proceed."

"I'm jest carryin' out the last wishes of a friend that died. You and Crockett kin amuse yourselves tinkerin' with this property. It'll take your mind off the hot weather next summer. Now about that boat, Cato . . . will it take me 'n' these honeymooners to Buenos Aires?"

"Not unless I go as skipper and we pass New York where I can pick up a blonde lady that's dizzy enough to be my wife."

"I dunno if I kin stand two sets of lovey-dovey idiots, but a man can't have everything. That car of mine is primed fer goin'. Say we pull out as quick as Bill and

Joe gits back from he'pin' Lannigan to the States with his prisoners? Crill's hired them two wild Injuns fer life."

"Did the map pan out OK?" asked Cato.

"Finer'n frawg hair. You kin have it fer a souvenir. You always was hell fer crossword puzzles."

The *mozo* brought drinks. Crockett looked happier than he had been for years as he made some excuse and left the room.

"Give us a toast, Crill" — Cato grinned — "and don't make it 'To the ladies,' either. Something different this time."

"I pass. Colonel White is on his feet. Shoot, Colonel. Both barrels."

"We'll drink to something worth all the gold in Mexico, boys," said the colonel, his eyes misty with memory of reckless youth, "that thing which can't be sold or stolen or killed, once it grows strong. It's the thing that brought us here tonight. It will always hold us together, regardless of distance, time, or even death. Yolanda, gentlemen, I give you . . . comrades!"

And as Colonel Tom White drank, his fingers touched those of Crill and Cato and Yolanda where they lay on the treasure map of *Don* Francisco's dead dreams.

ABOUT THE AUTHOR

Walt Coburn was born in White Sulphur Springs, Montana Territory. He was once called "King of the Pulps" by Fred Gipson and promoted by Fiction House as "The Cowboy Author." He was the son of cattleman, Robert Coburn, then owner of the Circle C ranch on Beaver Creek within sight of the Little Rockies. Coburn's family eventually moved to San Diego while still operating the Circle C. Robert Coburn used to commute between Montana and California by train, and he would take his youngest son with him. When Coburn got drunk one night, he had an argument with his father that led to his leaving the family. In the course of his wanderings he entered Mexico and for a brief period actually became an enlisted man in the so-called *gringo* battalion of Pancho Villa's army.

Following his enlistment in the U.S. Army during the Great War, Coburn began writing Western short stories. For a year and a half he wrote and wrote before selling his first story to Bob Davis, editor of *Argosy All-Story*. Coburn married and moved to Tucson because his wife suffered from a respiratory condition. In a little adobe hut behind the main house Coburn practiced his art and for almost four decades he wrote approximately 600,000 words a year. Coburn's early fiction from his Golden Age — 1924–1940 — is his best, including his novels, *Mavericks* (1929) and *Barb Wire* (1931), as well as many short novels published only in magazines that now are being collected for the first time. In his Western stories, as Charles M. Russell and Eugene Manlove Rhodes, two men Coburn had known and admired in life, he captured the cow country and recreated it just as it was already passing from sight.